To gizom,

Metin

Işık Bookstore Publications
No: 146

Meeting Sister
Novel/2025

Writer:
Metin Murat

Typesetting and Cover Design:
Barış Argus

Front Cover Artwork:
From painting by Güray Altun

Printing:
Mavi Basım Yayın Ltd.

Tel: 0533 863 19 57
Nicosia - Cyprus

ISBN:
978-9963-267-79-8 (printed)
978-9963-267-80-4 (ebook)

Also by Metin Murat
The Crescent Moon Fox

Meeting Sister

Metin Murat

IŞIK KİTABEVİ

*This novel is dedicated with love to the village of
Balalan/Platanissos, to its dead souls and to its living, to
its descendants around the world and those still to be born.*

ACKNOWLEDGMENTS

Writing, like boxing, is not quite the solitary art that the casual observer might think it is. Invariably, in both professions, there are a cast of important characters behind the scenes whose support is invaluable. In my case I need to thank the following for their particular help with this novel: Claire McGlasson, my writing coach from Faber Academy; my Turkish Cypriot 'sisters' who nagged me and encouraged me throughout to make sure I finished writing this story: Ciğdem Turan and Şenel Beliğer; Naciye Demirel who provided invaluable insights in to the real 'Zeki'; my friend Ipek Ozerim who has supported me in various ways with this novel and the previous (*The Crescent Moon Fox*); Okşan Atılan whose support and considerable efforts helped get this book into print; Nahide Merlen my publisher; the poet and artist Nafia Akdeniz whose work inspired some of the scenes in the novel and who contributed the photograph that inspired the artwork of Güray Altun that you see on the cover; Sonya Karafistan who provided me with some excellent advice relating to the handling of some of themes in this novel; and lastly, my beloved relatives and extended family from Cyprus – those still alive and those who have passed into the 'other room' – who helped shaped my sense of being a Cypriot, and a proud Turkish Cypriot at that.

PREFACE

Meeting Sister was written partly because so many of the readers of the first novel, *The Crescent Moon Fox*, wanted more of Aydin – originally supposed to be a minor character in that novel. I hope that in this one I have now brought him to rest. But partly because I realised that I had unfinished business with the fictional village of *Bamyaköy* and the questions of identity that we Turkish Cypriots face. Undoubtedly, I will once again be asked questions about the 'truth' of the novel. As with the first one, I stress that this is a work of fiction and a product of my imagination. However, what is certainly true is that a few of the characters are distantly inspired by real people. For the record though, my own beloved mother, and beloved stepfather, are not reflected in this story in any shape or form.

The question of Turkish Cypriot identity and fealty is a complex one. Our community has a wide spectrum of opinions on these matters, ranging from ardent Turkish nationalism to ardent Cypriot nationalism. Whilst I have some emotional sympathy with those who argue that it suffices to believe that you are Turkish to be Turkish, I personally don't think that is sufficient to give yourself a national identity. In my own particular case for example, I freely admit to liking Turkey, to liking Turks in general and to being an admirer of the great Kemal Atatürk. I also believe that, as tragic as it was for my fellow Greek speaking Cypriots, the Turkish intervention in 1974 did save my community from the possible threat of extinction. The short-lived Presidency of the murderous Nikos Sampson is all too often forgotten these days... But despite these favourable sentiments that I have for Turkey they do not make me a Turk. For my identity I rely on history, geography, and the study of genetics. Any serious study of these fields will clearly identify that those of us who are of pre-1974 stock are brothers and sisters to our Greek Cypriot compatriots. And that we Cypriots – be we Armenian Cypriot, Greek Cypriot, Maronite Cypriot or Turkish Cypriot – in all our incredible and rich mosaic of DNA, are part of a wider Levantine world. Our genetic cousins, before you reach the family tree of modern-day Turkey or Greece, are Syrians, Lebanese and Palestinians. Some of our social practices and customs are even to be found as far afield as the islands of Sicily and Malta – not surprising when you consider the ancient maritime trading routes. The Eastern Mediterranean is most definitely our world and our heritage. Not the modern Republics of Greece or Turkey. A simple consideration of distances will further bring this point home: 87 miles separate Cyprus from the shores of Syria; 150 miles separate Nicosia from Beirut (same as the distance between London and Cardiff incidentally); 236 miles separate Larnaca from Gaza. In comparison, the distance between Nicosia and Ankara is 326 miles; and between Nicosia and Athens, 578 miles.

The historical reasons for disunity and civil strife on the island of Cyprus are varied. They are not as some like to believe because of a clash of civilizations or religions. Cypriots, however they identify themselves, are very close to each other culturally. Turkish Cypriots practice a moderate form of Islam, if they practice at all – so religion is not a factor. The reasons for our disunity can be laid squarely at the door of competing education systems with different political narratives – as a consequence of the Ottoman policy of giving administrative and educational autonomy to different religious communities. Thus, for hundreds of years there has been a systemic 'othering' of people from different groups sharing the same little piece of land. This was exacerbated by the rise of nationalism, in all its ugly forms, in the 19th and 20th centuries. Men, and it was by and large men, latched on to these heart-stirring, but in my view, intellectually limited ideas for political ends – with the tragic consequences that we know today. I would further argue that, as a result of the myopic leadership of Archbishop Makarios III, the first President of Cyprus Republic, our island lost the one single major opportunity, provided by independence from Britain in 1960, to create a non-denominational national identity and society. It is doubtful that this chance will come again.

However, I still believe that a better future is possible for all Cypriots and that we can overcome some of the wounds of the past. I do not underestimate the pain of individual tragedies on both sides but if we consider the context of the wider experience of our Syrian, Lebanese, and Palestinian cousins, our collective suffering is tiny when compared to theirs.

How do we move forward? It will certainly not be through relying on politicians. The political class on both sides has largely failed us Cypriots. It will be through intercommunal dialogue, through sharing personal stories and perspectives, looking for what unites us and a conscious policy of 'de-othering'. Hence the importance for Cypriots, of all backgrounds to write and share their perspectives and to be read by the other. The first step to truth and reconciliation is, as they say, to be understood by the other. I am proud to say that in my own close circle of Cypriot friends, there are Greek Cypriots whose fathers were nationalists and EOKA supporters and yet they themselves have abandoned those hateful ideas to make peace with Turkish Cypriots. I have learnt from these friends. So, on my journey I too have come to embrace a Cypriot identity without renouncing my Turkish Cypriot heritage, nor my willingness to speak up in defence of my community. This novel is my own further contribution to sharing a Turkish Cypriot perspective and to putting up a mirror to some of the ills blighting our society. I hope it will encourage other Cypriots to express their own points of view.

Trigger Warning

Some readers, but certainly not all, will find some aspects of this novel disturbing and unsettling. However, the majority of advance readers of this novel took it in their stride and accepted the view that a novelist's role is also to challenge and provoke. I invite you to withhold judgement until the last page. My own views are clearly expressed in the Afterword following on from that.

CHAPTER 1

There is little more inconvenient than a funeral in summer. Particularly in a village like Bamyaköy where, even today, the season's heat imposes its own strict and time-honoured roster: sheep to the hills as day breaks; household chores until nine; the return of the shepherds and their flocks by mid-morning. Then, as the sun reaches its apex, a closing of shutters and a foot-shuffling retreat to the sweaty cotton mattresses where the villagers lie in a state of reptilian torpor – neither sleep nor wakefulness but a third condition of sluggish being.

It is only when the sun has dipped over the brow of the hill that some semblance of life can return. For the dwindling number of men left in the village, this is the signal that they may now amble to the coffee shop; for their wives it is the time of day they throw open the windows of their kitchens and start preparing the evening meal. Even, in the gummy heat of early evening, potatoes need to be fried; okra, onions and tomatoes need to simmer. The wealthier households will have lamb or chicken to add to the pot. And so it is that later, the smell of cooking wafting across the village will remind the men, like a genie calling them, that it is time to return home. The only patrons left behind in the coffee shop will be the hopeless drunks who will carry on drinking rakı or whisky until the early hours of the morning, until their ash trays have overflown and the last salted peanuts and clementines have been eaten.

But this funeral, that had come to upset the circadian rhythm of the day, was different. Not only for me. Not because it was for my uncle, Ismail. Not because of the new things I learnt about my long dead father and, in the same brush stroke, about myself. But because it seemed to me that we as a community had also come, in our own way, to bury ourselves. Though few would have realised, this was our end also. People and politicians had travelled from the four corners of our little strip of land to proclaim their love for my uncle, like raised hands of allegiance to a flag. But the imagined pennant fluttered over a waste land. We are no more. My people no longer exist in any meaningful sense. We are shadows of what we should have been. The British Empire left us, and another power filled the void and told us we were safe. But our new fealty meant that we could no longer just be Cypriots, we had to be something else.

There were many stories told about my uncle. Some of them were even true. Soldier for the British during World War Two? True. Prize bare-knuckle fighter? Also, true. Member of the TMT resistance movement? As much as the rest of the men in the village. Scourge of the Greek Cypriots? A little fanciful, perhaps. The story was starting to become more complicated. Avenger of the martyred? No, just a reluctant participant. Honest shepherd and fine upstanding member of our community? Despite all the affection I have for the deceased I couldn't check that box for I was the recipient of his confession as he lay dying in hospital. But the day of his funeral was a day for wallowing in our collective nostalgia, not for telling the truth. In today's world who cares for that anyway? So here it was, in death, uncle Ismail was the symbol of better days, of what it was when we had hope, when we stood tall.

There was only one other person who knew the truth about Ismail. And that was Aydin. He was sitting opposite me and smoking his usual Cuban cigar; his eyeliner heightened the impression of a chameleon lounging in the sun as he sat opening and closing his mouth with a smacking of lips as he drew on his Cohiba. He only removed the cigar so he could blow out the rich smoke that mercifully cancelled out the smell of the cheap cigarettes the other men were smoking.

If I was there at all, in that little village on the long finger of Cyprus, the Karpaz as we call it, it was because of him.

Some days I don't know whether I should be grateful to Aydin or not. Until I met this old man, two years before, back in London, I was deliberately unaware of who I was. It's not that I was special or anything. It's just that I was happy to go along being the person my mother, Caroline, and her husband, Hugh Bligh-Smith, had fashioned in their own likeness. Despite the very obvious physical signs to the contrary – green eyes, dark hair, olive complexion, stocky peasant build – I was brought up to think of myself as an Englishman, with all the conceit and handicaps of someone educated at a very minor public school. I had been christened Alexander, which was later abbreviated to 'Sandy' and my family name switched from Aziz to Bligh-Smith. So, on paper there was nothing Cypriot about me. My life until I met Aydin, had been a predictable trajectory of school, university, comfortable well-paying job in a second-tier merchant bank, marriage to a girl from Royal Tunbridge Wells and a few years later, predictably perhaps, a divorce entered into with the same nonchalance as the original walk down the aisle. I accepted that life of mine without a second thought, because I hadn't expected anything more from the world. However, in what was supposed to be a business meeting, this strange man, better known to the City of London as the Chairman of Famagusta Trading Company, recognised not just that we shared the same ethnicity but guessed that I was the son of his long dead friend, Zeki Aziz. So started a long journey that led me to taking a leave of absence from my job and going to Cyprus, to my real father's village; to find out about him and live as a Cypriot. Until that day of the funeral, I thought I knew everything there was to know about Zeki and the world that he grew up in. I liked to tell myself I was a real expert on my father. Quite something for a man who would never have the chance of meeting his genitor.

Drinks were served by the never-ending trayful as a recompense for the time the male funeral guests had spent sweating in line while waiting to pay their respects to my uncle. The women had opted not to join us, out of respect for tradition. Instead, you could see them, with children in tow, wandering around our largely abandoned village of Bamyaköy, peering into the vacant derelict houses through half broken windows and trying to get a glimpse of what life used to be like. For all intents and purposes, they could have been on a day's outing to a historical theme park.

My own role as host, as the senior remaining male in my family, was to make sure that Burak, the coffee shop owner and a cousin of mine – we are almost always cousins over here, the only question being to what degree – maintained the generous flow of rakı and beer until I decided that it was enough. His diligence paid off, for the conversation soon meandered away from my uncle. It went to tales of the civil war, the Greeks, or any of the other martial topics those men like to opine upon. They then turned to another subject they fancy themselves experts upon: women.

'As soon as they get a taste for foreign girls, they're done for...' said one, ruefully and apparently out of the blue. But I knew what he was referring to. As did all the other men. They were now nodding their heads in solemn agreement. Some even sucked their teeth to add emphasis. One blew smoke through his nostrils onto his nicotine-stained moustache. No one looked at me even though I was, in effect, the ultimate subject of the statement. It was not meant unkindly. Not really. But the inference was clear: if my father had not married an English woman, he would not have had the misfortune of being shot in the head. That, at least, was their wishful hypothesis. It never occurred to them to think about my mother, weeks away from giving birth to me, cradling my father in her arms, his skull blown apart, blood pouring onto her dress. No, they never considered that. But I did. By then, at least.

Since I first came to the island to learn about my father, I had thought about that a lot. I had thought about my mother and what she went through. She never spoke to me about that day or her relationship with my father, not in any consequential detail. She had turned the page – for that I don't blame her – and settled into the life that had been rightly hers from the beginning.

I had almost completely tuned out their conversation with my thoughts of her when a faint change of inflection signalled to me that there was something to pay attention to. And I was not the only one who was concentrating at that point. I looked over at Aydin. His eye lids fluttered, stopped, and widened as he heard the comments from another of the men who had, by now, decided to join the conversation: 'Well, it wasn't right him getting her knocked up, was it?'

'And when you think about it, he'd just got married to that posh English woman,' said another.

All the men save for Aydin shook their heads. Only he, of all of them, was now staring at me.

'You know of course, Sandy?' said one of the men to my right, slapping me on the arm.

I nodded although I had no idea what he was talking about.

'So, what happened?' said another.

'Well, they got her married off in a jiffy to some fellow visiting from London. It was just a few weeks after Zeki was killed.'

'That's right, now I remember. He was older than Fatma and had already been living over in England for a few years. A nice man. An accountant or something.'

'If you ask me, if Zeki had waited for Fatma, instead of marrying that English *kadın* he would still be alive today...'

'...and could have been President or something.'

'But what happened to Fatma?'

'Well,' said Turan, the man who had introduced the whole topic. He leant forward and lowered his voice. 'She had the baby in London. Just a few months after Zeki *Bey*'s death. It was a girl. And her husband, Ziya Necati was his name, didn't mind. In fact, what I heard from my wife's cousin who lived near them up in

North London, not only was he a good husband – no fooling about or nothing – but he was head over heels with that little girl. They named her Defne. Nice Turkish name. Apparently, no one would ever have guessed that Ziya wasn't the real father, the way he used to dote on her.'

'So that's it then? Fatma stayed in London with her husband and Zeki's child?'

'Well, not quite.' Turan lowered his voice again. 'I heard she also went on to get all these diplomas and ended up teaching in a university. And after her husband died a few years back she returned to Cyprus but,' he said, scratching his chin with his thumb, his cigarette held between his index and middle finger, 'she's over on the 'other side', teaching at a university in Nicosia'.

There was a sharp intake of breath from the men.

'What, teaching on the Greek side?'

'Yes.'

After confirmation of such treachery there was a dumbfounded silence. From the way they struggled to come to terms with the idea that somebody from our village had gone over to the 'other side' and not even dared to show their face back here after so many years away, you could have been forgiven for thinking someone had invoked the name of the devil.

A little moment later the conversation re-ignited, and they turned their attention to me.

'So, Sandy, you must have met her? What's she like?'

I shook my head. It was my turn to give a dismissive suck of my teeth, like a real native. I forced myself to stay poker-faced. But I could feel the weight of Aydin's gaze upon me. Inside my head, the whole conversation was slowly being replayed and conclusions were dancing around in sickening realisation of a new set of truths. For a moment I couldn't believe what I had just learnt.

These foolish old men were talking about my father in a way that they would never have dared when he was alive. I wanted to lash out. I wanted to shout and tell them to shut up. Could it really be true that my father, the man they all idolised, the one in whose shadow I lived, had cheated on my mother only weeks after getting married? Did she know? If she were to find out, what would she think about him, the young man she was married to so long ago? This disgust was tempered with a second, more intriguing thought: *I have a sibling. I'm not the only child I've always thought myself to be. I have a sibling.*

But pretty soon my ruminations were interrupted by the arrival of Burak. He had one of the funeral guests with him; apparently, he had been asking to meet me. I had noticed him earlier. He was a tall man who, despite being perhaps in his late sixties, or maybe early seventies, stood ramrod straight and looked as powerful and lean as an athlete. His eyes were blue grey and all the more striking because of the contrast with his tanned skin. His salt and pepper moustache, I noticed, was immaculately groomed.

'Here he is, Colonel...' said Burak.

With my peripheral vision I saw Aydin staring at the man. I detected hostility. For a brief moment, I thought I saw a family resemblance, but it was certainly not in the physical shape of the two men. Aydin's face was podgy, powdered, and his blue rinse hair was carefully blow-dried to give volume to the sparse strands that remained. But they had similar noses and cheekbones, and most of all there was something resolute in their gaze.

'I'm sorry, Sandy, for your loss,' said the Colonel. His handshake was too strong, too firm for good manners. I thought of squeezing it back harder, but I was not in the mood for games right then.

I nodded. But said nothing.

'We don't see much of you, young man. You should come and spend some time with us.'

I nodded again to be polite. I had no idea who 'we' and 'us' was – for all I knew it was a regal label that he gave himself – but something in his tone of voice suggested that he was referring to something more.

For my part, I just wanted him to go away. I wanted to go off and find a corner where I could lick my wounds and come to terms with what I had just learnt about my father. Perhaps I should have felt gratitude now that I had discovered that he was not perfect. But I just felt unbearable sadness for my mother. I was not close to her, but there, in that place, on the day of my uncle's funeral, I wanted to put my arms around her and comfort her over a betrayal I hoped she would never discover. And then, of course, I had to come to terms with the fact that I had a sister.

CHAPTER 2

It was this thought, *I have a sister*, that I took with me the next morning as I headed off to the hills behind Bamyaköy. Those early morning excursions were a habit I began in the company of my uncle Ismail – during those first few months I was living in my father's village, trying to learn about him, about my community, about being a Cypriot. I am not sure that we ever shared much of a conversation, the old shepherd and I, except perhaps that last one on his deathbed, in his broken English. Even then, I am not sure that it qualified as conversation. Confession is more accurate, I think. During that last hour I spent sitting next to him in hospital, he said many things. He spoke of his wife, my Aunt Aysel, who had recently died; his eloquence not in the words he chose but in the intonations with which he repeated her name, like a religious chant. The rising and falling octaves of a lifetime of love and closeness. She had been his wife since he married her at sixteen. More than sixty years of life together.

Then, somewhere between a shudder and a sob, he unburdened himself of his guilt at having murdered Aydin's father, Mehmet; for having stolen his sheep; and finally, for having blamed the whole wretched affair on the Greeks of the neighbouring village. He asked if I could make things right for him with Aydin, as if I might have had special powers of intercession. But my poor Uncle Ismail never understood that no one cared about the murder. Least of all, Aydin. Why should he have cared about the killing of a man who used to beat him for not being 'a man'? A man. My God, the stupid things we Turkish Cypriot men spout when we talk about masculinity. In my time in the village, I have been lectured on the concept of manhood until I am sick to death. I have listened to flabby pot-bellied men relate fighting, and sexual prowess with a prostitute, to being a 'real' man – as if Mars and Cupid were the only deities that define our gender.

But the stealing of sheep, and thus depriving a needy family of valuable income, is a sin for which Ismail must surely have paid dearly at his day of judgement – if you believe in such a thing, that is. As indeed he must for blaming the murder on our Greek neighbours. Such a reckless thing to do, yet so plausible back in those days when both communities were at daggers drawn and the internecine killings were starting to happen. After centuries of peace, the imported forces of grandiose, romantic nationalism had come to pollute our little island.

We Cypriots are a simple people, big-hearted emotional people. Strip away linguistic differences – Greek vs Turkish – forget religious affiliations – Christianity vs Islam – and we were, in those dying days, as a minor colony in the British Empire, still 'A People': an ethnic papier mâché of layer upon layer of different DNA, from antiquity to modern times. Minoans, Mycenaeans, Phoenicians, Ptolemaians, Romans, Arabs, Crusaders, Venetians, subjects of the Ottoman empire in all their diversity – and all the many others whose origins and history are scarce recorded. Our love for family, celebrations, traditions, our easy way with foreigners, is what used to unite us as Cypriots. Even today when it comes to language there is sometimes a blurring of lines – with Greek and Turkish spoken in the same breath. Especially up here on the Karpaz where 'Turk' spoke Greek, in some cases as fluently if not more so than the beautiful Ottomanised version of Turkish that is particular to Cyprus. And as for religion, the finer points of doctrine seemed all too often forgotten, with many of the Muslims of Cyprus drinking alcohol with a thirst equal to their Christian compatriots. So, for Ismail to falsely lay blame at the door of a neighbour was to add fuel to the fire. A fire that was starting to consume Cyprus and that would ultimately rip our land apart after the departure of the British in 1960. But it was not my place to judge my uncle. I took him at face value as the man I knew for that short period of time and for the things I learnt from him.

And so, that day after the funeral, I made my way along the narrow flinty paths that are ordinarily the purview of sheep and goats. Because of him I knew where there was fresh spring water to be found. Where to find shade at different points of the sun's arc. I knew where to shelter from wind, from rain. I learnt from him the habits of a shepherd. I carried his heavy stick – not to chivvy along sheep but in case I needed to fight off the pack of feral dogs in whose territory I dared venture. They were the descendants of those who were left to fend for themselves when their owners died or moved away. Their untamed ferocity just another marker of our community's decline. Secured safely in my trouser pocket was my fine American Buck knife. But I freely admit that I only carried it for show. For, unlike my uncle, I did not know, nor did I really care to know how to set a collar for a rabbit, fleece it, cut it, and cook it with wild herbs over a small fire. Having this expensive knife, which doubtless he would have admired out of the corner of his eye, was just me pretending to be somebody else. By this time, after having been in Cyprus all those months, I could see more clearly the disguises I had worn so often in my life.

There was no plan when I had set out, earlier that morning, but my legs carried me up in automatic pilot to what I had christened 'Eagle Rock': for at a distance, I liked to think it resembled the majestic hooked beak of a great bird of prey. Up there I sat my back against the stone. It felt good just to sit there. Below me was the sea, our precious *Akdeniz*, that stretches all the way to Turkey. In the hazy distance I could make out the Taurus mountains. This view should have been enough to calm even the most restless of souls, if only for a moment. It should have been enough to make me think that this beauty was all I needed from life. And perhaps it may even have been true for my uncle. But that day, I was overcome by a strange feeling – a mixture of anguish, uncertainty, fear, regret, anger. This unsettling cocktail of emotions was of course triggered by the previous day's discovery that I had a sibling. That I was not alone. With all that it implied for me and for others, both the living and the dead.

That fact, for I assumed that it was thus – for no other reason than by then I wanted it to be true – felt like the final unravelling of who I once thought I was. Three years before I was safely cocooned in the assumptions and perceptions forged since my childhood. I had been unquestioning about my identity. But within a year I had met Aydin. It was he who forced me to confront the truth of who and what I really was. With this latest revelation at the funeral, I felt like I had taken one step further and been thrown into a void where I must examine the details of my solitary childhood. I saw it all so clearly, how my mother and stepfather fashioned me as if I was made from clay, into some rough figurine approximating an Englishman. An effigy they infused with all the snobbishness of the British upper middle classes. They gave me a religion different to my father's and, without thinking, turned me into an apostate. Until I came to Cyprus, my unquestioning and easy acceptance of the Church of England had posed no existential problem for me – but that was soon replaced by a profound unease. I used to wonder what my father would make of his son's lukewarm practice of religion in the Anglican Church; the religion of our British colonisers. Sometimes, I like to think that as a devotee of the great Atatürk and all the secular values he brought to Turkey, he wouldn't have minded. But religion is a touchy subject and you never know how people will react.

I had built walls around myself for so long, to protect me, to hide who I was from the world. But all of a sudden, now, there rose the possibility that there was another person out there like me, of the same father, maybe somebody with whom I could let down my guard.

But then I thought: *What if I don't like her? What if she has some strange and disturbing habits that I can't abide? What if we have nothing in common? What if she doesn't want anything to do with me – just as I'm preparing to open up and make myself vulnerable?*

As those questions went through my mind, I felt conscious of the presence of another person, as if they were standing behind me.

It happened to me often in Cyprus – not just when I was out in the hills surrounding Bamyaköy but when I went to my father's old house. It was not something spooky or scary. I don't know how to describe it. I want to say it was like the presence of an angel, but that is of little use as a description if you don't believe in them. Let me try different words: when it happened, a sense of solemnity and weight filled the air and enveloped me.

The identity of that other 'person', if he were more than just a wishful thought, was not a mystery to me. It was, of course, my father. Had he come to check in on his son? Was he there to guide me? To comfort me? Was he leading me to my sister? Encouraging me? Foolishness, but…

I looked around as quickly as I could. In the hope that maybe, just this once, I would catch him, catch a glimpse of the young man who had been my father. He too must have walked this way, herding his family's flock of sheep from one sparse clump of grass to another. But as usual I drew a blank. The same disappointment that always came over me. Then came the petulant anger and bitterness – why could he not have tried harder to reach out to me? I forgot in those moments that we can expect nothing from the dead.

The mid-morning light came flooding back into my consciousness. And for a moment the hot air was cooled by a saline breeze coming up from the sea. I found myself calmed and I felt a certainty that everything would be alright; that it was only right for me to go and find my sister. But I would need help. And there was only one person I could turn to.

CHAPTER 3

He didn't say anything for a long while. A chunk of ash fell from his cigar onto his lemon-yellow trousers, and he let out a sigh. I wasn't sure whether it was prompted by the grey smudge on his knee or because of what he considered to be the absurdity of my request.

I was sitting opposite him on the wooden veranda of his newly built colonial style mansion, up on the crest of the hill above Bamyaköy. This perfectly chosen location had a view of the sea on one side and the valley, that leads to Malatya, on the other. Next to him sat his personal assistant and live-in companion, Frankie. To all intents and purposes, she was engrossed with knitting a child's sweater. She didn't break the cadence of the clicking needles when I asked Aydin for his help in finding my sister.

In the eternity it took him to answer me, I looked around, taking in every detail of my surroundings. Everywhere there seemed to be highly polished wood. I think he told me that his architect had taken inspiration from the home of a famous American clothes designer. Although the house would not have looked out of place on the pages of a magazine, up there on the Karpaz, where the summer sun was so harsh and low stone houses were the norm, the carefully nurtured teak and high ceilings looked incongruous. But that was not something to bother Aydin. And perhaps by that time I had gone a little native in my perceptions.

Before he spoke, the only sounds were the whirring of the big wooden fan above us in its feeble albeit elegant attempt to cool us down, and the metronomic clicking of Frankie's knitting needles. I remembered he had once told me that he had been inspired to build a place "back home" after meeting me, Zeki's son. It had made him think it was time to return to the island, to have a place to come to in the summers and escape from London every now and again. Why he had not been back home in more than forty years, he never explained. In the past, when I had pressed him on this, he changed the subject. Just as I turned my mind to his relationship with Frankie – Francesca, in reality – he cleared his throat, took a sip of rum from the tumbler next to him and said more gently than I expected, '*Oğlum*, I understand why you might want to do this, but don't think it will be easy. And think about the impact on her. Just because you want to find her doesn't mean that she wants to be found by you.'

The idea that my own flesh and blood would not want to meet me seemed inconceivable.

'I can't not do this, Aydin. I have to believe that my sister would want to meet her brother.'

He looked at me over the end of his cigar and said, 'Well then, I'll take you to see her mother. I've not seen the girl in years. Not since before Zeki died and the Greeks attacked the village.' He counted on his fingers and said, 'She must be sixty-four or five now. You know, they wanted to marry her off to your father. And believe me he thought about it. She was the cleverest girl in the village. But she was too young. Would you believe they offered her to him when she was fourteen? Her mum and dad were good people. Now, let me try and remember… what were their names? Kemal and Bessie, that's right. Hard working decent people they were. And they had lots of land. I wonder what happened to all those fields of theirs? Anyway, no matter… you see Fatma was an only child. But in any event, your dad convinced her parents to keep her in school. It was a shame really. It would have been a good match.'

'Was she pretty, Aydin?'

'Well…?' As he hesitated, I saw Frankie look up from her knitting and give him a smile. And for a moment the clicking stopped.

'Come on, you must be able to tell me something.'

'Seriously? She was fine looking. Quite tall compared to the other girls. Long legs. Dark hair. And like so many of us from this village, she had big beautiful green eyes. You know that don't you?'

'What?'

'In the village we have two distinguishing features. First, unlike most Cypriots, the majority of us have green eyes. Your dad always used to say it was proof that we were descended from the Crusaders or something. God bless him, he was always talking about our history.' He stopped, took a gulp of his rum and looked into the distance. His eyes were bloodshot and rheumy.

'And the second thing?' I said.

'What?'

'You said we had two distinguishing features.'

'Oh yes… right.' He grunted. 'She knows,' he said, motioning his head towards Frankie. 'Go on, love, show him what I mean.'

'He doesn't want to see your ugly feet, Aydin.'

'Of course he does. Go on, show him.'

To my surprise, she got on all fours and pulled off the black slip-on shoe from his right foot. And then she peeled off his thin pale blue cotton sock to reveal a broad pudgy foot. He wiggled his neatly pedicured toes for my benefit and pointed to his small toe. It was slightly shrunk and curved in awkwardly. I looked at him. 'Are you sure this defect is common to the village?'

'As God is my witness, son.'

He could have been right for I had exactly the same deformity. As had my aunt. And, apparently, as had my father.

CHAPTER 4

There is a border for us to cross in our own land. No sea, no mountain range separates us; instead, men have built two lines of white metal barriers, splitting our tiny island in two. And between these barriers, which each side decorates with their own flag, and a second flag that proudly proclaims allegiance to somewhere else, Greece in one case, Turkey in the other, there is a no man's land. It is made up of barbed wire, pock-marked buildings, and the sky-blue huts of the UN forces who have a mission to keep us Cypriots – 'Greeks' and 'Turks' – from breaking out into schoolyard fights.

A few days after our discussion about finding Defne, we found ourselves at the border, ready to make the crossing to the 'South', in reality no more than a few hundred metres or so from where we were having breakfast – supposedly to fortify ourselves. But Aydin did not touch his food. In front of him, the slices of squeaky white halloumi, pink watermelon wedges, small torpedo like cucumbers, bright red tomatoes, peeled boiled eggs, sesame covered soft bread rolls, butter and jam, remained listlessly untouched. His tea had gone cold. The spoon was still standing in the miniature tulip-shaped cup. He had not bothered to stir in the sugar cube that had long since fallen to the bottom and settled like sediment on the seabed. He just sat without talking, puffing away at one of his beloved Hoyo Epicure #2s. One of his "short smokes" as he liked to refer to them. It was his second since we had arrived at Hamur.

This little restaurant was famous on Trip Advisor for serving fine Turkish breakfasts, and richly-filled meat and cheese puff pastries for the rest of the day. Drinks on its neat little patio under the protection of a giant orange awning, were just another reminder of our island's tragic past. Once, it would have been an elegant family home built during the British mandate. It sat on a street that goes past the once glamorous Ledra Palace Hotel – now boarded up with plywood and metal protection – and on towards the Armenian cemetery. But it will never be a residential street again. Too many guns have been fired, too much destruction, too much hatred has seeped into the pores of every stone, brick and piece of mortar. The restaurant was close to the taxi rank, which itself sat next to the border control-post. At all times of day, a steady flow of pedestrians with business on one side or the other hurried past, haunted by the walk through that strip of ghost land. We should have been going, but I sensed that something other than our cross-border excursion was weighing on his mind.

I had long since finished my share of the breakfast and was scrolling through messages on my Blackberry. Nothing much of interest: word from a few friends who occasionally enquired after me, or general invitations to an art gallery showing. So, what I was doing was for show, to allow Aydin time for his thoughts. Then he broke the silence and said, 'Do you know why we came to this specific crossing point, Sandy?'

'No,' I shrugged my shoulders. To me it didn't matter one jot which crossing we used but I was aware that in Lefkoşa there were three possibilities to get to the Greek side, to what is better known in English as Nicosia: one – by car, if we had the right paperwork, and two – on foot. I looked up from my screen and around the restaurant in case the clue might be staring me in the face. But nothing was immediately obvious.

Aydin reached into his pocket and drew out a substantial wad of cash, held firmly together by a Hermès silver money clip – the H very much in evidence. He peeled out a few notes – more than enough to settle the bill plus a generous tip – and laid them down on the table. He secured them from the wind with his cup of tea and then slowly stood up, his joints cracking out loud. 'Come Sandy, come for a walk with me first. There is something I want to show you.'

Instead of heading to the Turkish checkpoint we turned right into a quiet residential street. There was little sound except for the distant noise of traffic, the tapping of Aydin's walking stick on the chipped pavement, and his laborious wheezing. Eventually we came to a piece of wasteland.

At first all I could see in the foreground were piles of bricks, empty rusting cans, and a dozen piles of dog faeces in different degrees of decomposition. 'Aydin, are you sure you meant for us to come this way?'

He pointed his walking stick to the corner of the plot of land. And there I saw the remains of a building. Possibly, it had been a large villa once upon time. There was a hole through the roof as if it had received a direct hit from an artillery shell. Its once whitewashed walls were scarred and disfigured with ugly graffiti in at least three languages. We carefully made our way through the high grass until we came to the steps. On the ground was a faded peeling sign, perforated with bullet holes. I could make out some letters. I reached down, picked it up and brushed it clean with the side of my hand. It read, 'Nikki's'.

'Do you know this place Aydin?' I turned and looked at him. To my surprise tears were coming down his cheeks. Big glycerine-like drops. He tried to motion to the side of the building, but hardly had the energy to lift his hand. I stepped forward and saw that rubble had buried a staircase going down. As I peered over the detritus, I saw that, at the bottom, there had once been an entrance into what looked like a vast underground area.

'Aydin what was this place?'

He took a long breath, exhaled, and said, 'It was the last place that Tassos was happy. I haven't been back here in more than fifty years.'

'Tassos?' I said the name as gently as I could, for I had noticed the tone of reverence that he used. I was concerned that the slightest of missteps would plunge him back into his sorrow. I was not used to seeing him like this. Aydin, always the tough man, even in his femininity. Always the brawler; the shrewd trader by all accounts. But here was someone else. In that light, the lines of his face had tightened, and I saw a younger man, no less sorrowful, but a glimpse of what he might have looked like.

'Who was Tassos?' I asked again.

'The man I loved *oğlum*...' His voice choked as he spoke.

This was the first time he said something that I had guessed at long ago. Since our first meeting two years before. Not that he particularly hid from me who he was, but here it was, out in the open.

'Tell me, what happened.'

He shook his head. Not in the manner of someone saying no. But as if he was trying to shake off the pain, the bad memory. 'It was a place for people like us. There was nowhere else for us to go and have a good time. We came here to have fun and be safe.' He wiped his cheeks with a silk handkerchief. 'In those days, I was working all the time. You know it was my first proper business – I had a pastry shop, with display cabinets full of fresh *baklava*, and I was going to open another.' For a moment his voice recovered some of its usual confidence and the young man I glimpsed in his face a few moments ago was back. I saw him, as he was, on the cusp of success, with all his vitality and ambition to make something of himself pumping through his veins. 'Anyway, Tassos wanted me to take a break and told me about this place. We didn't have a car or anything like that. We had to catch the Saturday afternoon bus from Famagusta to here. Sandy, you can't imagine what it was like for someone like me, from Bamyaköy, to come somewhere like this. The music, the dancing, the men having fun. No one cared if you were 'Greek' or 'Turkish'. There were even Tommies. You know we had so many of them in those days – over for their National Service. You can imagine what a cushy posting this was for them. So much better than Malaya, Kenya or anywhere else the British were involved with back then. Even when those EOKA fellows started on them. But anyway, you won't believe it now,' as he said this, he patted his stomach. 'Tassos even got me to dance a little.' He laughed for a moment and then looked down at the ground. 'You know, Sandy, I imagined I could have an establishment like this. Right there and then I started working out all the money they were making. It was so exciting to think of the profit they were raking in… and then…' He sobbed, his chest heaving. He wiped his nose and eyes with the cuff of his yellow linen jacket leaving a trail of wet mucus. 'And then, the police came and beat everyone up with sticks before carting us off to a police station way out on the outskirts of Nicosia. That's when I made the worst mistake of my life.'

'What did you do?'

'I spoke out against the policeman in charge. He cottoned on to the fact that Tassos was with me and that I had a bit more money than the others. He took us away to the cells…' His face creased with pain. He was no longer with me. His mind was fixed on flickering images of the past, but he came to and started to speak again. 'The next day…' he paused for a single gasping breath.

'Come on let's walk, Aydin.'

He shook his head. 'No, you might as well hear it.' I reached out for his hand, but he pulled back. His whole body was quaking. 'Next day, his sprit was completely gone – all that was beautiful and lovely about him… they took it from him. The policeman in charge did terrible things to Tassos right there in front of me. They'd chained me to the walls. I closed my eyes but I could hear it all.' Aydin reached up and wiped his eyes again. 'Trust me, I got the better of that policeman in the end. But it was never going to bring my beautiful boy back. A few days after the prison thing, Tassos hanged himself.' Aydin looked up at me. Now his gaze was defiant. 'So now you know about old Aydin.'

I wanted to say something like 'thank you', but the words

seemed silly and inadequate, so I just stood next to him in silence.

After a few minutes he said, 'If you're ready, *oğlum*, let's go and find Fatma.'

CHAPTER 5

It was Aydin's first time inside a university. At first, what worked for him elsewhere worked for him there: a twenty euro note peeled from his money clip and slipped into the palm of the security guard at the entrance of the Kallipoleos campus of the University of Cyprus bought us our own tour guide. However, as we were led through the maze of the different faculties – Applied Sciences, Social Sciences, Engineering, Economics, Letters – he fell silent. He seemed timid, almost. I saw his lips moving as if he was reading each and every sign to himself, slowly, so as to make sure he understood correctly what was written. Occasionally, some of the female students turned to look at him and giggled as they walked by. But mostly, they rushed past, paying us no mind. I noticed his gaze lingering on some of the young men. He tried smiling at them, but he was of an age where such acts of charm no longer worked. If they had stopped to look at him, they would not have imagined in their wildest dreams that they were the grandsons of men he went to war against. They might have thought of him as some soft creature, an object of ridicule. I reached out for his forearm. Ostensibly to guide him but somehow, however clumsily, I wanted to give him some comfort, some solidarity.

Finally, we made it to the Faculty of Humanities. Our tour guide, the security guard, Mr Andreas, had become Aydin's friend. He was chatting away happily explaining to us about all the distinguished professors who taught at the university. He stopped at the faculty office and spoke in hushed tones to one of the secretaries there. We saw her pick up the receiver. She uttered some words in Greek, then turned back towards us and nodded her head at Mr Andreas. He led us towards the lifts and took us up to the Department of Turkish and Middle Eastern Studies. We found ourselves in a nondescript corridor with bare brick walls. The only hint of colour came from the odd poster held up by Blu Tack. In silence, we followed behind the security guard until he finally stopped in front of one of the office doors. The name plate read: Dr Fatma Necati.

Aydin stepped forward and knocked on the door, but I thought that he did it too fast, too loud, like a hotel worker making sure the coast was clear to enter a guest's room. This was not how Aydin, the CEO and Chairman of Famagusta Trading LLC, should be conducting himself I thought to myself.

A woman's voice gave us leave to enter. For a moment, I wondered if she thought we were students come to petition her.

He turned the aluminium handle and walked in. His frame filled the doorway. I followed him in.

'Fatma… *nasılsın*… do you remember me?' he said warmly.

She did not get up to greet us. She stayed sitting behind her desk and looked Aydin up and down until eventually she said, 'Yes, I do. *İyiyim, siz?*' My rudimentary Turkish was enough to notice that she had responded to his informal use of 'you' with the formal version used for strangers and officials. I wondered if he had noticed too.

If he had, he gave no sign of it and said cheerily, 'I can't complain.'

'So, what have you been up to all these years? Still selling *baklava*?' Before he had the chance to respond, she continued. 'How long has it been?'

I noticed that Aydin's eyes hardened a little. 'It's been since Zeki died. You were still a teenager back then. You haven't forgotten him, surely?'

There was not the least flicker of emotion at the mention of my father's name. Instead, she said, 'Yes, you're right, that must have been it. I married soon after and moved to London.'

'And I haven't sold *baklava* in a long time. I left behind the bakery and coffee shop after that business at the enclave.'

'Yes, I heard that you were quite the hero, although...' and here she paused for a moment, 'there were some strange stories about you.' She raised an eyebrow in a quizzical fashion as if she was expecting him to elucidate.

Aydin ignored this and motioned his hand towards her bookshelves. 'So you're a teacher?'

'I'm a university professor.'

'Well, that's good. Especially for a girl from Bamyaköy. Your mum and dad must have been proud. And Erol, the schoolteacher – remember him? – he and his wife Zainab would have been proud of you too.'

'You didn't hear about my parents, Aydin?'

'No, what happened to them?'

'They were killed in reprisal for the raid against Avrigadou? You must remember what happened at Avrigadou, Aydin? Surely you of all people must remember that?'

'Yes, I remember that, Fatma,' he said slowly. There was coldness to his tone now. I saw her drop her eyes from his gaze. There was something that I had never seen before in his look – pure and utter menace. I think I may even have shivered a little. 'But...' he continued, 'I am sorry about your mother and father. I didn't know. You know what led up to Avrigadou? What they did to Erol and to the others? Surely you haven't forgotten what Erol did for you and all the other girls in the village?' His voice grew louder. But then he took a deep breath, regained control of his emotions and, in a lighter tone of voice said, 'I haven't come to talk about the past. No, I wanted to introduce Zeki's son to you.'

All this time, she had not looked at me once. Now she turned her gaze towards me. Her face was unsmiling. Her eyes looked like little dull green pebbles.

In the absence of anything better to say, I said, 'Hello, my name is Sandy, Sandy Bligh-Smith. Pleased to meet you.' I leant across her desk to shake her hand, but she did not move. Instead, she just looked at my outstretched arm as if I had committed some great impertinence.

'Why should I wish to meet Zeki's son?' she said, turning back to Aydin.

Instead of answering her question Aydin said, almost desperately, 'He's really posh, really well educated. You know he used to be one of those fancy investment bankers.' I was touched by his sense of pride in me. I hadn't realised that he felt that way.

'Aydin, why should I wish to meet this man?'

'Well because…'

'Because I think your daughter might be my sister. Well, my half-sister. And I would like to meet her.' Judging by the look of horror on her face I realised that I had completely made a mess of things.

'What are you talking about?'

I couldn't retreat so I said, 'I heard that maybe your daughter is also my father's child.'

Behind her I saw a silver-framed colour photograph. It was of a woman with dark curly hair and big green eyes; a broad forehead and high cheekbones. In the picture, she was laughing. I was sure that I could see a resemblance with me. I was convinced that this was indeed my sister. I scrutinised every inch of the image. There was something familiar about the backdrop of the photograph. There were trees, and a tarmac covered path that led towards a large red brick building with huge white chimneys. It dawned upon me that she was standing in Battersea Park, only a few minutes from where I had lived much of my life. The Thames must be to her left, outside the camera's field of vision. And, if I had it right, the photograph was taken just beyond the Peace Pagoda.

'Only you know, Fatma,' said Aydin softly breaking the silence that had overcome the three of us.

I pointed to the photograph, but Fatma did not turn her head. 'I would like to meet her. She lives in London, right? If you could just tell me her whereabouts. That's all.'

'Out of the question. I don't know who you have been speaking to, but I don't want to hear another word about this. Now, please leave.'

I tried one last time. 'Look Fatma, I lost my father before I was born. I never knew him. I have spent my whole life trying to be someone I am not. I am done with that now. If your daughter is my sister, then she never knew her real father either. But at least give us the chance to know each other. At least let us be brother and sister. Please. I am not here to judge what you did with my father. I just want to meet my sister.'

She turned to Aydin and then back to me. There was a look of revulsion in her eyes. Then she picked up the receiver of her desk phone and said, 'Athena, call security please.'

CHAPTER 6

I was torn between staying in Cyprus and returning to London where I would properly be able to start the search for my sister. And more than that, start to find something meaningful to do with my life again. Over the previous weeks, I had become increasingly prey to a nagging sense that there, in the village, I was going soft, succumbing to the easiness of 'island life' – as I was starting to refer to it in my private monologues.

But Cyprus is a hard place to leave. It drives you mad at first with its heat, humidity, mosquitoes, and the haphazard, shambolic, nature of life – where nothing seems to get planned or properly organised. Then slowly you become inured to all that. Something else takes over. It is the beauty of the landscape, the daily changing contrasts of sky and sea against pastel beige rolling hills and outcrops. It is the smells that change throughout the day. In the early morning, it is the fresh breeze coming up across the olive and almond groves. Midmorning, the iodine tang of the sea. By afternoon, wood burning ovens cooking bread and roasting meats. And then, at nightfall, the heavy air that is full of jasmine and bougainvillea. Then there are the people... big-hearted, generous, always ready with a smile and laughter. For all these reasons, I dreaded the thought of returning to London and giving up what I had come to love. So, I put it off without a fixed date in mind.

I told myself that I could begin trying to find Defne from where I was. No need to return to England just yet. I could also take more time to think about what I wanted to do with my life. I was lucky, I thought, that I was sheltered from financial cares. Twenty years in investment banking had allowed me to put together a substantial investment portfolio – not counting my nest egg of shares and stock options in Braithwaite & Wilkins, my erstwhile employer, from whom I had taken a leave of absence – one that had long since expired.

However, if I was postponing my return to London, Aydin certainly wasn't.

'Some of us have businesses to run,' he grunted between mouthfuls of charcoal-grilled seabass. We were sitting in my favourite restaurant, *Kemal Hussein Lokantası*, in my favourite place on the whole island, the hidden cove below the little town of Dipkarpaz. Nowhere else in Cyprus, and perhaps nowhere else on earth, could be as perfect as that place. Yet all Aydin wanted to do was talk to me about business. If I remember correctly, he wanted my advice on optimising his balance sheet. But I wanted none of that. I just wanted to enjoy the moment, and being where we were.

As restaurants go it was not much to look at: stone floor, wood beams, long sliding window panels that opened directly over a sheer little cliff. The tables had checked tablecloths, and each one carried a white plastic napkin dispenser, a bottle of olive oil and matching salt and pepper shakers.

But the experience of the 'restaurant' did not start with the restaurant itself. It started miles back, if you know how to look, and detect the signs of past empires, that is. For alongside the potholed tarmac road that makes its way along up the finger of Cyprus, the Karpaz, to its very tip, there is another road hidden in the sands. It is the one built by Roman legions – the greatest of all our colonisers. After a while, it bifurcates, leaving the modern road to make its way up the hill. The ancient one, rather more sensibly for the traveller, contours the curves of the terrain and leads you through a magical landscape of bamboo groves, dried out streams and fallen trees until, at last, it arrives at another milestone of our history: the grottoes carved out of the hills by early Christians. Hideouts safe from the rampages of pagans and pirates. The entrances to these dwellings look down on you like so many dead eyes. It takes a brave man to look back up at them. But when finally, you have shuffled past this hidden encampment, another more beautiful vestige awaits you. Two churches lie side by side; one completely broken and open to the sky and the elements, revealing only mosaic floor and the outline of an altar. Historians have dated this Byzantine structure to the Fifth Century; a few years after the Council of Nicaea and the beginning of established and codified Christianity. Its sister, older by five or six centuries, still has a little roof left. Burnt candles and empty match boxes on the ground suggest that from time to time it is still used as a place of worship. Indeed, there is much of God's creation to worship here. Stepping out from the shadows and the shade of the church through the side door, you see the restaurant.

It is all alone on a small peninsular of its own, next to the churches, and three palm trees – invariably swaying in the wind, the most perfect weathervanes. Yet it has one more surprise for the hungry guest. Below its perch, the trained eye can make out the outline of a Roman harbour. A dreamer can spend a happy moment imagining the comings and goings of flat-hulled boats and all the trading activities of antiquity, while his host grills seabass or grouper cooked on the open charcoal fireplace in the kitchen for his delight. Before the fish arrives, he will be served with meze and a large plate of freshly sliced salad drenched in pomegranate dressing. The salad will be bright from carrots, red cabbage, beetroot and tomatoes. Only one further item will be served: a bowl of chips cut by hand from the Cyprus potato. 'Chip' sounds so banal and may conjure images of mass-produced offerings but those made from our potatoes are a gastronomic delight of an altogether higher order – so crispy and golden is the outer skin, and so fluffy inside. The taste of that transformed potato is that of Cyprus. Of home.

But Aydin would not be deterred from talking about his businesses. 'When you're back in London, I want you to come over to meet me again, properly. I want you to look at my company's books. Tell me what you think. See if I should be doing something more.'

I nodded my head agreeably, but I didn't really want to get involved with his businesses. In any event, the subject lapsed, and we turned to talking about my sister, my father, the past. Always the past, in Cyprus.

CHAPTER 7

My investigations and attempts to locate my sister drew a blank. Of course, I was not working with much. Just a name: Defne Necati. And I was still trying to do it from Cyprus. In my frustration, I began a hunt for a suitable private investigator. I found one online, a Martin Erickson. He said he had experience in this field so I gave him the details, as best I could. A girl of Turkish Cypriot parents probably born in London in 1965. I wired him the first part of his retainer fee and he promised to report to me in a month's time, at the end of September.

I was glad to have given this problem over to someone else for I was starting to worry more and more about the state of the stock market. Something strange was afoot. Nothing was being said openly in the media, but as I read the FT and watched the BBC and CNN business programmes, courtesy of Aydin's satellite dish, I could feel a certain tension creeping into the banking world. CEOs of big banks seemed to be working particularly hard at reassuring the investment community that everything was fine. Consumer spending was good, house prices were still on the increase. The pundits were still talking with excitement about emerging markets – Brazil, Russia, India and China. The slogan bandied about by the media was 'Shanghai, Mumbai, Dubai or goodbye.' But none of this made sense to me and I realised how far away I was from the heart of the action and, worse, that I was getting old by City standards and out of tune with what was going on. I tried to call a few chums back in London to find out, but nobody seemed to know anything. And then it happened.

Over one weekend, Lehman Brothers went bankrupt. All hell broke loose. On Monday morning, September 15, there was a blood bath. As hard as I tried, I couldn't get out of any of my investment positions. By the end of that day, my stock market portfolio was down by twenty per cent. I was desperately hoping for a rally. But none came. By the end of the following week, I was down eighty per cent on my investments. In some cases, there was absolutely no chance that I would ever recoup my losses. Many of the companies in which I owned shares had gone bankrupt. But worse was still to come. The following week, I learnt that Braithwaite & Wilkins had folded. All those years of hard work and ambition had gone up in smoke. My stock options and shares in my former employer were now worthless. I was, in effect, insolvent. I had a few thousand pounds in my deposit account, though certainly not enough to make my alimony payments in the months ahead nor my mortgage instalments. I felt profoundly ashamed. All of a sudden, I was a failure. My narcissistic little journey into finding about my father and my roots was over. I didn't explain to anybody around me why I had to leave Cyprus in such haste.

After I finished booking my flight back to Heathrow, I received an email from Erickson. He had an update for me. Apparently, he had found a record of a Defne Necati attending Hornsey School for Girls, in the 1970s and early 1980s. Certainly, the school dates added up, as did the neighbourhood – for that is where so many London Turkish Cypriots lived, and still live today. I should have felt some brief elation that he had found something apparently so tangible about my sister. But it only added to my depression. For as I was by then bankrupt, I couldn't see how I could face her.

I arrived back in London on a Wednesday, the first day of October. The weather was dull and overcast. Already this was enough for me to miss the vivid colours of Cyprus. When I entered my apartment, I did not feel the same sense of familiarity and ownership that I had before. I felt like an imposter. Perhaps it was because I knew that at some point in the near future it would be repossessed, and I would be homeless. But that was a problem for another day.

I unpacked and tried to make some sense of what had happened during my absence. I looked around trying to see what was not right. It was spotlessly clean. So, I couldn't complain that the cleaning lady had not been doing her job. My mail was neatly stacked in piles on the living room table. Nothing for me to worry about there – they were all settled by standing order. As I flicked through the envelopes, month by month, I didn't see anything personal. Not even a birthday or Christmas greeting. I told myself that it was just a sign of the times. The personal handwritten note was dead. It was all email or BBM messenger by then. Mostly, the letters that I sliced open were of a promotional or informational nature. After a while I gave up and threw them all in the bin.

I looked in my wardrobe. There, hanging in front of me, was an array of suits – all either grey or blue – a dinner jacket for the opera and club functions, a blazer with brass buttons. On the shelves were stacks of double-cuffed white shirts; drawers of white boxer shorts and black knee length socks. My suitcase from Cyprus was open on the bed, revealing neat piles of white T-shirts, blue jeans, khaki shorts and an assortment of Tod's loafers and canvas sneakers. My lack of originality in work and leisure dress had never before been so obvious to me.

Thankfully my bathroom still had some of my favourite Moulton Brown black pepper shower gel. The towels were ready for use. In an hour, the water was hot enough for a shower. I still had some creature comforts.

The kitchen cupboards were empty except for a glass jar of spaghetti, some tins of sardines and a packet of lentils. My wine rack had a few bottles of red left. I opened one of the Côtes du Rhone and went to sit in the living room. At least the bookshelves there gave me some comfort. My books were as I had left them, lovingly classified by subject, by author, save the for the biographies and autobiographies – those went from C for Camus by Olivier Todd, to L for Primo Levi by Carole Angier, to S for Stalin by Stephen Kotkin. The wine and contemplation of the books soothed me. I put on a CD from my classical music section. At random, I chose a selection of Schubert sonatas. But the melancholy of his 'Twentieth in A' set me on edge again. Over and above my fears about the future, something felt wrong. It was not until my third glass of wine that the real problem dawned on me. I was what was wrong. My skin was now darker and had thickened by being outdoors so much. Whereas I once had smooth, soft hands, I now had calluses and splits in my nails. The apartment was not meant for the son of Zeki Aziz. It was meant for that other person, the Sandy one. The one whose name I now hated more than anything. I needed to acclimatise, I told myself. Get used to London. And when I was back on my feet, I would find my sister. I debated opening a second bottle of wine but instead I went and lay on my bed and fell asleep in my clothes.

Chapter 8

'Sandy, how are you?' I could hear from Aydin's voice that he was in a good mood.

It was 23 November and, had he been alive, it would have been my father's birthday. I was feeling anything but joyful.

I tried not to let him hear how I was feeling so I said, 'I'm all right Aydin. Just considering my options.'

'Didn't that posh bank you used to work for want you back?'

I knew he was aware that Braithwaite & Wilkins had gone bankrupt because he would have seen it in the FT, which he read assiduously six days a week.

'No, Aydin. I'm looking for a job.'

'Well listen, don't be so down in the dumps. There is something I want to discuss with you. In fact, I had been expecting you to call me.'

'Discuss what?'

'You come and join me for dinner, and we can talk face to face. See you at Bibendum at 7 p.m.'

So it was that, a few of hours later, I was sitting opposite Aydin at his favourite restaurant. He didn't seem to notice that it was deserted. Life was, apparently, as normal for him. He ordered a Puligny Montrachet to accompany the lobsters he ordered for us both. In fact, he chose the whole meal and even refused my request to take a look at the menu.

Pretty soon he ordered a second bottle. And each time my glass was filled I downed it in three gulps.

I thought the lobster was all we were going to eat but there was more to come. To follow the first course, he had ordered Britanny rabbit along with a bottle of Château-Neuf-du-Pape. I went slower on the wine.

'So, what's up with you?' He said at last.

I shook my head. I didn't want to be a cry-baby and whinge about my troubles in front of him.

'Well, you look a bit glum, if you don't mind my saying.'

I watched him forking rabbit into his mouth and then, exasperated, I broke my silence. 'How the hell can you sit there so calmly when everything is falling apart?'

'Is it? Don't be silly, son.'

'Haven't you been following the news?' I think by now I must have been slurring my words.

Aydin lifted his head and raised an eyebrow at me. 'Oh, you don't want to be worrying about any of that.'

I took another gulp of wine. 'Well, I am. I've lost everything.' And there, out loud, I had admitted my failure, my humiliation.

He stopped, fork poised, ready to shovel its contents into his mouth. 'What, everything?' The question sounded like he was accusing me of having been careless. 'That's not good, *oğlum*. So, what are you going to do?'

'Well, I'll probably have to go back and live with my mother and her husband, Hugh...'

'Well, that's all right then. At least you won't be out on the street.'

'Aydin, I'm forty-three years old and facing the prospect of having to live with my parents again.' I took yet another gulp of wine and put the glass down harder than I intended. It was empty again. I knew Aydin had noticed this. But there was a half-smile on his face. He called over to the waiter to refill both our glasses.

When the waiter left, Aydin took his napkin from his lap and wiped his lips. 'Listen, Sandy my boy. There's something I have been wanting to discuss with you for some time. Only you haven't wanted to hear me out. This time you are going to listen.'

I looked at him. And now I could see that he had his serious face on. His business face. His voice was as sharp as if he had been drinking orange juice all evening.

'I want you to come and work for me.'

The penny dropped. At that precise moment, I knew that he had been planning this for a while and had just been waiting for the right moment. And, of course, he had timed it perfectly. I was desperate for a job but, nevertheless, for the sake of my pride, I tried some half-hearted resistance. 'Me, Aydin? Thank you, I'm flattered but what do I know about your kind of businesses?'

'Don't be such an idiot, Sandy. Business is business. You buy cheap, you sell expensive. And my businesses are good businesses. Cash businesses. And now's our time. We can make a fortune. Listen, I have a plan. And I think you can make it better.'

CHAPTER 9

From: Fatma Necati

To: Daphne Neil

My darling Defne,

I hope you are well and making good progress with your latest novel.

I thought I should let you know that someone might try and contact you and want to meet. A few months ago – I have hesitated to write to you about this – two men came to see me in my office at the university. The older of the two was someone I knew a very long time ago from Bamyaköy. He was – how should I put it – even back then, a very strange person. The man who was with him is about your age. A bit lost, it seemed to me. Anyway, they seem to have got some strange ideas into their heads about you. If either of them should reach out, I suggest that you ignore them. Of course, I said nothing about who you are or what you do but I have a feeling that they will try quite hard. Don't worry I don't think they are dangerous, just a bit delusional.

Anyway, I will try to come back to London at Christmas so that we can spend the holidays together.

Take care Defne. Very proud of you.

Love, Mum.

CHAPTER 10

At first, Aydin didn't want to talk about his plan. But I could see that he had carefully thought through my initiation to his businesses and how he intended to make use of me initially.

The first task he gave me was to sort out his financial investments. Before finally agreeing to take this on, I reminded him how badly I had done with my own. He just shrugged his shoulders and said, 'Well you won't make the same mistakes twice, now will you?' He must have seen me looking doubtful, so he continued. 'Son, I trust you. You'll get it right this time. Don't worry. You'll look at things differently now. I promise. After all you've been through. Not just this crisis but the past couple of years…' I didn't know what he saw in me, but I was determined to do the best I could and repay his faith.

When I finally dug into his investments, I saw that he had a good quality portfolio. Their details and market valuations were kept in a leather-bound ledger that Frankie updated weekly with a silver propelling pencil, using data from the FT's Companies and Markets section. Admittedly, he had lost a bit in the crash, but far less than most people. Apart from equities, he had quite a few UK Gilts, precious metals – gold mostly, from which he had done very well – and a number of real estate investments in student residential properties. When I added up his whole investment portfolio it came to about fifty million pounds in value. This alone would have been a remarkable achievement for someone from Bamyaköy. But I had yet to see his operating companies.

Suddenly, as if by magic, he produced another twenty million pounds from an account with Pictet & Cie, a private bank in Geneva, which he gave me to invest in the markets. With this additional sum, I increased his exposure to US blue chips and, counter-intuitively perhaps, I bought into US banking stocks. I figured that the ones that survived the crisis would rebound one day. In particular, I took a large punt on JP Morgan. I'd always liked the bank and knew that they consistently had good quality management.

At the end of my first three months, I went to Aydin with a PowerPoint presentation; a beautiful set of pie charts indicating his exposure to different asset classes and geographies. I detailed the price movements and gains he had made in the last quarter. To my surprise, he seemed little interested in the gains or the quality of information that I had prepared for him. All he could say was, 'Well that's all very good, Sandy, but we need to get down to the real stuff.' As if the returns I had generated were a mere rounding error in the big scheme of things.

For a moment, I was a little disappointed. I thought that he might appreciate the leap from paper ledger to Excel and PowerPoint and, most importantly, the healthy gains achieved. But I knew that he meant the real money was in his operating companies. I also knew that I had been avoiding getting my hands dirty with this real source of his wealth.

His two main businesses were amusement arcades and massage parlours. There may have been other businesses he didn't want me to see but I couldn't swear to that. Certainly, these two streams alone had made him a very wealthy man. They were cash businesses earning him tens of thousands of pounds every single day of the year, except for Christmas.

I mention Christmas because it's one of those things I discovered about Aydin, and what remained sacred to him. Although he was Cypriot, he had been in England for so long – since his thirties – that a part of him had become British. In a way, he had been British all his life. He was born at a time when Cyprus was a newly-minted British colony. And he left the island for Britain, five years after independence. This deep attachment for the country extended also to his deities whose photographs adorned the walls of his office: Her Majesty Queen Elizabeth II at her coronation; Sir Winston Churchill armed with a tommy gun; Margaret Thatcher at her first election, dressed in blue and with her arms wide open. He had a proprietary sense of being British and resented foreigners who lived off the welfare state or attempted to impose their culture on the country. This attachment to the Crown extended to an obsession about "paying his way". For him, that came down to settling every last penny of taxes that he owed. I think it was his way of earning his place in Britain, of showing his loyalty to the monarch.

His amusement arcades – he had twelve of them – were dotted around Greater London: Green Lanes, Shoreditch and Catford. They all operated under a single, if ironic, brand name, 'Jacky Gets Lucky'. Each operation had its own P&L with the manager taking ten per cent of the monthly profits in lieu of salary. Typical staff numbers were five to six at any one time – not counting two bouncers permanently on call to manage any trouble. Invariably, there was a pasty-faced money changer who sat in, what I was later learnt was, a bulletproof cubicle. Through letterbox openings in the Perspex, they took worn notes from equally pasty-faced teenagers and young adults. In return, they handed back paper cups full of coins and tokens. The remaining staff were cleaners. Mess, untidiness, spilt popcorn, and stains from fizzy drinks were things Aydin couldn't abide. He insisted that the chrome of the machines was polished clean of greasy palm and fingerprints twice a day.

It was on a Thursday night, in the comfort of his chauffeur-driven Bentley, that he first took me to visit one of his arcades on the Stanstead Road. As he explained, he did these visits randomly so that none of the managers could guess when he might drop by. He was even known to call on the same establishment three weeks in a row – just so that no one could ever get comfortable or think they were safe.

The windows of the arcade we went to were sparklingly clean.

On the bottom right-hand side, just beside the entrance, there was a large white sticker that stated, *Licensed by the United Kingdom Gambling Commission*. Already, I felt some comfort with the fact that we were entering a professionally-run business.

My first impression, as we entered, was of a glorified playroom with row after row of shooting, racing and dancing games; all with absurd electronic sound effects, strobe lights and techno music – the combination of which appeared to induce a zombie-like trance in the gamers. However, I noticed that when we stepped inside, and as soon as Aydin was spotted by the staff, the music level suddenly dropped by several decibels, as if by some pre-agreed protocol. A few gamers looked up to see what had happened but they turned back almost immediately, unperturbed by the sight of this tubby man wearing a camel coat, a maroon silk scarf tied around his neck and a blue rinse in his hair. These formal clothes, the hairdo, the large ears, the mascara-lined eyes, and the powdered wrinkled skin give him the air of a latter-day Nosferatu. Apparently, I was the only one struck by his appearance amongst all those flashing lights.

'Now you see, Sandy,' he explained with quite some enthusiasm, 'this is how you bring them in and hook them. At first, the kids… they just want to play on the arcade games. But see over there?' He led me to an area that looked as if it could be roped off. Up on the wall there was a sign that read, *Over 18's only – no exception.* 'This is where we make the real money.' He waved his hand towards the rows of chrome-covered fruit machines and smiled with something I can only describe as satisfaction. Children, teenagers and young men stood in front of the machines, feeding in coin after coin, hitting buttons and pulling levers. 'You see up there, Sandy?' He motioned to a large plastic dome that sheltered a dozen or so cameras. 'Those are the eyes of the command centre.' He then took me through a side door into a room which, as it turned out, had a reinforced two way mirror several inches thick looking on to the gamers.

'How are we doing tonight, Roy?' he said to the man sitting

behind a vast console of screens and buttons.

'Very well, Mr Öztürk.'

'This is Sandy. He is working for me on a few things. So, show him your tricks.'

He looked at Aydin quizzically, as if to say, 'Are you sure?' The old man nodded slowly, and Roy responded. 'Anything you say, Mr Öztürk.'

With the pride of an orchestra conductor, he proceeded to show how he could remotely control the fruit machines. Mostly he put them into losing mode. However, if he felt one of the punters was about to give up, he would allow a little win. And so it was that he managed crescendos and lulls until the punter had not only lost all the money they had come in with but borrowed more from whichever mate was close by. Or gone out... and done God knows what, to get more cash.

But this was not the end of Roy's artistry. 'Now see here Mr Sandy...' As he spoke, I could see his eyes shine with the excitement of the kill. 'You see that fellow over there?'

I nodded.

'That's our decoy. See, every now and again we have him go in and win big. This way the punters hear the coins spewing out and they take heart again.' He fluttered his fingers in the air as if he were playing a trumpet. 'Course you got to be careful,' he sniffed. 'You don't want the punters to think that the luck's gone out of the room. It's a very fine balance. A very fine balance indeed.'

'You're a real maestro, Roy,' said Aydin.

'Thank you, Mr Öztürk, thank you,' he said, beaming with pride.

Before I could control myself, I blurted out, 'But is this legal?'

They stopped and turned to look at me; staring at me intensely, as if they had come across some yet undiscovered species of insect.

It was Aydin who broke the silence. 'Don't be naïve, Sandy. We have money to make here. How do you think we pay your salary?'

'But surely there must be rules – you have a licence for God's sake.'

Aydin rolled his eyes and then said, 'Listen my boy when the inspector comes, we switch the machines back to the normal random number generator so they deliver the official RTP.' In response to my blank look, he clarified. 'That's the 'return to player' which is supposed to be set at ninety-six per cent.'

'So, what, that means that the punters are supposed to get back ninety-six pence in every pound they play? Ninety-six pence for every pound that they put in?' I said.

'Well, yes... but where's the profit in that, Sandy? I mean – seriously?'

'Yes', said Aydin 'where's the margin in that I ask you?

'So, what are you normally running at?'

Aydin turned to Neal who answered for him. 'Mostly, like we've agreed with Mr Aydin, we're running at an RTP of 50%'.

'But doesn't anybody realise they're getting ripped off?'

'Sandy, Sandy, my boy... do you really think any of that lot,' he said pointing out towards the floor, 'have the wherewithal to figure out what's going on?'

'But what about the inspectors?'

'Oh them – a few quid in their top pocket, a good meal in a fancy restaurant and a visit to one of my massage parlours... and everything's as right as rain.'

CHAPTER 11

The week after the amusement arcades, we went to visit one of his massage parlours. In the intervening period I had analysed every single one of his gaming outlets. It was hard to see how any more profit could be squeezed out of them without playing around with the accounting policies, which were, if anything, a little too conservative in my opinion – particularly with regards to depreciation. But I had started to understand Aydin's Darwinian approach and, I confess, I was intrigued to see what this other side of his business empire looked like.

The massage parlours also had their own unique brand name: 'Lotus Flower Valley Spa & Massage Centre.' He had located each of these establishments near a good flow of traffic. The one we visited was on Old King's Road and was his most profitable unit, generating at least three times the amount of the others.

'You see, Sandy, what with Chelsea football ground round the corner and the Broadway just up the road, there's always plenty of walk-in customers,' he explained.

The windows were black and opaque, but the doorway was brightly lit and a Chinese lantern hung over the front step. As soon as we stepped inside I wanted to retch, so strong was the smell of rancid massage oil tainted with, what I can only describe as a fish tank odour. Aydin did not appear to notice. To the contrary, he was all smiles. I don't recall any other time seeing him in such a good mood.

'Lettie!' He called out with delight to a middle-aged Asian woman – Filipina as I shortly discovered – dressed in a light grey two-piece Chinese style suit tied at the sides with two bow knots.

'How are you Mr Aydin?' the woman asked, with what seemed to be genuine affection.

'Can't complain. How's your boy? Jason isn't' it?'

'He's good, Mr Aydin. He goes to college next month. He wants to study accounting. He's very quick with numbers.'

'That's very good, Lettie. You tell him from me that being an accountant is a very good career. And if ever he wants a job during his holidays he should come and see this man,' Aydin said, pointing at me.

I left Aydin talking and went to take a look around. The whole place was dimly lit by a red neon light that blurred the sharpness of every angle and created the impression of a submarine: no sense of day or night, season or weather. Two distinct noises overlapped: the constant whirr of the ventilation system, and a feeble attempt to replicate oriental music overlayed with the sound of flowing water. I made my way down the narrow corridor. On either side, numbered doors gave on to 'therapy' rooms. One of these was open and I stepped inside, out of curiosity. But instead of the massage table that I expected there was a thin mattress on the floor with an equally thin pillow. In the corner, stood a large supply of towels, tissue boxes and jumbo-sized dispensers of massage oil.

I heard Aydin calling my name and made my way back to the reception. As I went down the corridor, a therapist came out of one of the rooms. I heard a man cough from inside. She was wearing the same uniform as Lettie but on her feet, she wore white socks and flip-flops whose thongs were lodged awkwardly between her besocked toes. In one hand I noticed she was holding a mobile phone. It had a protective cover with two black plastic cats' ears coming out of the top. As she shuffled past, her eyes focused on the ground in front of her feet, I saw the phone light up and there, on the screen, appeared a picture of a baby boy. She must have sensed me looking at her for she shot me a furtive glance and then hurried past me and somewhere off to the back of the building. As she disappeared, I caught the smell of perspiration, garlic and sperm trailing in the air. It was then that I understood what this business was really about.

CHAPTER 12

The next morning, I woke up at four-thirty. My mouth was parched. Try as I might, I couldn't get back to sleep. As I opened my eyes, all gummy, I saw that there was a half empty bottle of brandy on my nightstand. On the floor, where I was about to put my feet, a tumbler was lying on its side. I sat on the edge of the bed for a long while, undecided whether to go to the bathroom or force myself to have one more shot at sleeping. Eventually, I made my way to the kitchen to make myself coffee. All night long I had been haunted by foul images of Aydin's massage parlours. I had the dreadful realisation that I was earning my living from the lowest form of gambling – and illegal at that – and from what was, essentially, a chain of brothels. By association I was now a pimp. How could I ever explain to Defne, my as-yet-not-met sister what I did for a living? At least as a banker I had had a recognised place in the world. Now I was working with Aydin in businesses that appalled me. For a while, until my coffee went cold, I tried to reconcile the man for whom I felt so much affection with the reprehensible nature of his business activities. And then, when I could make no more sense of anything, it dawned upon me that if things went bad, I could end up going to jail. 'This won't' do,' I told myself. Even if it meant being unemployed again. Even if it meant I would really risk losing my apartment, this time. I think I may have mumbled something to myself about 'integrity'. But what is certainly true is that I went to fetch a pen and notepaper. I sat at my breakfast table and wrote my letter of resignation. It was not an easy task. The first two versions ended up as balls in the sink. The third and final version was finally crafted in both tone and content. I began by expressing gratitude for the opportunity – that was the easy part because it was true. The hard part, and hence the different iterations, was the explanation of why this was not for me. I didn't want to sound superior and precious. After all, I could anticipate

Aydin telling me that money is money, that it has neither colour nor creed and, so long as you pay your taxes, it doesn't matter how you make it. I knew he would gloss over the criminal nature of his activities. For him it was all fair game. In the end, I simply wrote that I didn't feel the Famagusta Trading Company needed someone like me. After that, I felt better, and I showered and headed off to the bus station as quickly as possible.

By 7.30 a.m. I was sitting at the Berkeley Street Starbucks. My *grande caffè latte* had gone cold and I thought about getting another one. I needed the coffee to ease my hangover. For the last half hour, I had been thinking about my options when I left Aydin's employ. It was not as if I'd had many. I even thought about leaving England for the west coast of Scotland, to see if I could find work in some remote community on one of the small islands in the Inner Hebrides. Bury myself there and hide away from the world. Forget about everything, as the old song goes. Forget who I was, or used to be; Cyprus, my father, Bamyaköy. Even succumb to defeat and give up the search for my sister.

My mind drifted as it tried to establish the things that were truly important to me. The list was terrifyingly small. My mother and stepfather? No. Not anymore. Since the whole Cyprus business, I felt estranged from them. Somewhere inside, I blamed them for having brought me up in ignorance of my identity. But in truth I was being unfair to them. For I hadn't asked about it. I was all too conscious that I had become a 'linen-cotton person', as they like to say in Cyprus; not one thing nor the other – set on a journey to reconcile two irreconcilable halves. London? Perhaps. But only with money. And I was not really talking about London. I was thinking of the few square miles I frequented – from the City, to Piccadilly, to Pall Mall, to Mayfair, to Knightsbridge, to South Kensington and Chelsea. That was my little bubble. How limited I had become. Then I thought about Cyprus. How could I turn my back on the island? How could I not finish searching for my sister? Did I not stand for anything, I asked myself. So, I resolved to stay in London until I had tracked her down. Even if at the end of the road she wanted nothing to do with me. Even if I lost everything and had to live with my mother and stepfather.

I was getting myself ready to go into the office and see Aydin, when I was interrupted by the arrival of Paul; Paul Andrews. He'd never been a friend at Braithwaite&Wilkins – just a well-respected colleague who was never so unsuccessful as to be fired, although neither did he cover himself with commercial glory. He stood front of me in a navy raincoat that had a film of grease around the half circle of the collar. Under his left arm, he carried a copy of the FT, which I noticed was folded open to the appointments page and there were blue circles around some of the ads. His left hand was holding a cup to go. His right hand held an old leather briefcase that looked suspiciously thin. His eyes were bloodshot and his face looked more lined, his cheeks redder, than I remembered.

'Hello Paul, how are you? Won't you join me?'

He shook his head. 'No, I must be on my way.' But he did not move and continued, 'So, what are you up to these days, Sandy?'

At first, I was not sure what to say but I gave an answer that could be shared with former colleagues and allow me to save face, 'Well, I'm heading the investments for a diversified conglomerate.' As I spoke these words I could feel my chest puff with pride.

'Aren't you the lucky one?'

It was then that I remembered how it was Paul's sarcasm that prevented us ever becoming friends. But the lack of bite in his tone alerted me to the fact that something was not right with him.

'You?' I said as kindly as I could.

'When the bank folded, of course we all lost our jobs. For a couple of days there was a rumour flying about that we'd be bought up by HSBC... but that came to nothing in the end, so we were all out on our ears.'

'Sorry to hear that. What have you been doing since?'

He looked down at his brogues then off to one side of my face and said softly, 'I've been looking for a job. I suppose something'll turn up. But right now no one's in the market for someone of my age. Or for anybody, for that matter.'

'I am sure things will pick up soon.' I said this in the absence of anything better to say. I didn't believe it. Neither did he. As he turned to leave, I reached down to my jacket pocket to feel my letter of resignation still there. I knew then that I would not give up my job. That I was too much of a coward to be without a steady income, even though there were some very big risks to staying with Aydin. I'd had a taste of what it was like to lose everything. I told myself that I would get stuck into Aydin's businesses after all and maybe, when the markets came back, I could think about something more suitable. I told myself that the job would look good on my CV, if I positioned it well (already the idea of listing myself as Head of Investments for a diversified conglomerate on LinkedIn was catching my imagination). I told myself that every minute of my spare time would be given over to looking for my sister.

CHAPTER 13

I began to earn well with Aydin. Within a few months he increased my salary, without me even asking for a raise. I think he was pleased with the early returns I generated on his investments.

I soon came to terms with my moral dilemma by mentally reducing Aydin's businesses to numbers on a spreadsheet. One tab for the amusement arcades; a second for the spas; and a third in which both were consolidated. This way, I no longer thought of human beings. Instead, I saw data. I saw growth, profit. The whole combination was hypnotic, so that I came to cherish my little entries and the fancy graphics I had made of the businesses.

We were coming to the end of the fourth quarter of 2009 and Famagusta Trading Company was doing better than ever before. Around us, businesses were going bankrupt. People were having their homes repossessed. There was talk that the ATMs would no longer have money in them. Pundits were talking about the Great Depression of the 1930s and the Second World War – as if X would lead to Y. But in all this misery, our companies were thriving. It hardly seemed rational to me that people would waste their money on what we offered, especially when times were so tough, but I think it was because we provided playgrounds where our customers came to forget and to escape.

We were about to close for Christmas, and I wanted to give Aydin the latest update. I was going to have another go at showing him my financial models. It was part of my plan to move him away from his old-fashioned ledgers and paper-based accounting. But he was not having it.

'No, don't show me the figures. I already know how we're doing.'

I closed the lid of my laptop. He must have seen the disappointment on my face for he said, 'You're doing good, son.

And I am glad you're modernising the business. But I'm too old for these tricks. You know me,' and here he used his index finger to tap his temple 'I keep everything in my head. All our records are only for the auditor and the tax man.'

He didn't say anything else for a while. He looked tired.

'Are you sleeping okay, Aydin?'

'Me? I'm fine. But there's something I want to talk to you about.' He put up his hand as if to shush me and then picked up the phone, 'Frankie, bring us two cups of coffee. Yes, that's right, Turkish. Sugar for me. And without for the boy.'

'What's on your mind, Aydin?'

'That's a very good question, *oğlum*,' he said with a big smile. Before I could press him for more, Frankie knocked and walked in without waiting for an answer. She had a tray with two little *cezve* with the steaming coffee in them, two small coffee cups, two glasses of water and two dishes of pistachio Turkish delight. We stopped speaking. Not because she shouldn't be privy to our conversation but to show due respect for the ceremony that was unfolding. She poured each cup carefully. The smell was rich and reminiscent of freshly roasted and slightly burnt beans. I thought how pitiful my daily Starbucks was by comparison. She had made sure there was a good layer of foam for each cup.

'Frankie, what a good Turkish wife you would have made,' Aydin said.

'And where would that have left you, Mr Aydin?' She gave him a smile, and he returned it. This was not an employer looking at an employee. These were two people that cared for each other. As she left the room, she gave me a wink.

When we were alone again, he pulled out an envelope from the top drawer of his desk. Inside was a one-page letter on beautiful thick cream-coloured paper. I could see that Frankie had typed it for him, so she already knew what was afoot. I read it. And then again. And then I put it down. 'You can't mean this?' I said to him.

'Well, why not?'

'I just would never have expected—'

'Listen, Sandy, there are conditions...'

The letter stated that I was to become Chief Executive Officer of Famagusta Trading Company, effective 1 January 2010.

'What conditions, Aydin?' I said softly. My heart was beating faster.

'Look, I brought you into the business because I want you to do something big... and then for us both to be done with it. This is not a game for you in the long term, we both know that. A posh boy like you. You think about things over the holidays and show me what you have in mind in January.'

I nodded. Ideas were already racing around inside me. I felt a wave of exhilaration taking hold.

'Now tell me... where you are with finding Defne?'

His question about my sister brought me back to earth.

'I've been using the services of a private investigator.'

Aydin raised one eyebrow. 'And?'

'So far, he found a Defne Necati who was at Hornsey School for Girls. Apparently, she got four A-Levels there in 1982. Which would make her my age. So that seems plausible. And...' I couldn't help a sense of pride creeping into my voice, '...pretty good grades too. A* in English Lit, A in History and A* in Maths.'

'Well, what do you expect, her being Zeki's girl and all? But really nothing after that? How strange.'

I shook my head. 'He's checked all the universities and there's no sign of her. Nothing in the records of deaths. She just disappears.'

'She can't have just disappeared, Sandy.'

'Well, I'll keep looking. But if only Fatma would help us.'

'Maybe, I'll try her again. I know people who might help talk some sense into her. Anyway… you get to work on that plan *oğlum*.'

What I didn't tell him was that I had known all this about Defne for some months but hadn't had the courage to pursue it. Largely out of embarrassment over the nature of my employment. But now I had been given the CEO role, I had regained some status. And besides, I intended to turn the businesses legitimate.

CHAPTER 14

I spent Christmas alone.

Caroline and Hugh had decamped to mid-Wales for a few weeks. Earlier that year they had bought an eighteenth-century slave trader's mansion near Aberystwyth for a bargain price. I was impressed at how little they managed to get it for. Apparently, the previous owner had gone bankrupt. But that did not bother them. They had fallen in love with the property and decided to retire there. The place sounded a bit gruesome to me, although they assured me that it was 'really quite exquisite', had marvellous views of the Irish sea, and Caroline was quick to point out that Hugh's ancestors originally came from that part of Cardiganshire. So, she explained, it was a genuine return to his roots. It occurred to me to talk to them about Cyprus and my connection to the island, but my mother had refused to engage with me on the subject the first time I brought it up, so now there seemed little point. I also decided not to tell her about my elevation to CEO. They were on their journey and the less they knew about mine the better. I think I promised to go and visit them over the summer. But in the event, I didn't, and they didn't invite me again.

It might seem strange, but I looked forward to Christmas by myself. It gave me time to work on my plans for Aydin's business. My only frustration was that the gym would be closed for a couple of days during the holiday period. I had started working out again. It had become a little obsessional as I was, by then, training every day. I even engaged the services of a boxing coach who put me through my drills three times a week. Slowly, I started to recover some of the skills and form I'd had as a young man. I told myself that when I finally met my sister, she would see me in fine shape, and I would be a brother to be proud of.

I spent Christmas Eve scribbling notes and sketching out different options. By the 26th, I had a solid PowerPoint ready in which I articulated all my ideas. I would never have said this to Aydin so clearly, but I had come up with a road map to turn his seedy businesses, as lucrative as they might be, into something clean, corporate and yet, in terms of financial opportunity, well beyond his wildest dreams of avarice. All my old banking instincts had been resurrected and like an alchemist I would show the old man how we would transform lead into gold.

The work consumed me, and for a while, I confess, even Defne was forgotten. At least, until New Year's Eve when for the first time in days I left my flat and its neatly stacked crate of empty wine bottles, to take a walk in Kensington Gardens. I set out with the intention of clearing my head of the fug that had descended upon me. I had been lost in an ether of 'what-if' scenarios, cashflow projections, valuations and potential exits for too long. At first, the walk did nothing at all. I remained in business-planning mode even as I made my way up Broad Walk. But at the top, as I reached the Round Pond, the sight of a bright yellow kite floating in the sky caught my attention. It was flying higher and further than it should. It was being carried away by the wind, well above the trees, towards Hyde Park. I heard a child crying and realised that it was his kite and that he must have lost control of the strings. His parents were consoling him. I watched them, and for a moment I was envious of this family.

Seeing this little act of love and care released the numbers swirling around my head and, all of a sudden, I was conscious of my breathing, of being alive, of being with other people on this winter's day. For the first time, I looked around properly. In front of me, ducks were paddling in the water, navigating around the toy boats that children, and some adults, were gently guiding by remote control. On the other side of the pond, older children were kicking a football around. And to my right, towards the bandstand, I saw a group of what I assumed to be students, playing frisbee and dressed only in T-shirts and jeans despite the cold. I sat down on one of the park benches and let the sounds engulf me. It was now that my mind turned to Defne. I wondered, as I had so many times before, what she was like. What she did for a living. Was she like me in any way? How did she like to dress? Did she have a good job? And then it dawned on me that she might be married and have a family of her own. That I might even be an uncle without realising it. But as soon as I expressed this thought to myself, I knew that I wouldn't want it to be true. I freely admit this was out of pure selfishness. I realised that this person who, so far, I had shaped according to my imagination, I wanted all to myself. I wanted to be her brother. I wanted her to be my sister. I wanted her undivided attention. I wanted to be able to walk in the park like this, on a day like this, and talk about anything; to feel connected. For once in my life, not to have to filter what I had to say or tailor the conversation to the person I was with. Maybe it was me pathetically searching for a world that belonged to happy families. And then I cursed the idea, shook myself off, told myself that I was ridiculous and soft and that it wouldn't do. But I was not convinced by my rushed self-dismissal. I told myself that somewhere out there was a better world where people could be close, where they could be safe, and loved by a sibling.

CHAPTER 15

'Well,' he said, wiping icing sugar from his mouth – Frankie had already, at his request, served him twice over with more pistachio *lokum* – 'I didn't imagine you'd be thinking this big. Do you honestly think it can be done?' I noted a touch of wonder in his voice, and was pleased to have impressed the old man.

'Easier to ask for the big amounts, Aydin.'

'But will they give someone like me that kind of money? Especially with all that's going on right now?'

For the last hour, I had run through my plans to separate out his two businesses, get big ticket investors and, with a substantial injection of capital, transform and grow them exponentially. We would take his amusement arcades and his massage parlours to every major city in the British Isles, and then float the two companies on the stock exchange as two separate entities.

'So, are you up for it, Aydin?' I said, looking him straight in the eye.

'It's a lot for me to take in, *oğlum*.' As he spoke, he fiddled with the pencil in front of him.

'Aydin, the market's crying out for good deals. Your operations, from an accounting point of view, are pure gold. No debt, cash businesses. Now imagine we get the money to turn them national, upscale the branding and start marketing them properly?'

He nodded his head. 'How much money do you think we could make?'

'It'll depend on the valuation for the stock market. I mean, you will lose equity in your company, but you can expect to make several hundred million pounds when the two companies float.'

Aydin brought out one of his longer smokes, a Cohiba Esplendidos, and said, 'Okay, let's go through your presentation again.'

An hour later, we were down to the stub of his cigar and the air in the room was grey with wisps of smoke. He spat out a strand of tobacco. 'All right Sandy, let's do it.'

As I closed up my laptop and gathered my papers he said, 'Oh, Sandy, I found out why you couldn't find anything more about Defne.'

CHAPTER 16

From: Fatma Necati

To: Daphne Neil

Kızım, I was sorry not see you over Christmas. I hope that means that you have finished your manuscript by now. (Have you sent it to your agent yet?)

I would have liked to talk to you about those men who came to see me all those months ago and why the younger of the two wants to meet you. But now you have to be told. A few days ago, the older man, Aydin, called me on my mobile phone. Apparently, he got my number from cousins of mine. The long and the short of it is we talked for almost an hour.

I realised that he was right. There are things I do need to tell you about. There is only one person among the living who could still be hurt by what I am going to tell you. That is, maybe aside from you. I don't know how you will react.

Ziya, *mekanı cennet olsun*, will always be your dad. But your real father was someone called Zeki Aziz. He was, like me, from Bamyaköy. I am sorry if you are shocked. I suppose you are shocked twice over. I imagine that you are wondering how I, of all people, could have let this happen.

There is no easy explanation. It's good that I write this down for you, else I might get flustered, and things would not come out right. You need first to understand about Bamyaköy, as it was back then.

The Cyprus I was born into, as you know, was still a British colony. Today, people say all kinds of things about the British and their empire – and some of what is said is no doubt true. But for us Turkish Cypriots it was different. The British kept us safe and ran things honestly and efficiently. I know it's not fashionable to say that but it's the truth, Defne. I need to say more about 'us'. The terrible thing about Cyprus is that we can never be quite Cypriots, full stop. We are always a _something_-Cypriot: Armenian-, Greek-, Maronite-, and in our case Turkish-. The reality is that there's no pure anything on our island. We're all Cypriots but the only language we have in common is English. The majority of Cypriots speak Greek and we, well we speak Turkish, a beautiful form of the language that can be traced back to the Ottoman Empire. Most Turkish Cypriots when I was growing up were poor and lived in the countryside. In Bamyaköy very few people could read and write. My parents certainly couldn't. Hardly a single woman could back then.

Things started to change in the 1930s, just a few years before I was born. A new teacher came to the village, Erol Baysal, and he helped the boys get better educated and for the first time he encouraged parents to let their daughters to stay in school. You can't begin to understand how revolutionary this was. And this starts to explain Zeki and me.

Zeki, came from one of the poorest families in the village. His father died before he was born – as it happens, just like you – and he had a wretched stepfather of sorts. But Zeki was brilliant. And because of this, he won scholarships and was sent away to school. Pretty soon he came to the attention of the British who sent him to university in England. When he came back he was very different. People said later that he was secretly working for the British government. We never understood how, but when the British left, he became a member of the Cyprus Republic parliament. At that time, he did not have a wife but when his sister started looking for a bride for him, she talked to my parents. My mum was over the moon but my dad, who was proud of me, wanted me to stay in school. In the end, it was Zeki who encouraged my mum to keep me in education. I was just fourteen years old at the time. He told my parents that I too had the potential to go to university. Just like him. And that I could be one of the first Turkish Cypriot women to go that far. I wouldn't have minded marrying him. But I also wanted an education. I never forgot that he was the one who, in a way, made sure it happened.

Anyway, he eventually married some upper-class English girl who he'd known back in England when he was studying. All the men were very envious of him. Cypriot men can be so silly about blonde-haired women with blue eyes. Back then she looked like a film star. At least in Bamyaköy she did. I was happy for Zeki. Really, I was. But by this time, three years into independence, things started to fall apart. And then in December 1963 we had the so-called 'Bloody Christmas'. It was during that time that Erol Bey was murdered. Of course, our men retaliated. But things were very ugly and Turkish Cypriots moved back to their villages or into enclaves. Zeki had already resigned from parliament and returned to Bamyaköy where he was put in charge of manning the defences for the village. One day, a group of Greek Cypriot soldiers came. It seemed as if some of our men had been involved in revenge killings up in Avrigadou, on the plateau above Bamyaköy. And one of those men was a friend of Zeki: a man called Aydin Öztürk. People said he'd done terrible things up there. Killed men in cold blood. So here were the soldiers coming to take revenge.

But we women of Bamyaköy were having none of it. Zeki's sister, Aysel, organised us all together and we marched down the street right up towards the soldiers. And in the end, believe it or not, they went away. Our men were embarrassed because they thought they should have been the ones to do something. Anyway, a few days later I saw Zeki go up to the top of the hill by himself. So, I followed him. I can't really explain why. I was just drawn to him. He was a handsome man, with such vitality. And when I found him, I sat next to him. And things just happened… It wasn't right. His wife was there down in the village. I found out later that she was also pregnant.

So, there you have it, Defne. The man who became your father in the end, Ziya, he was a good man. I told him about what had happened. He knew, I promise. He never held it against me. He was kind. He never asked much of me. I don't think he was too interested in the kind of stuff that men and women do together, which explains why I never had other children after you. But he encouraged me to continue my education. As soon as I'd given birth to you, I carried on with my studies. But by this time Zeki was dead. I'd have liked him to know that I had finally been educated. But the Greek Cypriots couldn't let a man like him live. They hated him. They couldn't stand the thought of an educated Turkish Cypriot who might speak out against all their lies and criminality. As he was boarding the boat for Britain, they shot him. So, he never knew I was carrying his child. And that I wanted it. I wasn't going to give you up. Not for anything.

Now you know the truth. I hope you won't judge me too harshly. As you have probably guessed by now, the younger man, the one who wants to meet you, is your brother – your half-brother.

I love you, Mum

CHAPTER 17

'Daphne Neil? Are you sure?' I said.

'Apparently, she changed her name by deed poll when she was eighteen. Which explains why there was no trace of her at university and why that investigator of yours lost the trail.'

'How did you find all this out, Aydin?'

'Well, I spoke to some people from Bamyaköy who live up in Green Lanes and who knew the father, Necati.'

'Where's Green Lanes?'

He looked at me impatiently. 'Don't you know anything, Sandy?' It's like Cyprus in London. It's a bloody joke if you ask me. It's full of Greek and Turkish Cypriots living together side by side. Ridiculous. Back home they can't stand each other but as soon as they get to London, they all cling together and their kids grow up as best mates, so I'm told. Ridiculous. Now where was I? Yes, that's right, they remember Defne as a child and how, as soon as she turned eighteen, she changed her name to an English first name and surname. Apparently, after that, she wanted nothing to do with the Cypriot community. Even though her dad... sorry, I mean her stepdad, had made sure she grew up speaking Turkish.' At this, Aydin sighed and looked at me. He fumbled around in his jacket pocket, leaving icing sugar fingerprints on his clothes in the process, until at last he found a scrap of paper that he handed to me. On it, in big childlike letters, was an email address for Daphne Neil.

'And these people had her email address?'

'Well, not quite.'

'So how did you get it, then?'

'I had another go with Fatma. I called her and we had a long chat. In the end, she agreed that it should be her daughter's choice whether you two meet or not.'

I thanked Aydin and went back to my office. The address that he had written down was a simple Gmail address. I thought about writing to her there and then, but I wanted to take my time so I delayed doing it until the evening. For the rest of the day, I worked through my list of prospective private equity firms to target. But later, when I had finished and the office was quiet and I was alone, I took out her email address again and started to type.

From: Sandy Bligh-Smith

To: Daphne Neil

Dear Defne,

I am not sure how to begin this email, so I'd better just jump in. I think you might be my sister – my half-sister, that is. It looks as if we have the same natural father, Zeki Aziz. I know this might be a bit of a shock to you. It certainly was to me when I discovered I might have a sibling. I assume you don't know anything about this man, but you can be proud of him. One day, I hope I can tell you his story in full.

I am sure that there is quite a bit for us to tell each other about our lives and this email is probably not the right place. But if you would like – I would certainly be very keen to – we could meet. I am (thought I was) an only child and I very much like the idea of having a sister.

I look forward to hearing from you.

Yours,

Sandy

I clicked 'send' and went home.

CHAPTER 18

From: Daphne Neil

To: Fatma Necati

Mum?! Why won't you answer my phone calls? We need to talk about this. Really, we do. You can't just dump this on me and then run away. And how could you? I never want to hear another word from you about who I see or what I do. I mean back in those days... I can't believe you did something like that – especially after all the grief you gave me when I was growing up. Mum, really. And this Sandy fellow – what a ridiculous name – I don't want to have anything to do with him. Somehow, he's found my email address and written to me. Tell me it wasn't you, Mum? Please. I hope he doesn't know who I am. I don't want anything like this leaking out into the press. I've had so much bad coverage recently. I can't afford the hint of another scandal. My agent is worried enough about the damage to my personal branding as it is. Call me back, okay?

CHAPTER 19

The response from the private equity firms was encouraging. I could see that most took our investment proposal seriously. Even when we were turned down, I detected a genuine note of regret. It was either because the deal size was too small or because it didn't fit in with their overall sector focus. A few alluded to their corporate reputation and to not feeling comfortable with being associated with our lines of business. In the end, the field narrowed down to three who were willing to invest the £80 million required to transform the two businesses and turn them national. I am pleased to say that it turned into a bidding war with each firm trying their hardest. As a consequence, we were offered better and better terms as the weeks went by. Finally, we chose a firm called K-Capital which was backed by the Qataris. Not only did they offer us the best deal, but they were the ones who conducted the least amount of due diligence.

Their lead partner, Harry Eid, did not overly impress us at first. I think it was the nature of his attire, which featured the logo of every possible high-end brand like a walking billboard. And then there was the strength of the smell of his aftershave – it was as if he had sprayed himself a minute before coming in to see us – that took us aback. However, over time, we came to appreciate his abilities and hard work. And the fact that he was Lebanese – 'a cousin of ours' as Aydin liked to say – meant that the old man was more comfortable than if Harry had been a bona fide Englishman.

CHAPTER 20

A week went by without a response from Defne. I did all the things you do when you are waiting for an email that doesn't come: I checked my spam, I refreshed several times a day. I even double-checked that my own email wasn't stuck in my outbox. Nothing.

I felt deflated. I started to worry that I hadn't got the tone right and she'd taken offence. That somehow, I had misjudged things. For the first time, I felt old and middle aged. But a day or so later, while I was sheltering from a rainstorm at the bus stop by Green Park tube station, I came to understand why she might be so protective of her privacy and not want to engage with a stranger – despite all the claims that I made about our family ties.

It was the big advertising banner on a number 14 double-decker bus going up towards the Royal Academy, that caught my attention: *The House on Stilts* by bestselling author, Daphne Neil. There she was – a glammed-up face on the side of the bus. Her skin was makeup smooth, and her teeth seemed unnaturally white – but there was no mistaking who it was. This was the person whose photograph I had seen in Fatma's office months ago. So, my sister was a writer. Hiding in plain sight. I felt like an idiot for not having figured out who she was before. It never occurred to me that I would have a sister who was so famous. Maybe I didn't imagine that a Turkish Cypriot woman could make it so big.

As soon as I reached home, I switched on my computer to see if now, knowing who she really was, I could do a better job of locating her. Predictably, she was ex-directory and all online searches for her address and whereabouts drew a blank. But next day, I found a list of literary agents and was quickly able to find the one who represented her. So, care of her agency, I wrote again. The introduction where I asked for my message to be forwarded was a little self-conscious, but I couldn't see why a decent human being would not pass it on.

Again, I waited for a response, but in the meantime, my every waking hour was taken up by the business and our dealings with K-Capital.

CHAPTER 21

By this time, Harry Eid had deployed his post-acquisition team. As a consequence, we were now being inundated with all kinds of experts and professionals brought in to help us achieve the growth plans for the businesses. They insisted that we have a proper corporate office and appoint proper management teams for each company. And for this, Harry called in a head-hunting firm. After a first meeting with the consultants assigned for the recruitment exercise, Aydin decided he didn't want anything to do with them.

'Bunch of ponces!' was his assessment.

When Harry tried pointing out that we needed their skills to make the businesses grow and to have a credible line up for the stock market listing, he just sighed and said wearily, 'Sandy, you deal with them. I am too old for all this malarkey. I don't understand these kinds of people who've never run a business in their lives but who are trying to tell me who I need to put in place to run my business.'

But the truth was that we did need them, and they did bring us an impressive set of executives. And what I had sketched out all those months before on a PowerPoint was now becoming a reality thanks to the new management teams.

However, the irony was that Aydin and I found ourselves with more time on our hands than we were used to. We had become advisers rather than day-to-day operational executives. But worse for Aydin, was that he was now banned – of course this was not how Harry framed it (I think the expression he used was 'suboptimal for the new chain of command') – from visiting either the original amusement arcades or the spas. I think it was this that prompted him one day to tell me, 'Sandy, I'm off, back to Cyprus, my boy. For good. I want to enjoy that fancy old place I built back in Bamyaköy and enjoy it all year round. It's the right moment, son. I'll close up the house in London. Which, by the way, I want you to sell when the markets improve. So, I'll probably be gone in a couple of months.'

'But come on, you need to see the IPO through,' I said.

'No, Sandy, I don't. You're here. That's enough. I am done with the UK. It's been good to me. But it really is time to go home.'

I nodded my head. In my heart I knew he was right. And that there really was nothing more for him to do with the businesses. I hated to see him aimlessly wandering round the office.

But the conversation didn't end there. Just as I was about to leave his office, he said to me, 'Listen, at some point I'll ask you to do something for me, but – in case I don't make it for any reason – Frankie has all the details. I'll trust you to handle the matter.'

'Of course. Don't be thinking about things like that.'

'Oh, with regard to Frankie, that reminds me, you will need to find another PA for the office.'

'Harry doesn't want to fire her?' I said suspiciously. Anything was possible these days with all the changes going on.

'No, of course not. You think I'd let him do that? Come on, Sandy.' He looked at me, an eyebrow raised. His face turned hard. 'No. She's agreed to come with me to Cyprus to take care of me. You know she's like a daughter to me. After all, she's been with me since she was eighteen years old. And when she's done with me, she'll be fine. She won't have to work again. Maybe she can find herself a husband at last.' He paused for a moment and pointed his finger at me, 'You interested?' Then he laughed, good naturedly, and certainly not at her expense.

Actually, it was not an unreasonable thought. Frankie was an attractive woman. I tried not to look at her in a way that could be considered inappropriate but, try as I might, I couldn't help sometimes noticing how curvaceous she was, how flawless her skin looked and what piercing amber-flecked brown eyes she had. She was always dressed immaculately in expensive clothes and perfume to match. This was all thanks to the Harvey Nichols charge card that Aydin had given her. He once told me she was of Italian origin and that her father came over in the fifties to work in a restaurant in Goodge Street. So, in his eyes it made her a cousin. Rightly, he often spoke of a wider Mediterranean culture. It was one he understood and felt comfortable with. But over and above that connection and her good looks, I also liked the fact that she did her job well, that she was efficient and had a good head on her shoulders. Nor did she ever let her privileged relationship with Aydin affect the way she interacted with others, even though she was utterly devoted to him. It was not beyond the realms of possibility for me to think about getting married again. After all, I had been alone for so long. But I put the thought to one side. I needed to see the businesses floated on the stock exchange and I needed to find my sister before I could think about a romantic relationship again.

CHAPTER 22

It was coming up to the end of June and I hadn't heard anything from Defne's agent. I had even picked up the phone and called the agency. Messages were taken, but no one ever called me back. The receptionist was so familiar with my voice that she used to cut me off before I could finish my sentence. So, I came up with another plan. I was ashamed of it because it smacked of desperation, of being a stalker, but I couldn't see another way. Given that Daphne had a new book out, from what the announcements on her agent's web site indicated, she was in full swing of promoting it. And she was soon to be at Hatchards, just up by Piccadilly Circus. I decided that I would queue alongside her fans and have her sign a copy for me. At least I could be assured of meeting her, if only for a minute or two.

Since I had discovered that my sister was a writer, I had ploughed through a selection of her recent novels. She had written fifteen at that point. From what I could judge, that meant one a year since her first success. I was not used to reading commercial fiction, but I could see why she was so successful. Her stories were engrossing, quick-paced and always had satisfying endings. I had been finishing one every three days. Normally a piece of fiction lasted a week or so with me. But hers, I just couldn't stop turning the pages. I was racing through them, hunting for any clue that might tell me what she was like. Although it was foolish of me to think that I would recognise the true her since, objectively speaking, I couldn't possibly know what she was like. Her characters revealed nothing. I suppose I was disappointed that there was never any reference to Cyprus. But who was I to judge? If I had to guess, without knowing her origins, I would have said she was pure Home Counties English. Certainly not someone of Turkish Cypriot origin. And wasn't that just how I had tried to portray myself? Both of us trying to fit in.

In my naivety, I assumed I was going to be able to just walk in, give her my copy of her book to sign, and then start a conversation. But when I arrived at Hatchards, there was a long queue just for her, that went all the way past St James's Church and up to Waterstones – which I imagined was rather galling for that other bookshop although I did notice that their display window also had The *House on Stilts* prominently displayed. So it was that I found myself at the back of a line that was moving along the pavement at a snail's pace. I was taken by the patience and bonhomie of those queuing. Some of whom, quite sensibly, had brought sandwiches and Thermoses of tea. I realised these were not novices but Daphne Neil afficionados. The talk was all about the 'marvellous ending', but everyone was doing their best, as if they had signed the Official Secrets Act, not to reveal what actually happened. For my part, I found the slow pace of the queue pure torture. I was getting ever more nervous and tense. I could feel the palms of my hands turn sweaty. I was worried that my forehead would look greasy and that, overall, I might look a little shifty and unwashed. For a fleeting moment I thought about giving up, but in the absence of more reliable strategies on how to meet her, I stayed the shuffling course.

At long last, I found myself in the brightly lit and humming foyer of Hatchards and she was there just a few steps in front of me. Only two fans separated me from my sister.

CHAPTER 23

My sister was not beautiful, in the flesh. At least not in the classical sense. But she was lovely. My God, how lovely. I was now just one person away and could study her properly. Hers was a face that was used to smiling, judging by the fine web of lines around her mouth. I could see our family resemblance in the forehead, cheekbones and the chin. We had the same hair colour and the same hazel eyes. But what she had, that I didn't, was warmth. She just radiated it. She was listening to the man sitting opposite her, with intensity, as if he was the most important person in the world at that moment.

Even at that distance, I could smell her perfume. It was like nothing I had ever smelt before. I think I detected floral notes, and musk, and then something I had no adjective for. It triggered in me a sense of wonderment as if I was discovering myself to be fully alive rather than just existing. She was dressed in an elegant black dress that stopped just a fraction above her knees. She wore a necklace of large and beautifully imperfect pearls; and hanging loosely on her wrist, a rose-gold man-sized Rolex. I thought of my aunt back in Bamyaköy and all the Turkish Cypriot women I had met up until then. My sister was nothing like them. For a moment, I wondered if Zeki would be proud of her, of me, at least for what we had become professionally; for the distance we had travelled from village life. I think Defne noticed I was staring at her for she looked past her adoring fan and sized me up. I smiled at her. She smiled back but I felt she was doing it to be polite. I realised that I was still anonymous, as yet. Perhaps it would have been better for her if it had remained that way for ever.

So now, after an hour of queuing, it was my turn. I sat down opposite her with my copy of *The House on Stilts* in front of me.

Here I was at the point I had wanted for so many months and I couldn't utter a word.

'Would you like me to sign that for you, sir?' she said, in a manner suggesting she had concluded I might be slightly simple.

I pushed the book across the table.

'What is your name, sir?' she spoke gently and encouragingly, as if coaxing a nervous primary school pupil.

Finally, I spat out my name and, as I said it, 'Sandy,' I hated how it sounded coming out of my mouth. In my self-consciousness, I felt it was not a name for me, for who I was, and that my father would never have chosen such a preposterous name. For a reason I couldn't fathom, I felt compelled to explain it to her. 'Alexander, is the full thing, but my mother and her husband abbreviated it to Sandy.' Why the stupid detail about having a stepfather? I guess I wanted to telegraph my loss. In hindsight, how ridiculous of me.

But the explanation did nothing to alter the black cloud that descended on our little bubble. I was conscious that there was a line of people legitimately waiting behind me to have their copies of her book signed. Her face hardened. I could see that she had guessed who I was.

She looked stern. Her smile, the one she lavished on her adoring fans, disappeared. 'Why have you come?' she hissed.

'I didn't know how else to meet you, Defne.' The use of her birthname earned me a flared set of nostrils which I interpreted to mean, 'You wretched little traitor, you.' My spirits sank lower.

Here I was in front of my sister, and I felt foolish. I had an overwhelming urge to tell her that I didn't want anything from her, at least, nothing material. That I was Sandy. That I was her brother. I felt an emptiness and defeat start to surface, one that I normally kept boxed away. My shoulders slumped. I had been naïve, delusional even. How could I possibly have imagined she would want to meet me?

'I am sorry, Defne. I don't want to inconvenience you. I just wanted…' As I said this, I could feel the people in the line behind me stirring with impatience; and they were right, my time with her was up. 'I'd better leave you.'

I got up to go. I needed to go. I could feel tears coming to my eyes. I had failed completely to connect with her.

'Sandy, your book,' she said.

I looked back and saw that I had left my copy in the no man's land of the table where at which she was sitting.

But now her voice had changed and softened. Her face was no longer hard and suspicious. 'Sandy, I tell you what, if you can spare the time, let's have a drink after I am done here.'

My heart was pounding, and I felt a rush of blood to the head, 'All right, where?'

'At the French House, just up the road on Dean Street. 'I should be finished in an hour or so.' Before she let me go, she took back my copy of her book and scribbled something inside. Then she smiled, pushed the book back towards me, and said, 'See you properly in a little while.'

CHAPTER 24

I was almost a bottle of Chablis down by the time she arrived. The 'hour' had turned out to be two. But I didn't mind. I was fortunate enough to have found a corner place to sit in. From that vantage point, I could observe my fellow drinkers. Most of them spoke loudly and laughed often. I guessed by the prevailing air of flamboyance that they were artists or actors or other creative types. Though I am quiet by nature, I felt at ease there. Occasionally, people turned to look at me as if trying to figure out whether I was one of them. Whether I fitted in. But even if I didn't, they smiled at me. It wouldn't have taken much to start a conversation. I decided that I liked the place and that, even if nothing materialised with Defne, I would come back. Apart from the patrons, I liked the décor: the wooden bar, the old black and white photographs, the possibly contrived loucheness that gave the impression that nothing had changed since the 1950s. The whole environment suggested that here, at least, one could be without pretence, without artifice. It was in that little fuggy cocoon that I sat, patiently reading her book, waiting for her arrival. I flicked back several times to the handwritten dedication: *To Sandy, despite myself.* I wondered what she meant by that. Perhaps, I would ask her when she came. It didn't cross my mind once that she wouldn't show. Simply because she said she would come. And, if she was anything like me, if she was really my sister, then her word was binding.

When she did finally arrive, no one turned their head as she pushed her way through to the bar. At first, she did not see me. I should have stood up and waved. That would have been the right thing to do. But for a moment, I was just content to watch her. She was no longer the successful and self-confident novelist. She looked left and right with little darting sparrow-like movements of her head. She seemed fragile; even more lovely than she had in the bookshop. Then finally she saw me. She stopped. I could have sworn that, just for a moment, a beam of light connected us. In that instant there was no more noise. There was no one else. Just the two of us. I stood up as she approached my table. As she reached me, I leant forwards and kissed her on the cheek. Again, it was that smell of her perfume that sent my senses tingling – now it was magnified by the warmth of her skin. A bat squeak of something I shouldn't feel flowed through me. I felt emboldened. My self-doubt disappeared. I felt like now I was back again, not as a supplicant, but as the man she had come to meet. Her brother.

But then a little voice inside me said, *Sandy, don't forget this is your sister, not a date*. Impatiently, I dismissed it. *Yes, of course, I know that!* I snapped back at my better angel.

'How did it go?' As I said this, I poured her a glass of wine without asking if she wanted one.

'Oh, you know, the usual...'

'Why do you have to do these things? I mean you're famous enough as it is.'

'It's about building the rapport with the readers and helping the bookshops. If the fans come in for an event like this, they usually buy more than one book and then they get used to coming in.'

Then our conversation stopped. We looked down at our glasses. We knew that this small talk was not what we had come for. So I plunged in.

'I hope it wasn't too much of a shock finding out about Zeki and your mother.'

She looked me straight the eyes and said, 'For a while, it was horrible, sickening, to think that my poor dad, Ziya, was not my father. And then I got to thinking that it didn't really matter. Because Ziya was my real father. Because he loved me. In fact, more than that: he was like a mother and father rolled into one. He was always there for me. He did everything. He picked me up from school. Cooked me dinner. Proper Turkish food that took ages to prepare but always better than the restaurants. He made sure I did my homework. And, at night, he read me stories before I went to bed. All the classics. Do you know he even read me Lord of The Rings, all three volumes? He read every single one of the Narnia Chronicles. And all Oscar Wilde's short stories for children. Sometimes I would laugh at him because of his accent. He couldn't quite say some of the words right. And then I'd try and teach him how to say them and we'd repeat the words together.' She looked away for a moment. Her eyes were glistening. I was not sure if it was the thought of her stepfather or the wine.

In an attempt to change the subject, I asked, 'Is that how you got the bug to write?'

But she ignored the question. 'On weekends he took me to museums. He was determined that I should have every opportunity.'

'What about your mother?'

'She was not a motherly mother, if that makes sense. She was studying all the time. Just after I was born, she signed up to go to university to do a degree. And then she got a master's and then it was on to a PhD. Dad used to say that she had something to prove for the women left behind in her village. He never minded. He was proud of her. But she never had much time for me... or for him. I think that's why we were so close.' Her glass was empty. I refilled it from the bottle in the ice bucket. As I did, I spilled big splashes of iced water on the wooden table. I saw her look at the stains and took my handkerchief from my pocket and wiped the table dry, thinking I had done something wrong.

But she had other things on her mind. 'So, what about you?'

'What about me?' I think my tone of voice was more defensive than I would have liked. I told myself, *Sandy, you have to relax. It's okay.*

'Well, did your mother know about Zeki and my mother?'

'I haven't told her. I mean what's the point? It doesn't exactly put Zeki in a good light. But the thing is, I don't know if now, after all these years, she would care. She's never really told me what she felt about him. I suppose if she did really love him then this would be terribly painful.'

'What? So, it's okay for you to take the risk of blowing my life apart but not your mother's?' Her words cut me to the core. I knew she was right, of course. I hadn't considered that aspect. All of a sudden, I felt embarrassed and selfish. I put my glass down and passed my hand over my forehead and eyes.

'I'm sorry, Defne. I wanted to meet you. Like you, I grew up an only child and I was completely taken with the idea that I would have someone who was close to me. A sister. I didn't think everything through. Particularly not the impact on you. I'm sorry.'

'It's okay. So now you've found your sister you'd better tell me about *your* family life. I've told you enough about mine.'

'Well to start with it, was nothing like yours. Zia sounds like an angel of a man. I don't mean that there was anything wrong with my stepfather. And I always knew he was just that – a stepfather. So, emotionally, there was always going to be a distance. He was the kind of man that my mother should have married in the first place. You know, they always looked like they matched. If you saw them at a party, you'd have picked them out as a couple without knowing them. They spoke the same. Liked the same things. They were very close. Still are, for that matter. I guess I felt excluded… you don't think about that when you're a child. And anyway, they sent me away to boarding school as soon as they could. Bloody wretched place. Not a posh one. Sort of second-rate. All the teachers wore greasy club ties and thought we wanted to hear about their experiences in the Second World War all the time. One of them even used to say, "What we need is another good war to sort things out." Jesus, can you believe that?'

'I'm sorry,' she said, and she put her hand on mine. I felt its warmth.

'No, don't be. Nothing too bad. No funny stuff from the teachers. Just a sense of not being in the right kind of public school. And after that, you end up with some frightfully affected accent only you don't have the credentials to match.'

I had let out rather more bitterness than I would ever normally have admitted to. I shouldn't have started on the second bottle of wine. But it was too late. Once I started to drink, I didn't seem to have an off button. My only comfort was that she was already on her third glass now. Her eyes were shiny. Her face was full of gentleness and concern, so I continued. 'Hugh and Caroline were determined that I should be an Englishman. There was never any mention of Cyprus. Never any mention of my father. I'm embarrassed to admit it now, but I didn't mind. When I was growing up, I don't think I was once curious about where my father had come from.'

I ordered another bottle of wine. Defne was matching me glass for glass by now.

'Do you know, in a strange sort of way, Zia wanted me to be English also. I mean we weren't like you.'

'What do you mean?'

'Posh. I mean, Dad was just a high street accountant. But God Almighty, how he loved Britain. He never took me back to Cyprus. And now it all makes sense – why that must have suited Mum too. Every holiday was somewhere in Britain: Cornwall, The Cotswolds, Yorkshire, Wales, or the west coast of Scotland. When I was sixteen and starting to think about university, he even paid for me to have elocution lessons. He didn't want me speaking with a North London accent like all the other Turkish Cypriots around us. In fact, it was him who encouraged me to change my name.'

'Why would he do that? Defne is a lovely name.'

'Probably for the same reason your mum called you Sandy... or is it Alexander?' She giggled. 'So I could fit in. Dad knew enough about Britain in those days, that with a funny name and an accent you had little chance of getting ahead. I know things have changed now but back then in the eighties it was hard for North London Turkish Cypriots to get ahead, to be taken seriously. Particularly by posh people... people like you... people like your mum and dad. They probably thought that all Turkish Cypriots worked in kebab restaurants.'

I was about to deny this when the barman called time and people started to leave. We got up to go but as she stood up she caught the strap of her handbag on the table and was yanked right back. I reached out for her hand to steady her. She did not let go. We walked out of the pub hand in hand. I could feel my heart pounding. On the pavement I moved my fingers between hers. I felt her thumb gently stroke the side of my hand. I reached up to stroke her face. I leant towards her and kissed her on the cheek. She did the same back to me. I felt her lips on my cheek. I could smell her perfume. I could feel her breathing. We stayed like that for what felt like an eternity. It was probably only a few seconds but enough time for me to hear that little voice hissing away about right and wrong. And then, as if she had heard the same voice too, she broke away. She looked at me and said, 'Thank you, Sandy. It's been a lovely evening.'

'When shall we see each other again?'

'I don't know if that's a good idea.'

'Why not?'

'I don't want any more complications in my life.'

'We are brother and sister, there is nothing complicated about that.'

'Well, let's see how it goes then.' She leant forward, kissed me on the cheek then turned on her heels and walked off towards Shaftesbury Avenue. Even though that was the direction I should have taken, I didn't want to appear clingy or desperate, so I headed up towards Old Compton Street. I was impervious to the night life that was coming into its own now that closing time had been called all around and the next phase of Soho's night life was about to begin. As I walked, I thought about Defne and tried to make sense of things. I couldn't. I knew that something was not right about what I felt around her. Maybe she was right, I told myself. Maybe we shouldn't see each other again. At least not alone. Sometime around midnight, I realised that I had walked as far as Marble Arch, and ended up taking a taxi back home to the Fulham Road.

CHAPTER 25

From: Daphne Neil

To: Fatma Necati

Mum, I thought you should know that I met Sandy last week. I hadn't wanted to meet him, but he turned up at one of my book signings. At first, I was going to tell him to get lost. But there was something about him. Almost touching, vulnerable. So, I agreed to meet him for a drink. And it was so strange. I felt this connection with him. I guess it was the DNA kicking in. In the end it wasn't as bad as I'd imagined it could be. I'm glad I met him. Not sure if we will see each other again. I will tell you more in due course. Hope all's well with you.

Love,

Defne

CHAPTER 26

Harry Eid was going over the roll-out plans for our two businesses. From his laptop, he had projected a PowerPoint slide with the map of the UK on to the white wall of Aydin's office. All the cities with more than 100,000 inhabitants were highlighted. Seventy-seven, apparently. He explained how each one, constituted the right size of market opportunity. I heard words like 'fragmented', 'brand development', 'customer engagement', 'J-curve' 'maximisation of revenue opportunities'. I knew he was talking sense, but my mind was so full of Defne that I couldn't concentrate. It was ridiculous.

You're not a teenager, I told myself. *For God's sake... she's your sister. Just you remember that.* I nodded at the little voice inside my head. Conveniently, Harry took it as assent for what he was presenting.

At the end of his presentation – I knew it was the end because he had the good grace to slap down the lid of his computer – he said, with a hint of triumph in his voice, 'So what do you think Mr Sandy?'

I am not sure if he saw me cringe at the '*Mr* Sandy' but when I responded by saying 'Well... it seems fine,' the flesh around his jaw tightened as if he was clenching his teeth. I realised too late that I should have said something more encouraging, for I had no doubt that he had done some fine work.

'Do you not see what it represents in terms of opportunity... and revenue... and potential market capitalisation?' I heard the frustration seeping through.

'Like I said it seems fine. I tell you what, if you email your presentation to me, I will take a look at it and come back to you if

I have any questions.'

'You've done a good job, Harry, looks very nice, your presentation, I just hope you can deliver on it,' said Aydin. He could see that a mollifying tone was required to assuage the financier's consternation in the face of what he assumed was my indifference.

Harry went to leave us. As he reached the door he said, 'Mr Sandy if there's anything you are unhappy with just call.' He made the gesture of a phone call with his hand.

'Yes, of course, Harry. And thank you,' I said, more kindly.

When we were alone, Aydin said 'So what's up with you? I was watching you and you didn't listen to a word of what he said.'

'Sorry, was it that obvious?'

'You were miles away, Sandy. What's got hold of you?'

'I had things on my mind.'

'I don't mean to be funny, Sandy, but what can be more important than this for God's sake?

'Defne. I met her last night.'

'Oh! I didn't know you'd managed to find her. When were you going to tell me?'

'It's a long story but we met up last night. Sort of by accident. At a signing of her latest book.'

'What are you talking about? What book?'

'She's a writer. She writes those blockbusters.'

'So, she's rich then?' His face was all smiles.

'I suppose so, but that's not the point. It was about meeting her.'

'So, how did it go?'

'It's not what I expected. She's lovely. I mean, in her own way, she's beautiful.'

'*Öyle mi?*'

'She's beautiful, lovely. I don't know what else to say. I've never met anyone like her before.'

'Well, that's nice that your sister is so good looking. So, what did you two talk about? I mean, how did she take the fact that Zeki was her dad and all?'

'It was a bit of a shock for her, obviously. At first, she was a bit funny with me but then we started talking about how we grew up and things got better.'

'So, when are you going to see her again?'

'Not sure. We're both still thinking about it.'

'What is there to think about, for God's sake? You're brother and sister. Don't waste time, is my advice. And tell her that I was a friend of Zeki, and I can tell her a fair amount about him.'

'Will do.' It was my turn to head for the door but just as I reached it, Aydin said, 'One last thing, son. Now is not the time to get distracted. We are on our way to making a bloody fortune if what Harry says is true.'

Chapter 27

It had been five days since I had met Defne at the French House. A weekend had passed, and I was clinging on by my fingernails, resisting the urge to message her. Saturday night was the worst. I stayed at home watching *The Sopranos* on DVD with a bottle of wine that eventually became two. The urge to tap something stupid and inane was unbearable. Thankfully, the battery on my phone died and, before I had a chance to re-charge it, I fell asleep on the couch, still in my T-shirt and boxer shorts, and with my big Samsung screen flickering faithfully on. I knew I would have to do something, or I'd go mad. But what? We had left everything hanging in the air. Was it up to her to make the next move, or me? But I couldn't wait any longer, the lack of clarity was eating me up. So I chose to be the one to make the next move. I had to frame it just right. I couldn't suggest dinner. Too intimate. Something out in public. Something intellectual so she'd see me as more than just a boring ex-banker. Desperately, I flicked through the pages of *Time Out* until I came across an ad for an exhibition dedicated to writers from the Levant and North Africa at the National Portrait Gallery. I tore out the page.

The next day at the office, instead of going over Harry's presentation, I went online and checked out the exhibition. Amongst all the featured writers one name in particular caught my eye. On the strength of it, I sent Defne an SMS. I was expecting an immediate response, but my phone remained painfully silent. Thursday, nothing. Friday, nothing. It was not until Saturday afternoon that I got the response I had been checking my device for every hour for three days: 'Okay, see you by Nelson's column tomorrow at 3p.m.' That was it. Nothing to suggest that she was pleased or, to the contrary, that this was a tiresome obligation that she should honour out of pity. My mind assumed the latter. But I'm ashamed to admit, I was prepared to settle even for that.

I sat on the steps just below the gallery with a whole view of Trafalgar Square in front of me. I was absurdly early but I wanted to be sure that I was the first to arrive. So, I sat there absorbing the sound of the traffic coming down Charing Cross Road. I watched tourists take photographs of themselves with the pigeons. For a while, I allowed myself the right not to think about anything. I remained seated in a reptilian state of patience. Keeping my heartbeat slow; trying to ignore the fear that was rising up out of my guts – that she might not come. Then finally, when the clock of St Martin-in-the-Fields chimed the half hour, I saw a figure dressed in black marching, head down, as if hunched up against rain. As soon as I saw her, I stood up and rushed down to the meeting point. She beat me to it and turned around, frowning, as if irritated at the thought I might have wasted her time and not showed or been late. And then she saw me. And she smiled. Relief went through my body. I didn't speak because I knew I would say something stupid if I did. Instead, I kissed her on the cheeks, but more briskly than at our last encounter, and led her back towards the entrance of the gallery.

I hadn't been to the National Portrait Gallery since I was a child. So, I had to look awkwardly around for the ticket office – already losing the advantage of seeming suave or in control – but I finally got the tickets, and we headed into the exhibition. As we went in, she stopped, placed her hand on my sleeve and said, 'What made you choose this particular exhibition? I mean, I wouldn't have taken you as somebody with an interest in literary figures from this part of the world?'

'I'm not. Well, not really. But I thought it would be interesting, given how you are a writer and all. And we are both, when all's said and done, from the Levant, ourselves.' I turned away from her quickly in case I betrayed the hint of a smirk and patted my jacket pocket to reassure myself that my gift for her was still there, waiting for me to bring it out at the right time.

We made our way into the exhibition, where the walls ahead of us were lined with photographs, mostly black and white. The introductory blurb told us precious little, save to say that they were displayed in alphabetical order by surname. Deliberately, I led her to the opposite wall, where the final photo of the exhibition was hanging. It was of a writer called May Ziadeh. The name meant nothing to either of us. But I noticed that Defne read the biography carefully. I could see her nod her head a couple of times. Thankfully, I had not professed any knowledge so, like her, I could just discover. Then we went to the Qs, to Nizar Qabbani, the Syrian poet. And there they had listed some lines of his love poetry. In the exhibition leaflet I gave him a tick with my pen as a reminder to order a book of his verse.

As we made our way, in reverential silence, from picture to picture – Asma Tubi to Nawal El Saadawi, Amos Oz and Albert Memmi – the ticks on my leaflet multiplied. On we went, leaving behind Sami Michael, for Naguib Mahfouz, Ghada Karmi and Tahar Ben Jelloun. For the first time, I was seeing my little community in a wider context, adding layers to my sense of the world. The first iteration of my identity was British: simple. Then there was Turkish Cypriot. Then Cypriot. Now, staring at the faces of all those writers, Palestinian, Syrian, Lebanese, Sephardim, Ashkenazi from Israel, Moroccan and Greek, I recognised a common DNA in wrinkles, foreheads, and eyes with dark patches under them that were staring at us from those portraits. We were closing in on the one image I wanted her to see. Ahead of us we still had Mahmoud Darwish and someone whose poetry I had actually often read: Constantine Cavafy. The Greek poet looked down at us, haughty and sad, with his thick round glasses. If Aydin had been more of a reading man, I would have given him a copy of the Alexandrian's most famous poems. Perhaps I might anyway. As a farewell present before he finally left for Cyprus. Perhaps he would find words that summed up his own feelings for Tassos more eloquently than he ever could, there in Cavafy's poetry. I put that thought to one side, for at last we had come to the portrait which had made me bold. We stood in front of the curly haired portrait of Taner Baybars, the father of Turkish Cypriot literature. In the picture he must have been in his twenties. He was gazing downwards, lost in thought, a fine angular nose, the shade of an adolescent-like moustache, a nattily splayed-open collar and a cabled jumper that looked like a ploughed field. His great poetry was yet to come. His stories of Cyprus were no doubt fermenting. The 'troubles' were starting to break out, but he was still a citizen of the British Empire; his image captured at a juncture where there was still hope for Cyprus. A dream that after thousands of years there would be independence, no more colonisers; that Cypriots could live as just that. A hope that was to shatter within years of the photograph being taken.

From my jacket pocket, I brought out a copy of Baybars' book *Plucked from a Far-Off Land* and, as I handed over the offering from my own bookshelf, said to her 'The words of one Turkish Cypriot writer for another'. I had written the same on the inside cover.

CHAPTER 28

After that Sunday at the exhibition, we started going out together several times a week. She was always being invited somewhere: to gallery openings, fashion shows, musical events, charity functions. And everywhere she went, she knew people. They came up to greet her as soon as she arrived. I noticed that she never explained our connection to each other. It was always just, 'This is Sandy.' Anyway, it didn't matter because I was invisible. No one ever said a word to me. They would smile politely and then turn all of their attention to her. But I didn't mind. I just liked looking at her. When people became too much and were in danger of intruding on our time together, she simply despatched them, in such a way that they didn't even realise they had been dismissed. In all these busy gatherings it only ever felt like the two of us. It was as if there was a magical shield around us. We talked all the time. It just flowed. Sometimes we couldn't get our words out fast enough and we quickly formed the habit of finishing each other's sentences – almost as if we were different sides of the same mind.

For the first time, I held back on Aydin. I didn't tell him that I was seeing my sister so often like this. I occasionally mentioned that I had seen her. I reassured him that we were taking our time getting to know each other. But I was all too conscious that we had begun some strange subterfuge. Defne admitted to me that she was doing the same thing, with her mother.

Why both of us should have favoured privacy, and a carefully curated account of our relationship, was not something we chose to explore. At least not then. What would someone spying on us have seen? Very simply, a man and woman laughing, in intense conversation, finishing one bottle of wine and calling for another, a couple walking arm in arm in the park, in the street, in fact everywhere. It was as if we had to be physically connected all the time.

But one thing we never did was visit each other's homes. We were always in public. I did think about inviting her over so that I could cook her dinner, but that little voice told me it was not wise. And I recognised the sagacity of the counsel. Because something that had been there, that first night in the French House, was ever present, bubbling under the surface. I was afraid each time we saw each other, each time we leant forward for the kiss on the cheek, that precise moment when I felt the warmth of her skin against mine and smelt her perfume, that I would lose control. That I would mess everything up. That I would do something untoward. That the court of public opinion would have me stoned and put in irons. But despite all that, I admitted to myself that I felt happy and realised that it was possibly for the first time ever. Everything was going well for once in my life. Even at work. I was kinder and more friendly towards Harry. I listened to his briefings more carefully and made sensible comments. I even made the effort to take him out to lunch from time to time.

Even Aydin noticed. In fact, one morning, he dropped by my office and said 'Sandy, are you seeing a girl you haven't told me about? You seem different. Happy. Never seen you quite like this.'

Quite truthfully, I denied it. Nor did I let on that my good humour might have something to do with Defne.

Then he changed the subject and said, 'Don't forget that I'm heading back to Cyprus next month.'

I had completely forgotten about it. All of a sudden, I realised to my shame that I had not yet introduced him to Defne.

Chapter 29

Aydin, as I had come to learn over the years, was a man of predictable tastes and a creature of habit. Thus, organising a farewell lunch for him required little originality of thought. The devil, however, was in the execution. Everything had to be just right. With this in mind, I made sure we had his favourite corner table at Bibendum. I had even been in touch with the restaurant's sommelier earlier in the week to make sure they would have his favourite wines available in sufficient quantities. For the white, I chose a 2000 Puligny Montrachet; for the red, a 1999 Gevrey Chambertin. Both of them premier cru. It was one of Aydin's little foibles that he did not like red wines from Bordeaux. He was always muttering about how they were adulterated with cheaper wines from Spain and that you couldn't trust them and were sure to be ripped off. But there was one Bordeaux he adored and that was his beloved Chateau d'Yquem. I pushed the boat out and went for a 1975 vintage. I knew that he loved to drink this sweet wine not just with dessert but starting earlier with his Roquefort – pretty much the only cheese he ate. Every now and again, he was known to take some mature Cheddar – but I suspect that was something to do with flying the flag for Britain rather than anything else.

I knew he wouldn't have minded if I had charged all this to my corporate credit card – he never once checked my expenses, modest as they were – but this lunch was the least I could do for him. I was going to miss seeing him as often as I did. He had become an integral part of my life. I am not sure at which precise moment the boundary between boss and adopted family member cum mentor became blurred. But by then it certainly was.

When I had first planned the lunch, it was to have been just for Aydin and me. But I decided it was a good occasion to introduce Defne to him and make up for having been remiss in not having done so before. Then Defne asked me if her mother, who was in London for a little while, could come. So, a party of two had become a party of four Turkish Cypriots of different iterations – two older ones born to that same little village of Bamyaköy on the Karpaz finger of our island, and two younger ones born, like the majority of us Turkish Cypriots today, in London.

Aydin and I arrived ahead of time. Without waiting for our guests, we started on the Puligny. During the first few sips neither one of us spoke a word. I noticed that Aydin was looking around. Even though he knew the restaurant well, there was a look of wonder and delight on his face. He nodded his head, and his lips moved a little as if he was talking to someone under his breath. Then finally, after a particularly large swig of wine, he turned towards me and said, 'Well, *oğlum*, I think I am leaving the business in good hands with you at the helm. And while you're concentrating on the stock market listing with Harry, I'll be enjoying the summer in Cyprus. You know, I might even buy myself one of those big fancy motorboats...' He looked into his glass which had only a finger of wine left in it and said, 'Can you believe it? I haven't lived in the village properly since I was a lad!' A silence. His mood changed, not definitively, but fleetingly in the manner of a cloud covering the sun. He grabbed his glass of wine with both hands, drained it, then once he had thumped it back on the table, he said, 'I don't know why I am doing this.'

'You said you wanted to go home.' My response was irrelevant. Conversation had changed to monologue.

'It was okay for your dad. Him being so clever and loved. But for me? You can't imagine. You know my own dad was old fashioned. He thought that a man had to be a certain way. He was forever beating me because he didn't like what I was. He knew what I was before I did. He thought that if he hit me hard enough, he could chase it out of me like the devil.'

I tried to interrupt his flow and lighten the conversation by introducing what I hoped might be a more pleasant topic, and said, 'What about your mum, Aydin?'

'Nothing she could do to stop him… he used to beat her too. She had no friends in the village. No one to go to, no one to rely on. She was a complete outsider. She didn't even speak Turkish,' He saw me looking puzzled. 'She was Palestinian. In those days, would you believe it, there was a fair bit of trade between Famagusta and Gaza. God knows how my father got hold of her. Anyway, she wasn't one for talking. She just gave that rotten bastard one child after another. Most of them died though. The only ones that survived were my two younger sisters… and a younger brother – a nasty bit of work he is.'

'You never told me that you had family,' I said.

'I don't, at least not in any real sense. My sisters left the village when they were young – twelve or thirteen – and were married off somewhere. I was away living in Famagusta at the time and when I came back no one knew where they'd gone. And my brother... I don't want to talk about him, right now. But at another time, oğlum, I should. So, you see, you are the only family I have now.' He placed his soft manicured paw on my hand. I didn't mind what anybody thought seeing me there with him, with his thin, blue-rinsed hair blow-dried into a bouffon, his pale-yellow checked suit, and his lemon-coloured shirt with a tobacco-coloured tie. I was beyond caring. At least this version of me was.

The cloud passed. He reached out for my cheek and stroked it. He smiled and said, 'You look happy, Sandy. Treasure whatever you have. You never know when you'll lose it.' He picked up his glass, which by now had been refilled almost to the brim, but changed his mind and set it down again and said more seriously, 'Who I loved was taken away from me in the physical sense, but he is always with me in my head. All these years I've been building and making money to show him. I say to him 'Look Tassos. This is what we have now. This is the life we could have had. I would have taken care of you. Here in London, we would have been safe.' Every single expensive thing I've ever bought was for him and because of him.' He looked at his left wrist and the gold Patek Philippe fastened around it. For a moment, I thought I saw a look of disgust on his face. 'You know, when Tassos first met me, I spent nothing on myself. He took me to Nicosia for the first time. I mean, it's just a small town compared to London, but going there was magical. It must have been some time around 1958. He made me go and buy proper clothes. He helped me choose them. It's like he brought me alive.' The old man's eyes sparkled. He was far away. His face softened. I was about to ask him to tell me more about his life with Tassos – this was only the second time he had ever mentioned him to me - when we were interrupted by the arrival of Fatma.

My heart sank. I shouldn't have felt that way. This was Defne's mother after all. This woman was once my father's lover. Someone who was presented to my father as a potential bride. Trying as hard as I could, I still failed to picture Fatma young, with full lips, or the curves that her daughter certainly had. But she must have had something. My father was a handsome man. In my wallet I still carry a copy of the photo I found of him back in his house in Bamyaköy. Sometimes I used to take it out to look at it. I knew every detail of the black and white image by heart: his Brilliantined wavy hair groomed to neatness with a pencil-sharp parting; his high forehead; the aquiline nose, thin elegant lips, and his strong, slightly angular chin. But the gaze… it was always off to one side. How many times had I wished to have a photo of him looking straight at the camera, with something coming close to a smile? So that I could imagine that he was looking at me, his son. Just for one second some acknowledgement from him that I was his flesh and blood. I only realised that I had become lost in these thoughts when I heard Aydin call my name. I blinked, confused, then I saw Fatma's hand extended in front of me, waiting for me to shake it. I looked into her eyes. She returned the gaze with the same condescension as before, except I noticed there was now an extra layer of scrutiny, almost curiosity. I took the proffered hand. It was cold and bony.

Once again, I studied her face trying to imagine what my father might have seen in her as a young woman. However, forty or so years of life that had flowed past had covered the tracks of what she must have been; as much as I tried, I saw nothing seductive, kind nor inviting about her. No glint of charm or coquettishness. All that was left of the face that once looked upon my father, were her eyes. These were like mine, like Defne's, like Aydin's, and so many others from Bamyaköy. They were green, speckled with tiny flecks of brown. A little scraping of DNA that we all shared.

CHAPTER 30

'Where's Defne?' Aydin asked me.

I sensed, from the distracted looks he gave the passing waiters, that he was tired of the effort of talking to Fatma. We had finished our first bottle of wine. Her own glass remained untouched.

I took out my Blackberry. No messages. At least none from that day. We were into the habit of texting most days. Not too much but enough to be connected. To share the odd thought, to confirm plans. Nothing more than that. I pulled up her number from my favourites and, just as I was about to press the green call button, she entered the restaurant.

It seemed to me that the dining room went through a climate change, as if a crackle of electricity had circuited through every atom, revitalising the universe around us. I felt my heartbeat accelerate. I couldn't take my eyes off her. She was her usual chic self, dressed in 'faux casual' mode. In contrast to my suit and tie, she was wearing faded ripped Levi's, a V neck navy blue cashmere sweater, gold coloured Valentino trainers, and her pearl necklace – the same one she wore the night I met her. In the light of the restaurant, it seemed to be glowing, as if reflecting the warmth of her skin.

'Hello, Mum!' she cried out, exuberantly, as she approached our table. She went over to her mother and threw her arms around the old lady. As she did, Fatma leant her head to one side like a boxer slipping a punch and then wrinkled her nose. My sister didn't notice. She went over to Aydin. For a moment she hesitated and was about to shake his hand but then he said, 'No need for that, kızım, you're family. Give me a kiss.' Once she had pecked him on both cheeks, it was my turn. She gave me just a single kiss on the cheek but rested her face against mine a little longer than good manners required. It occurred to me that she was smelling my skin. Part of me wanted to reciprocate but instead I pushed her away as gently as I could. In front of her mother, I felt shy. As Defne took her seat between Aydin and me, I caught, over and above her perfume, the unmistakeable toasted almond smell of champagne.

For a moment, there was a lull in conversation at our table, for Defne's arrival had triggered the appearance of our waiter with the menus. I knew from the gurgles coming from his paunch that Aydin was hungry and that he was eager to eat. However, out of consideration for his guests he made a show of reading the menu slowly and attentively. Of course, he knew it by heart. He had already established that there were Gillardeau oysters for starters. For the main course, I knew he would have the Beef Wellington. Followed by cheese. And then the Sicilian mango ice cream for dessert. But despite his best efforts to be polite and patient, they took too long for his taste. He grunted a little to help things along. But they failed to take the hint. So, he started to make suggestions and when that did not produce the desired outcome he said, 'Would you like for me to choose? I know all the best things to have here.'

'What a good idea!' said Defne shutting the leather-bound menu gleefully. Her mother, on the other hand, held out a little longer but eventually even she settled on what she was going to eat.

When we had given our order Fatma called time on the uneasy truce that had prevailed thus far and said, 'Where have you come from Defne?' The tone of her voice was sharp and held a hint of rebuke.

'Just meeting with some girlfriends for a quick drink, Mum.'

'But you knew we were going to have lunch with Aydin, and...' Instead of mentioning my name she motioned her head in my direction.

'It was just a couple of drinks, Mum. And his name is Sandy.' As she said this, I could feel her knee up against mine. It was the first time she had done anything so intimate. At first, I was taken aback, even a little shocked.

'There's no harm, Fatma,' said Aydin. Then to throw the older lady off balance, he went on, 'You know who I was thinking about the other day?' She shook her head. 'Turgut,' he said. Neither Defne nor I had any idea who he was talking about but mentioning this name had the desired effect of stopping her inquisition.

'The man who used to go around the village barefoot?'

'Yes, that's the one.' He turned to Defne and me and said 'You know, there was this fellow who used to live in the village – no family, no house. He used to do jobs for people and get paid in food, and they would give him space to kip down in their barn. But always smiling. Would do anything. Could build a dry-stone wall like no one else. I don't know why I was thinking about him. Whatever happened to him, Fatma?'

'He was killed, Aydin. One of the many.' And there it is, put us Turkish Cypriots together and at a certain point it just comes up in conversation, the war, 'the troubles,' the 'us' versus 'them'. The old lady continued, 'I think you had already left for England by then. He was out in the hills, apparently, and some Greek soldiers came upon him and shot him.'

'Why did they do that, Mum?' There was a hint of a slur to Defne's voice.

Fatma looked down at her place setting and said under her breath, 'Because he was a Turkish Cypriot. And that was enough to get you killed in those days. Being one side or the other.'

'And this is the place you want to retire to, Aydin?' I said in a bid to lighten the mood. The question I really wanted to ask Fatma was how, after all that had happened, she could live on the Greek side. But I decided to keep the question for another time. Too hostile. Too much for what was supposed to be a happy farewell lunch.

Aydin patted my hand and said, 'Those days are over, *oğlum*, we are safe in our part of the island thanks to what Mr Denktash did. And besides, Mr Erdoğan has our back now. It will be fine.'

The oysters came for Aydin, Defne and me. A dozen for each of us. Each platter accompanied by a silver sauce boat with mignonette, plates of fresh bread and Isigny butter wrapped in gold foil. Fatma on the other hand had beetroot soup. She refused the sour cream that was supposed to be spooned into it. The sommelier refilled our glasses. Fatma's was still untouched, I noticed. All she drank was water. I saw her looking pointedly at Defne who had just taken a big gulp of wine. Then she said, 'Defne, don't you think you've had enough?'

'No, I fucking well haven't, all right?' The expletive froze everything for a moment. Even the tables nearest ours went silent.

Aydin didn't bat an eyelid, and said, 'Sandy pass me the shallot sauce, there's a love.'

Fatma sat stone rigid in her seat. For a moment I even felt sorry for her.

Then Defne, realising what had come out of her mouth, said, 'Sorry, Mum, I didn't mean that.' For a moment it was the voice of a child, not the beautiful grown woman that she was.

I reached out for her hand under the table. I wasn't sure why. It was instinctive. As soon as I did, she took it. She squeezed it hard, almost viciously – as if doing so might expunge her sin – but when she turned to look at me, I could see her eyes were moist. At last, she softened her grip but continued to hold it, as if we had always been like this, in communion one with the other. No one, except for the waiter, could see us – and that was only if he chose to look our way. We broke off to eat but at the end of the first course we reconnected. And then again after the main course. There was no little voice this time telling me I shouldn't, so I told myself that it was all right. That it couldn't be wrong.

'Where's the Roquefort?' said Aydin. The waiter had just

wheeled over a trolley with a glass dome, under which was a luscious looking assortment of cheese. I nodded to the sommelier who, right on cue, brought us the bottle of Chateau d'Yquem. Aydin called the man over and put on his reading glasses. 'A '75, *oğlum*? Very nice choice. You're spoiling me.'

All eyes were on him as he took his first sip of the yellow amber elixir. He closed his eyes and took another, and said, 'That's the stuff. Lovely.' But just as he saw Defne about to take an enthusiastic swig from her glass he said, 'Gently does it, *kızım*, this wine is to be savoured.' She tempered her enthusiasm a little but nevertheless took a gulp exceeding the dictates of decorum. But then she giggled. And Aydin smiled and motioned to the sommelier to fill up our three glasses again.

During the main course, Fatma said nothing. But it didn't matter, for Aydin was on fine form telling us story after story about life in Bamyaköy – even some I hadn't heard before. But now that we were coming to the end of the cheese course, I saw her looking over at Defne, who by now had one elbow on the table and was laughing along with Aydin. For a moment, I said to myself that if I cut Fatma's sour face out of this picture, it would be a happy scene, a family lunch. But Defne's mother was there, in all her puritanical gloom and sobriety, doing her best to dampen the mood.

As soon as dessert was over – Aydin had two servings of his Sicilian mango ice cream – Fatma got up to leave. She came over to Defne and said, 'I wish you wouldn't drink so much, Defne.' And after having said goodbye to Aydin, she left. She did not look at me nor had she said a word to me during the whole lunch.

The three of us remained seated. And then Aydin said to me, 'Come on my boy, order us another bottle of the D'Yquem – you know there won't be any of that stuff once I am back in the village.'

By the time we made it out of the restaurant, Defne and I were no longer hiding the fact that we were holding hands. I don't know if Aydin noticed, or cared, for when he came up to me, he said,

'You be good, *oğlum*. Keep me updated on the business and I will see you soon.' We hugged and he went off to his Bentley where his chauffeur had the door open for him. At last, Defne and I were alone. We looked at each other, and there on the pavement right outside Michelin House, with all the cars accelerating away from the traffic lights and up the Fulham Road, we kissed each other on the mouth. We kissed so hard and inexpertly that our teeth collided and clinked. We kissed for so long that when we drew back our chins were wet with saliva. And then we kissed all over again.

CHAPTER 31

We woke up with parched mouths and splitting headaches. But that was nothing compared to the shock of realising who we were waking up with. And, more importantly, what we had done the night before. So, for what seemed like an eternity, we both lay there silently patching together the blurred strands of the previous afternoon and evening. Eventually, she got out of bed and headed for the kitchen to make us coffee. At first, we couldn't look each other in the eye but after a while she said, 'What have we done Sandy? We're brother and sister. It's like we're animals who don't know better.' But her words lacked bite. At the time, I thought she said it like a disclaimer, to prove that she had voiced the appropriate level of remorse. 'Don't you think?' She went on but her tone of voice was unsure, and I felt she was looking to me for affirmation that we had broken the accepted moral code of the world and that all that was left for us was to hang our heads in abject shame and remorse.

I looked at her and remained silent, and then took her hand. What did I really feel at that moment? I knew it was supposed to be revulsion at having had sex with my sister. Half-sister. But something had blown me away. I just wanted her. And I knew that feeling was reciprocated. Whatever pangs of guilt we may have felt were cast aside by the simple fact that as soon as we finished our coffee, we went back to bed to make love all over again. By the afternoon, we knew that whatever moral compass we had strayed away from, we would continue to do what we had done. Nothing in my life had prepared me for this. Anything I had ever felt previously for a woman before paled into insignificance.

After that day, we did not refer again to our 'situation'. It was as if we relegated it to some dark little cell at the back of our minds.

Instead, we became one of those fortunate and rare couples who discover they can't bear to be apart. Dinner dates several times a week, theatre outings and visits to galleries and museums morphed into clothes left at her place and then into something else.

I wish I could tell you of some grandiose event that marked the next phase of our relationship. If I play it back to you like a film it goes like this: I came home one day from work, to her first floor flat in Onslow Square; I put one key into the top brass lock and then the other more complex key into the bottom lock, turned it and entered her apartment; she was standing there, waiting for me, a few feet from the door; we looked at each other, we knew, we just knew; I walked towards her and reached out for her hands and gently pulled her towards me, so close that our foreheads were touching. And then I said it.

It is a profoundly moving experience telling another person that you love them, and really meaning it. It is only when you do that you come face to face with the platitudes and insincerities of the past. In my case, I shouldn't have been saying it all. At least, not in the way that I meant it. But I couldn't help myself. When I did, I was the luckiest man alive because I didn't regret it, it didn't come out wrong. Then she said it back to me. It was the right thing, at the right moment. It felt, in that instant, as if two halves that had been separated at birth were now reconnected.

October came quickly. So much had happened in the previous few months, and already we were in autumn. In Cale Street, the pavement was thick with heaps of russet-coloured leaves. And, here and there, were splurges of bright green and mahogany of conkers fallen from the horse chestnut trees. Since meeting Defne, I had learnt to see the world anew and, dare I say it, with less cynicism and bitterness than before. I discovered that life could be fun and that there was beauty in the smallest of things. I turned right on Sydney Street and made my way towards Onslow Square.

It was three months since we had decided to live together. It just made sense since I was there with her most nights and steadily moving in more and more of my clothes. We were a good match because, besides a steady supply of starched and laundered clothes, my day-to-day needs on the domestic front were minimal. I didn't even miss my own possessions, for she had everything we needed. Most importantly for me, she had a fine selection of books – though almost exclusively works of fiction. Other than that, every one of her gadgets were high-end and elegant and she was happy for me to play with them, particularly her deluxe TV and Bang & Olufsen hi-fi. At first, I struggled with her coffee machine, one of those integrated bean-to-cup affairs, but apart from making coffee occasionally I really didn't have to do any chores. She had a cleaner who came in daily and kept everything immaculate for us.

I walked through the front door and into our first floor living room which overlooked the gated communal garden below. Everything was as I had come to expect: bright lights, the warmth of a thermostat turned to 23 degrees, her huge corner leather Poltrona Frau settee where she would be sitting, a book or a notepad by her side.

But that day she was crying.

'Sandy, I can't do this,' she said, as soon as she saw me.

I started to panic. My heart was beating. For a moment I was devastated at the thought that she might not want a moment more of what we had. I was sure that this was a 'we' thing. But then she said, 'I can't hide us from my mum.'

I put down my raincoat and briefcase and slowly walked over and sat by her side. Guiltily, I could feel my fear that she might feel compelled to give me up, subside. This issue with her mother was now simply another problem to be solved. It was not the end of our story.

'My love...' I took her into my arms and rocked her ever so

slightly. Over the fragrance of her shampoo and perfume, was the smell of damp salt from her tears. My fingers combed through her hair. I cradled her head as gently as I could. 'We will tell her if that is what you want...' I thought she was better and stronger than me. For I couldn't tell my own mother about Zeki, Fatma, and my love for Defne. I didn't have the courage. Nor the closeness. Those past months I had spoken even less than usual to Caroline. She knew no more about my life than that I was working with Aydin. And because she did not like him, she asked me nothing at all on our once-a-week phone calls. I sensed that she felt that I must have failed if all that I could find by way of employment was a job with 'that man'.

It's because we decided to tell Fatma about us that, a few weeks later, I found myself heading towards the Ritz for afternoon tea. It was December and Fatma was back in London for the Christmas holidays. The prospect of cucumber sandwiches and sponge cake washed down with cups of Earl Grey was strange enough for Defne and me. We didn't do such things in the normal course of events. But we wanted to get it right. Defne thought that Fatma would like a sober elegant environment for our meeting. We wanted everything in our favour. We agreed that Defne would have some time with her mother first and then I would come a few minutes later.

As I arrived at the Ritz, there was some commotion beside the cloakroom next to the main entrance. I could hear music playing. In front of me were various women dressed up as if for some formal evening event even though it was only four o'clock in the afternoon. I paid them no mind. Fortunately, I could see Defne and Fatma sitting a little way ahead of me. The music continued cheerfully along.

I pushed my way through the women who were walking back and forth at pace. Then Defne looked away from her mother and saw me coming towards them. She pointed at me and started to laugh. I hoped my arrival might have had a more dignified effect upon her, particularly given what we were about to discuss. I made it to the table where they were sitting and leant forward to kiss Fatma on both cheeks. For a moment I thought she was going to refuse but, after a slight hesitation, she allowed me to place my lips below each of her cheekbones. Kissing her was a disagreeable experience. Her skin felt doughy and clammy like raw pastry. Instead of greeting Defne with a kiss, I just nodded respectfully towards her. Then I sat down. My trousers were neatly pressed, and my shoes were shined. Earlier that day, I had gone to Trumpers on Jermyn Street to make sure that I was impeccably shorn and groomed. I hoped I would make a good impression on Fatma this time, although I had my doubts, given what we were about to tell her. Once properly settled in my chair, I looked back at the entrance. It was then that I understood what all the commotion had been about and why Defne had been laughing at me: I had just walked through a catwalk of models showing off evening wear. Fatma, true to form, did not look at me. Once again, I felt her condescension. For a moment I was tempted to say something nasty but, instead, I smiled politely and enquired about her trip over from Cyprus.

She wanted no small talk with me and got straight down to business. 'So, Defne, what is so important that you have invited me for tea here? And why does he need to be here?'

'Don't be like that, Mum? Why couldn't I just want to see you?'

'Nothing is ever simple with you, Defne, is it?'

Seeing the hurt on Defne's face I intervened, 'Fatma, we have something to tell you...' As I spoke, I was conscious of Defne watching my lips. I felt as if she was watching a car crash about to happen in slow motion, but I couldn't do anything different. I was accelerating straight into the wall.

'I'm sure my daughter can speak for herself.'

'Well actually, Fatma, it concerns us both.' My words came out harsher and more exasperated than I would have wished.

I saw the old woman's lip start to quiver. She turned to Defne

'What is it?'

'We've fallen in love,' I said.

'Yes, Mum, it's true' Defne whispered. 'I don't know how to explain… it's like nothing I've experienced before.' I reached out for Defne's hand.

The look on Fatma's face was not pretty. 'You both disgust me,' she said, spraying spit over our faces. I reached up and wiped my cheek and chin with my handkerchief.

'Mum, don't be like that. Can't you be happy for me? For once… I'm begging you.'

'You don't understand, Fatma. I love your daughter…' I could feel my voice breaking as I spoke. Then the flood gates opened. I tried to make her understand. 'She makes me feel special, loved. She is the only person I want to talk to now. I never have enough of her company. If I could, I would make her my wife.' Out of the corner of my eye I could see Defne looking at me. Her mouth was wide open.

'Do you realise what you are saying? The obscenity of it? How unforgivable?' said Fatma.

'There's nothing I feel for Defne that I am not proud of, Fatma. I pity you for never having felt what we feel, because if you had you wouldn't be sitting there trying to poison it.'

'Look, Mum,' there was a pleading tone to Defne's voice, 'It's not like we are going to have children. We're careful. I'm on the pill again.'

'If you hadn't known that I was Zeki's son it would have been all right, wouldn't it?' I said. Why couldn't she just understand our point of view, for just one moment?

'But I do know, Sandy. That is the whole point.'

'Be happy for us, Mum. Can't you?'

'Defne, this is wrong. You can't be doing this.'

'But we want to be together. We need to be together. Mum, can't you understand what we feel?'

The old lady's face was frozen, every crack, every wrinkle, graven deep.

'Defne, you must choose.'

'Choose what, Mum?'

'Me or him.'

I froze. For a moment I was back in the grasp of that same mortal fear that Defne was going to give me up. But then I felt her hand squeeze mine and my blood started to pump again.

'Mum, I can't give him up. I love him. This is not a one-off fling. Not like anything before. I promise.'

'You are both too revolting for words. I'm leaving. Don't come and see me until you have got rid of him, Defne.' She turned to me, 'You, have made my daughter unclean. You have contaminated her. I will never forgive you.'

'Mum, that's enough!' As she spoke Defne banged her hand on the table. Cups shook and the maître d' turned to watch us, wondering, I imagined, if he should intervene and ask us to leave. 'Who are you to lecture us? Really? I mean if you had controlled yourself all those years back, we wouldn't even be having this conversation now, would we?'

Suddenly Fatma started to sob. 'You can't speak to me like this,' she said. Defne tried to comfort her, but she pulled away. She wanted nothing from her daughter. I held Defne back as she tried to follow her mother. And then it was just the two of us. I had my arms around her. And there, in the elegance of the Ritz Hotel, there was only us, forsaken and damned. At that point nothing, nobody else, mattered to us.

CHAPTER 32

'The markets are looking good, Sandy,' said Harry. The financier was in the mode of a soothsayer divining the future. It was February 2012 and the world was indeed starting to look a little less bleak than at the height of what, by now, had been labelled the 'Global Financial Crisis'. 'We can start to think about stock market listings at the end of this quarter or beginning of next,' he said. The excitement in his voice was barely controlled. He could smell blood. He knew that our time was coming. And that he, like us, would make a fortune from the successful exits of our two companies.

Over the past year or so, there had been a massive ramp up of our outlets for both business lines. And in my office, bright pink and black pins were all over the map of the UK. Pink for the spas; black for the amusement centres. In my laptop was a spreadsheet that showed the revenue and profit and the quarter-on-quarter growth of every single one of our business units. I still briefed Aydin once a week by telephone, but his voice was ever more distant and our conversations always ended, 'When are you and Defne coming to visit me in Cyprus?'

On my next call, I planned to tell him that we would be there in a matter of months. As soon as the IPO was done. I would also tell him that we were not just coming for a visit but that we had decided to move permanently. But I wasn't going to tell him in what capacity we were choosing to move. Not yet. Not until I saw him face to face. I needed to do some explaining about Defne and me.

In fact, we had been talking, she and I, about making the move for some time. Until recently, more as a kind of wishful scenario oft explored during our evening's first glass of wine. In our gentle fantasy we thought about returning to our roots. To live as Cypriots. To live as husband and wife. To start our lives again. A blank canvas upon which we could paint the narrative we chose to display to the rest of the world. It may well have remained in the realm of speculation if it hadn't been for the events of a couple of weeks before.

We were at the opening of a new gallery on Albemarle Street – a favour to Defne's agent, Felicity – before going on to dinner at The Wolseley. By now, I was inured to these affairs. I was, to all intents and purposes, the dull spare part who allowed her to shine more brightly. I was quite content with this role for it allowed me to observe her interactions with others – and, as daft as this might sound, to admire her even more.

The reception, to begin with, was all I expected: poorly chilled South African Sauvignon Blanc, non-descript canapés with indecipherable toppings of different hues and, of course, a turnout of smartly dressed people speaking too loud and sniffing round each other.

Then Nick turned up. All six foot two of him. Blue eyes, blonde hair swept back, charcoal suit, blue shirt, brown suede loafers and, of course, a brightly coloured silk handkerchief flowing out of his breast pocket – with a casual elegance that I had never been able to achieve. Defne had not mentioned him before. So, when he came up to us and greeted her with particular familiarity, I was caught off guard.

'Daphne, darling, it's been such a long time since our last little get together. How are you?' he said, and as he did so, he turned and winked at me.

I saw Defne freeze. She didn't say anything back.

'Come on you must admit, it was fun,' he said.

By now I could see that she was blushing. In that moment, I understood everything. But I told myself that I was not going to judge her for her life before.

Then he focused his attention on me, looked me up and down, and said, 'Sorry, I'm forgetting my manners, Nick Moncrief… of Moncrief Antiques.' He held out his hand for me to shake and continued, 'And you are?'

Before I could respond, Defne jumped in and said, 'Sandy Bligh-Smith. She knew me well enough to know instinctively that I didn't like this man.

Then he turned back to Defne. 'So, Daphne when are we going to see each other again? You absolutely must come over to the gallery. We have just brought in an exquisite collection of eighteenth-century silver, and I'm sure there are a couple of pieces you will positively adore. How about next week? If you come towards the end of the morning, we can pop over to Wiltons for lunch.'

'I'm sorry, I really can't.' As she said this, she took my hand.

'Oh, how disappointing.' He looked down at her hand holding mine. From the expression on his face, you would have thought she had picked up a dead rat. He turned away from us without another word. I thought that was the end of the matter but a little while later I overheard him talking to someone else.

'God, what a disappointment. Did you see that little peasant she's hooked up with? What a waste. A serious sack-artist in her time. Don't know where I'll find another like her.'

The other man laughed and said, 'So, do you think you were the inspiration for the antiques dealer in her last novel?'

'Well of course, and you know that bit about—'

Before Nick could say anymore, I tapped him on the back. He turned towards me in surprise. 'Oh you. What do you want?'

'I want you to shut your mouth about Defne.'

'Go on, bugger off, there's a good chap, and trot back to Daphne.'

As he said this, he dismissed me with a fluttering of his fingers and then turned to resume his conversation. 'Now where was I? Ah yes that character in the novel, the one who is the most incredible lover, well—'.

I tapped him again but harder this time. In fact, so hard that some of his wine spilt from his glass. He turned back towards me again, but this time he was red in the face. 'You people are ridiculous. Do you know that? What are you, some kind of Taliban?'

A blind rage overcame me. All of a sudden, I ducked, spring-loaded my torso with a swift and precise rolling movement and then propelled myself forward with a left hook to his jaw. It connected. For a moment I saw disbelief on his face. He dropped his glass of wine. But I did not stop. I threw a right to his nose, and as I did so I could feel the cartilage crumple under my fist. Then I went in with a left jab to his right eye. He stumbled back and fell. I could feel broken glass under my feet. I stood over him, fists ready to unload again. He looked at me in horror. I looked up at the people around me. They were inching away. Their faces were drawn and filled with fear. I caught the gaze of one of the waiters. He nodded at me. He understood. Then I felt Defne take hold of my right hand. My knuckles were bleeding. She led me to the cloakroom to retrieve our coats, and we headed out into the Piccadilly evening. As we left the gallery, I heard people saying '*Call an ambulance. Call the Police.*'

Instead of going to dinner, we hurried off across Green Park. After a while, she broke the silence by saying, 'Sandy you can't be doing that kind of thing.'

'I know, I know. I'm sorry Defne. I really am.'

'So, if you know... what happened? He was just some pompous fool I made a mistake with once. Not worth your time. Not a patch on you, my love. No need to react like that.'

'I just go crazy sometimes. A red mist comes in front of my

eyes and I just need to lash out. It started when I was at school. At first, people – people like Nick – used to bully me. But one day, I exploded, just like that… and it stopped. Then it was like a safety valve was broken and I found it harder and harder to control myself.'

'Well, all that is over now. You have me. And you can't be behaving like that when we are together. Promise me?'

I nodded dejectedly. I was now covered with embarrassment and remorse. I knew that I had let her down. It was unbearable. I couldn't look her in the eye for a day or two.

In the event, there were no meaningful repercussions for me. But something had broken. Not between me and Defne. But between us and London. We took the altercation at the gallery as a sign that it was time to stop messing about with idle speculation about Cyprus and make it a reality. Once the IPO was done, there would be no business reason for me to stay in the UK. And as for Defne, an idea was taking hold of her. She said the genesis of it was the gift I gave her all those months back – the book by Taner Baybars. I think she said that to make me feel good. But be that as it may, she was talking more and more about writing something different. Something about Cyprus, as a Cypriot. As Defne Necati, not Daphne Neil.

To make our move to Cyprus viable, in the way that we conceived it, there was one further step we needed to take. And it was something we both wanted more than anything else in the world.

CHAPTER 33

June 9th, two days before the IPO, I got married again.

Defne and I were all alone for the ceremony at Chelsea Old Town Hall. There were no guests, and two members of staff stood in as witnesses. But as we came out into the bright sunshine of the King's Road, we couldn't have been happier. She was wearing a long figure-hugging cream-coloured dress. And around her neck the string of pearls that I had come to love so much. I was wearing a tuxedo, bow tie, white shirt and the solid gold Tiffany cuff-links she had given me a few weeks earlier. On her wedding finger she wore both her 9-carat diamond engagement ring and a simple gold wedding band. I had an identical band. In hers, my name was engraved. And in mine, hers. The registrar kindly took a photograph of us. But I knew that I would never need any reproduction image to remember that day. As we walked down the steps to the pavement, I had the feeling that, at last, my life was truly about to begin.

CHAPTER 34

Monday, 11 June 2012

'Turkish Cypriot businessman Aydin Öztürk takes his companies public' was the FT's main headline in the Companies & Markets section for that day. The IPO had been substantially oversubscribed. Aydin was now, officially, the wealthiest Turkish Cypriot who had ever lived. Everything he had earned before must have seemed like small change to him. And, thanks to his generous share grants to me, I was now wealthy in my own right and would never have to work again, nor depend on Defne for money.

I called him to share the news. But it was Frankie who answered the phone. 'Is everything okay?' I asked.

'Hello, Sandy. It's so-so. You know, he gets more and more tired these days. In fact, he's still sleeping.' It was 10 a.m. in Cyprus.

'Look, Frankie, I'll be there next month. Defne and I have our tickets ready. But do I need to come earlier?'

There was a long silence, then she said, 'No, I don't think so.' I heard a noise in the background. 'It's Sandy' she said, her mouth away from the mouthpiece. 'Here he is, Sandy, he is up now. There you go Aydin.' There was a rasping sound on the microphone as she passed him the phone.

I heard him cough and clear his throat of phlegm. Then, at last, he said, 'How are you son?'

'All good. A few things I need to update you on when I see you, but more importantly did you see the news, Aydin?'

'What news?'

'The IPO.'

'Oh that… how did it go?'

I ran him through the numbers. And told him about the money he had made.

'That's good, Sandy. When are you coming, *oğlum*?'

I repeated what I had just told Frankie, and he said, 'Well, you know what to do with the money. You know, talk to our friend at Pictet in Geneva and make the transfers. But I want you to keep back ten million pounds. I want you to take care of all the old crew. You make sure that Lettie and all her girls are taken care of. And don't forget Roy. Just the old timers. The ones who were there when you came.' I asked how much he wanted to give each of them. 'You figure it out, son. Just make sure they're taken care of. And help them invest the money. No silly pissing it away. But come soon, Sandy, okay?'

The weeks before we left for Cyprus were predictably fraught with getting everything ready for the big move. I made, as agreed, the presents of money to the old timers. The only one who was not happy was Lettie. When I gave her the envelope with her cheque, she did not open it. Instead, she said, 'How's Mr Aydin? Why he not come and see us anymore? It's been too long.'

'He's back home in Cyprus now, Lettie. You know that. He wants to rest… but please open and see what he's given you.'

'You tell him I say hello. All right? But he should have come to say goodbye.' Finally, she opened the envelope and took out the cheque. She looked at it for a while but did not seem impressed. As I turned to go, she said, 'Mr Sandy, you have a good friend with Mr Aydin. He is a good man. You tell him I told you.'

'I will, Lettie. By the way, what are you going to do with your money?'

'I'm going to buy a house and start my own business. Any

money left over will be for Jason… for his studies.' I realised that here was someone who did not need my advice. And somehow it seemed, out of that sordid business of Aydin's, some good had come. I pushed my luck and asked after Emma, the girl I had met on my first visit to the Spa.

'Stupid girl. She pregnant again. And will probably give all her money to that lazy boyfriend of hers.' She tutted then looked slyly at me, 'How come you never come for a massage, Mr Sandy?'

'It's not for me, Lettie.'

'But okay for you to make money from, no?'

CHAPTER 35

It was my final meeting with Harry Eid. I decided to hold it in Aydin's old office in South Audley Street; the one where I had first met him more than six years before. It seemed fitting that this chapter of my life should close in the same room.

There was still a slight smell of tobacco. The carpet looked a little frayed and the fine Turkish rugs had been rolled up and sent to storage. I was told that the landlord had already found a new tenant and refurbishing was to start on Monday. The brass plaque from the front door, the one that so proudly proclaimed 'Famagusta Trading Company' and that Aydin made sure was polished every single working day, had been unscrewed and laid on his desk. I told myself that I would take it with me.

Finally, Harry arrived. His hair had more streaks of white and the dark patches under his eyes were larger than before. But I noticed he had a new watch – even bigger than his last one. This one was a gold Panerai. A 'Luminor Marina', the logo on the dial proudly announced. It was so big that it hardly fitted under his shirt cuff.

'Harry, how are you? You must be pleased.'

'Very,' he said, smacking his lips.

For a moment, a wave of affection for the Lebanese financier came over me. Until now, I had never thought how hard he must have worked. How much he had helped us. All I ever saw in the early days were the slick outfits, and I got stuck there. I was embarrassed. But the feeling didn't last long. Eid had one of his big immaculate smiles on. And I was guessing he had something on his mind.

'So, what're you going to do now?' I asked.

'Well, we're already raising a new fund. And, in fact, that is why I wanted to see you.'

'I'm not sure what this has to do with me, Harry. We're done. No more companies to float.'

'Well, I was thinking you and Aydin might like to come in with us. Minimum ticket would be twenty million pounds each.'

For a moment, I considered it. I knew that, with Harry's flair and talent, the returns would be good. But part of me wanted to be out of the markets. I wanted to live my life differently. I wanted to be with Defne and no longer worry about money and the vagaries of the stock markets. But I also knew that I would have to invest the money I had just made.

'I'll think about it, Harry. I will see Aydin in a couple of weeks. And if we are interested, we'll get back to you.'

We shook hands and both went our separate ways.

Its only when I reached home that I realised that I had left the brass plaque on the table.

CHAPTER 36

'I've been so looking forward to seeing you, my boy. How are you? Where's Defne?' He spoke slowly and more quietly than when I had last seen him.

'Aydin, I'm happy to see you too.'

'But where's Defne?' he said, looking towards the door as if she might suddenly appear.

'Before she comes, there is something that I should tell you.'

He and Frankie looked at me intently. I saw worry lines across Aydin's forehead. All the warmth of the welcome had suddenly disappeared from the room and been replaced by a sterile, heavy air. Despite my apprehension, despite my fear that the old man would feel let down, I took the plunge. 'Well, I need to tell you about Defne and me...'

To his credit, he let me finish without interrupting. Frankie said nothing, though I noticed that her eyes widened quite considerably at the bit where I explained that I had fallen in love with Defne, as a woman, and married her. But when I finished what I had to say, his reaction was not what I expected.

'Sandy, it's done now. You've made a choice. You know it's risky, but I am not going to sit here and judge you. But son, you have to be careful. If people cotton on to who you really are to each other, there'll be no end of trouble.'

After a moment of silence, when all three of us seemed lost in thought, we moved on to more practical considerations.

'So where are you two going to live? Cos you can't live at your dad's old house.'

'I rather thought we'd stay at my aunt and uncle's place.'

For the first time, Frankie spoke up, 'Sandy, you can't stay there. Defne will loathe it. Far too small and poky. And besides, it hasn't been lived in for a while.'

'She's right. You should both come and stay here, with me and Frankie.'

'I appreciate the offer, but it will suit us fine being down in the village. We'll stay in the hotel while they fix it up. You know the time it takes a coat of paint and a bit of plumbing to be sorted out. And then we'll figure out what we do after that.'

Aydin sighed and looked over at Frankie and said, 'My goodness what a pair.' And as I took my leave the old man said, 'Son, it's good to have you here – don't you forget to come and see old Aydin often. I've missed you.'

CHAPTER 37

She wrote every day. There was no stopping her. Sometimes I worried that she hardly took a break. But every now and again, when I least expected it, she raised her head, saw me watching her and she would get up from her desk and kiss me on the mouth with all the intimacy and passion of our first embraces. It felt like her writing was an electric charge to her body and that the conduit of release was our physical intimacy.

My aunt and uncle's house in Bamyaköy was very different to what we were used to. Of course, I knew that from before but had never imagined that one day I would live there myself, even if only for a short while. However, there was something about the spartan nature of the house that appealed to us both. When it came down to it, there was all we needed: a bedroom, a bathroom and a work area. That is all. The floor was stone and needed only a bucket of water and mop to clean it. As for the kitchen, we mostly used it to make coffee because more often than not we ate our evening meals at *Kemal Hussein's*. Always the same freshly made mezze, the same grilled fish, olive oil fried chips, and salad. But each evening before sunset, we had an ever-changing, ever different seascape. Sometimes flat, sometimes hostile with white foamed crests. Sometimes turquoise, and sometimes metal grey. But always different. Very occasionally we saw dolphins curving in and out of the water. If I were to live a thousand years, I would never get tired of this little stretch of the Mediterranean Sea.

The workspace that we put aside for Defne was the box room that communicated with the adjacent, similarly shaped bedroom. It had an entrance door that, when it was open, gave on to a view of the valley below. From here, we could see the olive groves, fields and undulations that stretched as far the closest neighbouring village, Malatya. It was in front of this door, that she kept open until the mosquitoes launched their nocturnal raiding parties, that Defne set up her desk. I understood why she chose this spot to write from. Here, she was connected to the view. I liked to think she was drawing her creativity from our land, like an olive tree draws water from the soil. I too found myself mesmerised by the valley below us and often drank my morning coffee staring out at the fields. Sometimes I thought about our father, and sometimes about my aunt and uncle. But mostly I just admired the land. It was an experience of all the senses, for nothing in Bamyaköy could be simply one thing; it had to be many. There was, along with the visual, the repeating soundtrack of pigeons with their hypnotic cooing, supported by a myriad of smaller birds who made their own contribution to the morning chorus. I liked to imagine them as a jazz trio with each of the players coming in with his contribution as the mood and rhythm took them. These birds, that I cherished so much, returned the village to something that I liked to think of as a state of Eden-like grace – now that the population was reduced to a dying handful of inhabitants and nature had almost regained the upper hand.

There were also smells that I was already familiar with and that varied according to the hour and season. Mostly, it was the smell of the earth breathing that prevailed; fecund damp copper earth, that literally gives life and sustains. It was, for me, the essence of Cyprus itself. And finally, there was the taste of my coffee. I didn't drink it according to established protocol, I freely admit that. I should have sipped it from a thimble of a cup. But instead, I brewed my Turkish coffee in a pot large enough for six normal doses and then guzzled it out of a mug. But despite the American-sized portion, I was careful to respect tradition and never failed to take it to the boil three times before pouring it out; its taste lying powder heavy and gently bitter on my tongue.

Seeing Defne click away at the keyboard, day after day, made me a little envious, though never jealous. I wondered what she saw, what she absorbed, when she looked out. What alchemy occurred that led words to pour forth onto her computer screen? How was it that she had the creative gene, and I did not? Perhaps, I told myself, I should try watercolours. But I knew that was a ridiculous ambition. The reality was that I was a clumsy, blunt-skilled person.

Mid-morning generally found me high on the hill behind the village, sitting with Aydin on the terrace of his villa. Sometimes Frankie joined us. She never said much. She just listened to our conversation, to Aydin's repetitions. With her, it felt like we had been before... Before Defne entered into the equation. Before I fell in love. When we were our own little family trio. But by now Aydin was frailer, his breathing more laboured. He had no mind to talk about business anymore. Our conversations, or rather his soliloquies, were to do with Cyprus. They were of a world long gone: the island as a British colony, where peace and decency prevailed; of that time before the civil strife of the 1960s, when nationalist fervour was kept in check. They were of men long gone: Tassos, Zeki, and Erol, the schoolmaster of Bamyaköy.

In the afternoons, I often met with our architect and engineer. We had started the process of rebuilding Zeki's house and landscaping its garden – with the intention of making it our permanent home. I intended to keep the works on track and did so with rigorous cajoling, firmness and financial inducements, of course, – for this is what I knew, from my previous time on the island, to be effective. Defne and I decided that this new house should be more than just our home. It would be a memorial to our father: no one would be able to come to our village and not be confronted with his presence. The young man who died a year past his thirtieth birthday would have, in stone and blossoming bougainvillea, a testimony to his short life.

At night, over a bottle of wine, we would discuss our day. She looked over the plans I was working on with the architect and told me what she liked or disliked. I was always amazed by her sense of taste and had come to rely on it. Aesthetic enhancements that I suggested to the architect were, in truth, all from her.

Occasionally, she showed me a paragraph of what she had written that day. But I never pushed. I left her to come to me when she felt ready. But in what I read, I saw that it was Defne who was writing. Daphne Neil had been left behind like a discarded chrysalis. In the brief descriptive passages that I was privy to see, there were enshrined, in words more beautiful than I could conceive, images of the landscape we cycled through each morning for our daily exercise. It was as if I was seeing through the eyes of an artist: the ploughed fields, the planting of melon seeds, the miniature tornadoes of wheat chaff twisting away into the distance. I was seeing Cyprus anew. And our land, our precious land, resonated in my soul more than ever before.

Sometimes, if I was back early enough, we drove up to the top of the hill past the track that leads to Aydin's mansion and down to the sea below. We liked to swim from a private rocky cove that we informally appropriated. There was a small strip of sand where we liked to lie and make love, protected from wind and prying eyes. And afterwards, we looked out towards the mountains of Turkey, as the sun began its gentle descent; the two of us just sitting side by side, her head on my shoulder. We didn't talk much. The sound of the sea seemed to fill our souls, and I think we both found something close to peace. But over time, there was a change. It seemed as if our love making became more urgent, as if our bodies were willing us to break through into a final fusion where we would become like some strange god of antiquity; a new being set to be carried off on the foam of the sea lapping at our toes. When once, in those post-coital moments, we had said nothing, or but the merest of words, we started to talk with regret and pain at not having met earlier.

CHAPTER 38

I can't remember how it came about but somewhere towards the end of October we decided to hold a big event in Bamyaköy in the following spring, to celebrate the life of Zeki, short as it was. It would coincide with the completion of our house, with the big marble plaque upon which we would have inscribed words fitting for his memory.

In November, we hired a PR firm to make the invitations, solicit the appropriate ministers and generate press coverage. To our surprise we were, for a few weeks at least, subjected to almost feverish interest from the media. As Defne pointed out, this was simply because of the dearth of anything else newsworthy except for heart-breaking stories about failing crops and the rising cost of fuel and fertiliser. For my part, I would rather these issues had remained in the headlines, for I knew from my visits to Malatya and the cups of coffee I took with the mayor, how seriously they jeopardised livelihoods, and how much ordinary people were suffering.

Our newfound celebrity meant that all of a sudden, we found ourselves, much as we had in London, invited to every major social function going. Somehow, word about us, or more accurately about Defne, must have seeped south across the border, for to our surprise she was invited to teach a course in Creative Writing on the Greek side, at the very same university where her mother taught. Thankfully, there was nothing by way of name or physical resemblance to connect mother and daughter. But not everybody was happy about our new-found high profile.

'Sandy, you have to be stark raving mad to draw so much attention to yourselves.' The whole outburst cost Aydin a coughing fit that went on for the best part of a minute. It eased only after

Frankie brought him some water to drink.

It was the end of November, and I had come to tell him about the lecture that Defne would deliver the next day and to see if he could be persuaded to come with me to hear her. But he wanted none of that. In fact, he had hardly left his mansion since we arrived on the island. He told me it was because he wanted to make the most of every second back in his village after being so many years away.

'It's only a forty-five--minute talk. It'll do you good to get out of here for once.'

He waved the spoken invitation away with his hand. And then returned the conversation to Defne and me. 'If it gets out Sandy. If people find out...'

'No one who counts, knows. We've been careful. And if any of the old men talk, no one will believe them. People will believe that we are what we tell them – two Brits of Turkish Cypriot heritage who met in London, got married, and decided to move back to the homeland.'

'For such a clever man, you're a fool, son. You don't know some of the nasty people floating around this island. Not only will they want your money, but they'll want to hurt you if you don't do what they ask. You think it's all nice and relaxed here. Island life and all that. But trust me, there's a dark side to Cyprus that you don't want to discover.'

I was about to tell him that he had been watching too many films when I saw Frankie motioning for me to ease off. So instead, I said, 'Okay, Aydin, we'll be careful. I promise.'

His warning stayed with me and somewhere a nagging anxiety started to grow. I didn't mention anything to Defne. And in not saying anything, I realised that, for the first time, I was hiding something from her. I justified it by telling myself I was protecting her. She didn't need to be burdened with this – certainly not the day before she was about to give a speech.

CHAPTER 39

The 'Greek' Side was not a foreign land to us. Since our arrival on the island, we had become used to crossing the border between the two sides and going back and forth without much thought.

No one ever made any fuss. We accepted the contrasts. Mostly it was the prosperity of the South, the shops and the big IKEA that were the most obvious contrast with our own impoverished – although to my eyes, more charming and authentic – side. Every now and again, when we crossed over, I noticed the spray-painted symbol of ELAM. I suppose the logo first registered with me because it seemed so juvenile and absurdly Mussolini-like – with its glaive surrounded by laurel leaves. Friends on the Greek side told me that this newly established party should be taken seriously; that its far-right supporters were capable of great acts of violence. But I confess, that hearing this while seated in a taverna, drinking retsina, eating fish and discussing the ever more distant prospects for the reunification of Cyprus, made it all seem like it belonged to a TV drama – certainly nothing for us to be troubled by.

Anyway, that morning of Defne's speech was certainly not a day to be dwelling on such matters. It was her first time visiting the university where her mother was still in post. I knew that part of her would like to go and see Fatma. She was desperate to be reconciled with her. But the risks of another row were far too great. So, we just followed instructions that had been emailed to us for getting to the auditorium. These turned out to be unnecessary. As we reached the English faculty, I saw Mr Andreas, the security man, standing next to someone else who we discovered was the Vice Chancellor, Michaelis Florakis.

'Welcome to the University of Nicosia,' Florakis said, all smiles. He shook our hands in a two-handed clasp and made us both feel like we were the most important guests ever to cross the university's threshold. He led us to the auditorium himself and sat in the first row. My misgivings started to recede in the face of the warmth and graciousness with which we were received. By the time the lecture was over, I was convinced that all the stories I had ever heard about aggression towards Turkish Cypriots on this side of the border was paranoia and nonsense. Defne's lecture – on character development as the key to successful novel writing – was a great success, judging by the warmth of the applause and the line of young Greek Cypriot students queuing for her autograph or to petition her to read their own material.

We returned to Bamyaköy that afternoon full of hope about the possibility of reconciliation. All the talk of 'that side' versus 'ours' struck us that day as faintly ridiculous. We promised ourselves that, at some point, when we had time, we would engage with the various movements pushing for inter-community dialogue.

CHAPTER 40

One morning I got a call from Aydin. All he said was, 'Sandy, I want you to take me down to the village'. Then he hung up.

I should have been pleased that he wanted to leave his home, but I was worried about how frail he had become. Each day he seemed a little more diminished. It was as if the air inside him was escaping through a slow puncture. His once plump and cossetted face now hung loose. There were dark patches under his eyes, and he had given up applying eyeliner. I thought I detected in his look a man who saw the departed in every shadow and every corner – for his gaze flicked back and forth as if going from the real to the ethereal; perhaps uncertain which was which.

This sudden request was not what I had expected. I had been meaning to call on him that very afternoon to invite him down to the village for Christmas Day. I had persuaded Burak to cook a turkey in his mother's clay oven. And Defne had given instructions for roast potatoes and something approximating stuffing. From the 'Greek side', we had found suitable condiments. And I had ordered a hamper from Fortnum & Mason in London, and a mixed case of Aydin's favourite Burgundies from Berry Brothers & Co.

We were hoping that the weather would hold and that we could host him and Frankie on the terrace of the coffee shop on the 25th. It would be something like a family lunch. But when I arrived at his place and invited him, he didn't want to hear anything about all that. Instead, he just wanted me to take him down to the village, immediately.

It was only a short drive and the weather was not so cold, but Frankie had dressed him up for an English winter. He was wearing one of his best camel coats. Around his neck she had tied a maroon silk-on-cashmere scarf. And on his head sat a trilby with a small yellow feather tucked into the hatband. Whereas once the hat had fitted snugly on his head it now seemed a too big and the rim touched his ears.

When I put him in the car and closed the door, Frankie came up to me. She said, 'Take care of him Sandy. He's not himself.' She reached out for my arm. 'Do you want me to come with you?' I patted her hand and shook my head. I liked that she cared so much about Aydin.

He and I didn't speak on the way down. When we entered the village, I went to turn towards my aunt and uncle's old place, but he said, 'No, Sandy. I want you to take me to the house where I was born.'

It was with some embarrassment that I realised that, in all the time I had known him, I never once thought to ask whereabouts in the village he grew up.

He pointed towards the mosque. We drove by it and he directed me to go left down the hill, down an old track that had fallen out of use. I drove slowly, minding the potholes and mounds of rubble. Then, at the end of the track, I saw the remains of a dwelling built of mud and straw bricks. Even by the standards of the village, even when compared to the other derelict houses, it was a wretched and miserable carcass. The roof had gone. A piece of corrugated iron was propped up against the doorway.

'Sandy, move that away, I want to go inside.'

I didn't say anything. I just pushed the metal sheet to one side and went through. Inside, it was just one room with a hearth. There were broken bottles on the beaten earth floor. Grass was sprouting out in little clumps. On one wall were the remains of some tiles; almost as if someone, once upon a time, had made a valiant attempt to bring some beauty to this tiny, wretched dwelling. Aydin went over to touch them, almost lovingly, it seemed to me, like someone placing their hand on an icon for blessing and redemption. Then he turned and rested his back against them. Suitably shored up, walking stick in hand, he surveyed the room.

'This the house I was born in, Sandy,' he said at last. 'Not much to look at, is it? We all used to sleep in this one room. Me, my brothers and sisters. And my mother and father. I was lucky I got out when I did. Zainab, who later became Erol's wife, took me in. But the rest… they stayed in this pigsty until my dad was killed by your Uncle Ismail. You remember how he blamed it on the Greeks because he wanted to get hold of my dad's sheep?'

It was painful to be reminded of my uncle's treachery. I couldn't look Aydin in the eyes. But he didn't dwell on the matter.

'After his death everyone went their own way. My mum… I never knew what happened to her. Apparently one day she left the village, and no one ever saw her again. Do you know, Sandy, I never knew her name? She never spoke much and when she did it was in Arabic.'

I looked over at him. He was staring far away.

'How old was your mother when your father married her?'

'I don't know. I don't know anything about her, Sandy.' Anger and frustration gave his voice some strength back. He was speaking louder than I had heard him for weeks. 'All I know is how rough my father used to treat her. God knows why.' For a moment, his voice took on a reflective, thoughtful tone. Then he continued, 'He was making out like he was a good Muslim. He had that reputation in the village because he didn't drink alcohol… because he fasted during Ramadan. But in fact,' Aydin's voice cracked and wavered, '…he was a complete and utter cunt. You know,' Aydin was almost shouting, his voice was full of pain and anger. I could see tears coming into his eyes, and his fists were clenched as if he were ready to beat the dead man to a pulp, '…you know we'd have to listen to him as he took our mother. We could hear him grunt like a pig when he was on top of her.' His chest was heaving so hard that I was worried that Aydin was about to have a heart attack.. I made a step towards him, my arms outstretched in case he fell. But he brushed me away.

He spoke again and, as he did, I noticed his nostrils flare, 'I remember this one time when he was doing it to her.' Aydin pointed to the other corner of the room. 'And I needed to go to the toilet so badly I thought I was going to wet the bed if I didn't get outside in time. And he kept on going. Wouldn't stop. Anyway, I tried to make it out of the room without him hearing. See, the door to the back yard,' he motioned with his head to a low doorway across from where he was standing, 'was just next to their bed. And as I went by their bed, I was trying not to look but I couldn't help it… and she opened her eyes. My mum was staring at me, and the bastard had no idea that I was right there. And all the time he was banging away at her, she was staring at me. She never stopped looking at me.' He coughed then patted his pocket as if he were looking for his cigar case but, finding nothing, continued, 'When I came back, he was finished with her and he was over by the sink drinking water from a jug. Naked. He couldn't even be bothered to cover himself up. He didn't say anything… just made a step towards me as if he was going to hit me, and then he laughed because he saw I was afraid of him.'

Aydin shook his head and went silent for a moment. Then he said, 'My mother was always trying to comfort me. After my father had beaten me, and that happened a lot, she would come and take me in her arms and would speak her language. I think it was words from the Quran.' He closed his eyes and, to my surprise, he softly recited a prayer in Arabic. I had never known him to speak anything but English or Turkish.

I no longer recognised his voice. It became gentle and light. And there I was, watching him reciting the Quranic verses in the house where he was born, and it dawned on me that it was his mother that I was hearing; prayer and lullaby rolled into one. I felt as if she was speaking to me through him. And, although I didn't understand the words, something stirred me. For a moment, I was seeing a young child standing against the wall, comforted by his mother's love.

After that, we were both silent for a long while. Something I was not able to describe had entered the room. I am tempted to say that we had been joined by an angel and that for a brief moment we had been touched by God's grace. And then, at last, Aydin said, 'Oh my God, Sandy, I haven't said a prayer in a very long time. Haven't been to mosque since I was a boy. Never gone to Mecca. And what would I say at the Kaaba? Would God forgive me Sandy, would he?' He shook his head then said, 'In Islam they say that you never know which of your smallest acts of kindness will save you at the Day of Judgement. Did you know that?'

I shook my head.

'Do you think loving Tassos the way I did will be held against me? How I loved that boy. I still do. Never a day has gone by, Sandy, without me thinking of him, without me missing him.'

At this Aydin, doubled over, sobbing. Big tears fell on to the dusty floor, making damp little marks in front of his carefully polished shoes. He motioned me to leave. But I stayed with him.

After a while, he stood up straight again. His eyes were bloodshot and raw. He looked at me and said, 'Sandy, at the right time, you make sure you have prayers said for me and that I am buried like a proper Muslim.'

'I will. But let's not worry about that now.' I tried to move his mind onto something else and asked, 'What happened to your brothers and sisters, Aydin?'

He wiped mucus from his nose with the back of his hand and said, 'The oldest, Çiğdem, was married off at fourteen. It was the way it was in those days. And Özen... I don't know. You have to remember I was away in London by then. Hassan, my older brother, was killed by EOKA when he was out working in the fields.'

'And your younger brother?'

'You already met him.'

I wracked my brains to think who he could be talking about.

'Who, Aydin? I would have remembered if I had met your brother.'

'That soldier at your uncle's funeral.'

And then it dawned on me. He was talking about Colonel Kemal Kaynar. Apparently, his original family name dropped along the way.

CHAPTER 41

It was some weeks before Aydin and I spoke again about his brother. But the day we did so, it was to the smell of shit. His.

When I had reached his house, earlier in the day, I had found that he was in a worse state than I could have imagined. In the space of a few days – the few days I had been off the island on business with Defne – the old man had deteriorated terribly. I would not have thought it was possible unless I had seen it with my own eyes. It was his emphysema that had won the battle. The doctor told me that Aydin was stage IV and that there was nothing more to be done. I could see that every breath he was taking was agony. He must have known that the end was close. What was worse for this proud man, was that he was starting to lose control of his bodily functions. So much so, that they had put a thick plastic sheet on the bed.

In addition to the doctor, whose main purpose, as far as I could see, was reduced to administering oxygen from a big, badly scraped and rusty green cylinder, and ensuring a steady flow of opiates to his blood stream, three nurses had been hired by Frankie. They were there to take turns in attending to Aydin, day and night, in eight-hour shifts. Mostly their task was to clean him, turn him and change his bed linen.

Before they allowed me in to see him, they called Frankie. Ordinarily, she was unflappable. But when she saw me, she let go and fell into my arms sobbing. 'He's dying,' she said.

'I know, my dear. I'm here now.' I nodded at Defne, and she led Frankie away to the living room. Then I made my way to see my… at that precise moment I was at a loss as to which noun to apply to him. He had, in the years we had known each other, been so many things: business prospect; link to my father and his homeland; boss;

saviour; friend. But as I approached the dying man's bedroom, my stomach in knots, there was something else. Something that had been staring me in the face, but I had looked right through it. Because? Because all that I had been taught about the world had stopped me from seeing the simple reality – which was that Aydin, in his own way, had taken over the mantle that Zeki never got to wear, and that Hugh only partially carried. This man had loved me like a real son. He had challenged me, nurtured me, accepted me for what I was, what I had done and, most of all, for who I loved. He had, in his own way, set me free.

As I entered his bedroom, the nurse who had been dabbing at his forehead with iced water got up and left me alone with her patient. At last, I could see Aydin fully.

He was magnificent. Despite the pain, despite his humiliation, he was sitting up to receive me. He was dressed as I had never been allowed to see him. In the clothes that belonged to his other life. The one he never talked to me about, but I suppose I guessed at, imagined. As soon as I set my eyes on him, I knew that he was, in that moment, fully himself and was attired in the manner he wished to meet the Almighty. He was wearing a blonde Marylin Monroe wig. His mouth was bright with red lipstick. On his left cheek, Frankie – it could only have been her – had drawn a black beauty mark. Despite the wrinkles and the sagging flesh, he was, in his own way, glorious.

I sat down next to him. The smell of his bodily excretions mixed with that of naphthalene – presumably from moth balls used to preserve his wig – was overwhelming. Frankie had tried to mask the odour with regular squirts of his beloved Chanel No. 5. I could see the bottle up on the sideboard – it was almost empty. Another, still in its box and cellophane wrapping, sat ready for use. He opened his eyes, and his made-up lips extended into a smile. There were chips of lipstick on his tobacco-stained teeth.

'You've come, *oğlum*. You didn't have to bother yourself.'

'That's quite a wig you're wearing, Aydin,' I said, hoping to lighten the mood.

He reached for the hand mirror by his side and studied his reflection carefully, then he said, 'If only you knew all the things it has seen.' His voice was almost coquettish.

Sensing the slight lift in his mood I said, 'Go on then, tell me about its best outing.'

He meant to laugh but instead it turned into a painful wheeze. It must have gone on for a couple of minutes. I thought about calling in the doctor to administer a fresh dose of oxygen. But he recovered enough to smile at me. 'You don't want hear about any of that.'

'Just one story.'

'All right. The most glorious, you say. Let me see.' Some of the old Aydin returned. For a moment it was like we were back having one of our dinners, him about to regale me with one of his tales.

'D'you remember, I told you about all the enclaves where we Turkish Cypriots had to take refuge during the troubles?'

I nodded.

'Well, one of the biggest was Famagusta. I was living there at the time. I had a beautiful pastry and coffee shop. Lovely it was. I wish you could have seen it, Sandy. Right close to the port. At the time, there were so many people coming and going. I couldn't help but make money. But even so, we didn't let our standards slip… we served the best baklava on the island. Bar none, d'you hear me? Downstairs, we had the shop with glass display cabinets full of our pastries. Every kind you could imagine: pistachio, cashew, walnut. Some with cream and some with *künefe*. Beautiful it was. And then next to that, we had a dining area with alcoves. That was good for winter, but for spring and summer evenings we had this upstairs terrace with a fountain. And a canopy over it. Always full. A lot of couples and young people. In fact, that was where I first laid eyes on Tassos. I remember his smile. That beautiful boy. So beautiful.

One day he looked at me, and that was it.'

'You were wearing your wig at your coffee shop?'

My question shakes him out of his reverie.

'Of course not, Sandy. Come on, be serious, it's Cyprus we're talking about. In the nineteen-fifties. And by the way, I don't think much has changed come to that. No. The wig comes later.'

'So, what about the enclave?'

'Yes, I am coming to that. Give me a moment, will you?' He harrumphed by way of clearing his throat and continued. 'Well, after the Bloody Christmas of '63, more and more Turkish Cypriots started coming to take refuge inside the old part of Famagusta. At first, it was good for trade but then, eventually, I had to give up on the pastries and bake bread instead. Mind you I made quite a bit of money on that too.'

'What – you were taking advantage of the refugees?'

'Who do you take me for Sandy? No, of course not. I was robbing the Greek bakeries of their flour and then selling my bread at a discount. So, pure bottom line. You'd have liked that.' He sniffed and his face turned serious. Then he said, 'But even that was not enough. Terrible. All those people getting thinner by the day. The worst of it was to see it happening to the children and their mothers. But at least they were safe, I used to tell myself. Anyway, one day, the Greeks had had enough of us. I think they wanted to make an example to show people in the other enclaves what would happen if they didn't tow the line. So, they set up positions around the enclave – with mortars and Bren guns and all. And they had helicopters fly over to see what defences we had.'

'Did you have weapons?'

'The most we had were a few shot guns. And, as for our defences, they were just mattresses – *mattresses* for crying out loud! As if a bit of cotton stuffing was going to save anybody from a bullet – and whatever bits of furniture we could stack up.'

'But didn't you tell me once that the Turkish government was shipping in weapons to help the Turkish Cypriot resistance fighters? What did you call them, TMT?'

'That's right. But none of that had reached us in the Famagusta enclave. I, of course, had a couple of items. Business accessories really. But we had nothing that was a match for the Greeks. I mean they were the official army after all. Anyway, one morning, all the phone lines were cut. There was no way for us to reach the outside world. And then they sent in an officer to parley with us. Basically, he told us that we had to surrender the enclave or they were going to clean us out. Well, we weren't going to surrender now, were we?'

'With all those women and children wouldn't that have been the safest thing to do?'

'Sandy, we didn't trust the soldiers. We thought it better to try and hold out. Now, it seems ridiculous. But in any event, we were given our ultimatum and for a little while we were feeling pretty brave. And later, quite a bit scared. It's then that I had an idea. So, I went to see the defence committee and said I was going to try something. And to just leave it to me.' He paused and said, 'Go on son, give Aydin some water.' I held the glass to his lips as carefully as possible but, even so, some water dribbled down his chin. He didn't seem to notice. I took the glass back from him and set it down by his side. It had the lipstick imprint of his lips on the rim.

'Where was I?' He said.

'You were going to try something...'

He closed his eyes and smiled.

'Sandy, I don't have to spell out to you what I am. But you have to remember that, in those days, people like me didn't exist, not officially at least. There was nowhere we could dress up. I mean being what I was, in those days, was bad enough for most people. All those words they used about us – no end to all those names –

although, generally, no one said them to me.' His voice dropped a register. 'But,' he continued, 'at least there were bars we could go to, where we could have fun. Like that one I showed you in Nicosia.'

'Nikki's?'

'Yes, exactly. But nowhere where you could do the full Dolly Varden.'

'Dolly what?'

'Women's outfit, you chump. But see, I had a liking for that. Mostly I was dressing at home. Originally for Tassos. But what with him gone, I didn't have much chance anymore. So, I figured that if there was a possibility that I might die in that enclave, I'd do it on my own terms, dressed as I wanted. And, best of all, I could use it as a diversion to have a go at the Greeks.'

His face was radiant. It seemed years since I had seen him so happy, gleeful even.

'So, there it was, I spent the rest of the morning getting myself ready. You know, I shaved my legs. I had these beautiful clothes from Paris. Cost me a fortune, they did. And this wig. I loved Marilyn Monroe. I wanted to look just like her. So, I'd had this magnificent prosthetic bra made for me. I mean, keep in mind that I was quite a bit lighter than I am today.'

I looked at him propped up in bed. I tried to imagine the slender young man making himself beautiful for his outing that day.

'Every ugly hair was plucked. And Lord, my make up! Foundation, powder, blusher, lipstick. My lips... perfectly contoured. You know, I think with this wig I really could have won a Marylin Monroe lookalike competition.'

'Do you have any photos?'

'Don't get me started. One of the biggest regrets of my life. If only Tassos could have seen me like that. He'd have loved it.'

'How did your friends in the enclave react when they saw you?'

'Hah! You should have seen them. They were terrified. They didn't know where to look. But – here's the funny thing – when I showed them the Sten gun I had hidden under my shawl, and the pistol and grenades in my bag, and when I told them it was a diversion, they started to relax. And then I noticed that one or two of the lads started checking me out. Which I took as a compliment.' I noticed that his cheeks had become a little flushed.

'Okay, so now you were dressed as a woman, and I guess you were armed to the teeth, so what did you do next?'

'Next? Oh yes. Well, I walked over towards the Greek lines. Slowly of course. You know I pictured myself like a model walking down a catwalk in a fashion show. I think they thought I was a hooker got lost. God, how my feet were hurting. You know how wide they are. Can you imagine them squeezed into those high heels? I was telling myself all the while that I should have worn pumps. But anyway, as I got close – all the time I was waving at the soldiers making sure that I was moving my hips side to side – I think they thought they were in for a good time – I kicked off my shoes. Just drove them wild, the idiots. And then when I got into range, I pulled out my Sten gun and shot the bastards. And then I threw my grenades at the heavy machine guns. And anyone who was left, I shot with my pistol. There was one – the arrogant bastard who had come to ask us to surrender – who started begging me for mercy. He tried to hold onto my legs, but I wasn't having any of it. Up until then, all our side was cheering. You'd think we'd won the war or something. But when I dragged him into the middle of the square, everything went quiet. They could see he was still alive. Then I shot him in the face at point blank range. I hated those Greek soldiers. All that lot who had been talking about wiping us out. Well, they weren't going to wipe me out.'

There was spit on the side of Aydin's mouth. The conversation had gone somewhere dark and ugly. I wished that it hadn't.

We both fell silent. After a while, he reached out for my hand and said, almost as if he had guessed my thoughts, 'I've done a lot of bad things. I know that, Sandy. But those were bad times. Try not to think ill of me, son. You may hear other stories about me but remember I was doing things that I thought I had to; that war does terrible things to humans; I was being me, true to myself and to those that I loved. Never forget that.'

The whole effort of telling me his story exhausted him. His breathing was now even more laboured than before. Every now and again, it stopped but each time it kicked back in with a painful exhalation. I just watched his chest rise and fall.

After a while, he opened his eyes as if he had been gathering his strength for one last push and said, 'You're a good boy, Sandy. You've done good. Don't look back no more. Don't worry about all that stuff in your head. Don't do you no good. Your trouble is you think too much about things that don't take you anywhere.'

I nodded.

'But there are other things I need to tell you. Not stories about me dressed up.' He coughed and I reached out with a tissue to catch the phlegm he spat out. Seeing me look at him with concern, he said, 'See, all the cigars have caught up with me.' For a moment, it was the old Aydin flickering back on again. But then, more seriously, he said, 'Look son, I'm leaving all my money to you… but you knew that anyway.' It was true. I had been told by his lawyer back in December, but I had put it out of my mind. I thought we had many more years to go. Even just a couple of months ago, it seemed inconceivable to me that we would be having this conversation so soon. Aydin continued, 'But there are a couple of things I want you to do for me.'

'Anything,' I said. I was on the verge of saying *Baba*. it really was there on the tip of my tongue but the word just wouldn't come out. Even though just once in his life I wanted him to hear it. I wanted him to know that he had a son of his own. Something to give him comfort. But I needed to keep control of my voice. If I faltered, I knew I would be unable to control all the emotions that were threatening to break through and drown me. Already, it was bad enough that I could feel tears were coming to my eyes.

'I want a proper funeral for me and…' For a couple of moments, he did not speak and then finally he said, '…for me and Tassos. Use whatever money you need, son. Bribe whoever you have to. Frankie has the details of where he is buried.' Once again, he paused and closed his eyes. I watched his chest go up and down, wondering if this was the moment when everything would stop. He almost looked peaceful. Then he opened his eyes again, slowly, as if he was rationing the little strength he had left. 'Thankfully, his body is on our side… in one of those deserted Greek villages near Famagusta. You make sure we're together, me and Tassos. And I want the biggest mausoleum Bamyaköy has ever seen. No, the biggest for any Turkish Cypriot ever. Marble, Sandy. The best from Italy. You got that?'

'Yes, Aydin. It will be the very best. I know what you like.' I stroked his hand as I spoke. At that point I was unable to stop the tears coming down my cheeks.

He squeezed my hand and held the pressure, 'Look Sandy, you and Defne will have so much money now. So, I want you to do something useful. I know your first thought will be to invest it carefully, tight-fisted bastard you are. But I want you to spend whatever it takes to bring Bamyaköy back to life. Buy up the empty houses, bring businesses, build a school, give the kids free education, employ a doctor. Do whatever it takes to make Bamyaköy alive again. Sandy, promise me. Do good with all that money. If not for me, for your father. For all of us from Bamyaköy.' As he spoke, he shook my sleeve as if he feared that I might not have been paying attention.

'I promise, Aydin.'

He laid back on his pillows and looked up at the ceiling. His breathing started to slow right down. I thought about calling in the others, but I didn't want to lose a second with him.

'Sandy, last thing… be careful of my brother. He's mixed up in some nasty stuff.'

'What kind of stuff?'

'The Grey Wolves. Just be careful Sandy.' At this, he coughed, and his eyes bulged outwards and a look of fear crossed his face.

I saw that there was a copy of the Quran, in English translation, on the bedside table. There was a bright orange page marker in it. I opened it and saw that one of the verses was highlighted. He must have prepared it for me in anticipation of this moment. So, I read it out, as best I could, trying to keep my voice steady:

'O God, forgive him and have mercy on him, keep him safe and sound and forgive him, honour his rest and ease his entrance; wash him with water and snow and hail, and cleanse him of sin as a white garment is cleansed of dirt.'

A look of calm crossed Aydin's face. Then he started to speak, so softly that I had to lean up close to him to catch what he was saying. It was just one word, 'Tassos' repeated again and again until his hand went limp in mine, and he stopped breathing altogether.

I reached forwards and held him in my arms, rocking him back and forth like a child. The smell of shit, naphthalene and perfume were nothing to me at that moment. They must have heard me sobbing from outside because pretty soon the others came into the room. But I wouldn't let go of Aydin.

Later, I was told, that I held him for two hours or more, crying my eyes out. Apparently, no one could get me to unlock my arms that were clenched around him. All I can remember now is that at some point Defne led me away to wash all the powder and make-up that had rubbed off from his cold face on to mine.

CHAPTER 42

In accordance with Islamic tradition, I buried Aydin the next day – no more than 24 hours after he passed away. I planned to have him re-interred later when I had his and Tassos' mausoleum ready. Apart from Imam Hassan, there was only Defne, Frankie and me in attendance for the ceremony.

The funeral was made all the more desolate because the wind was whipping up dust and we had to cover our faces with scarves. But none of this deterred Hassan, who loudly and boldly recited the Quran in Arabic: 'God, if he was a doer of good, then increase his good deeds, and if he was a wrongdoer, then overlook his bad deeds. God, forgive him...' I lifted my hands to the prayer like Hassan had shown me. The other person that I once was, would have felt ridiculous making such a gesture. There, however, at the foot of the village, in the graveyard that lies next to the single, narrow, broken road that connects Bamyaköy to the outside world, with the wind howling through the poor wretched tombstones, it made sense to me.

I looked over at Frankie and Defne. They were holding hands. Both of them were crying. I thought about my uncle's funeral and how many people came to it. And how few had come for Aydin. But, if he could see from wherever his soul had gone to, I don't think it would have bothered him much. Those who really cared about him in his final years, and who he cared about, were there to see him out. The ones who could see beyond the money and the make-up. The ones who saw his capacity to love. Standing there in front of his grave, I remember expressing my own little wish, prayer if you like, that the life thereafter, the one we all like to imagine, the one where justice gets done and we are reunited with those we have loved and who have gone before us – where we meet those precious souls, they and we at our immortal best – would be true, at least for Aydin. I had to believe that a just God would see all the pain, all the hurt of the young child he once was and take into consideration what he made of himself. And that, like it says in the Quran, his sins would be counted and weighed not only against his good deeds but also against all the love and devotion that he gave to so many. That he would be saved, albeit after a brief reckoning, to enter another room and find Tassos waiting for him there. So that, at their reunion, he could give account of his life, day by day since the moment of their separation and that, in God's time, when this was done, they would lie down to rest and find peace.

I was glad that there was no line of people to help cast the earth onto his coffin. I shovelled it onto the casket myself, obliterating myself in the labour. With every shovel of earth, I repeated his name, my father's name, all the others of my family who had passed. Name after name, said again and again, like the prayer of a rosary – committing all those dead souls to the memory of the wind as it blew down the valley and on towards Malatya and the hills beyond.

CHAPTER 43

After the funeral, I did everything he had asked of me. I set in motion the various projects that were so dear to him. I even resorted to bribery when I felt it was the only way to make things happen. I was not proud of that. But I wasn't going to let Aydin down.

By the beginning of March, I had delivered on the first of my promises. The one that was most important to him; the mausoleum for him and Tassos. In the late afternoon light, it looked particularly beautiful. The long rays of sunshine brought its ivory marble alive with hues of pink and orange. The design had little originality as I had largely copied Italian Renaissance designs that I found on the internet. But it was no less elegant for all that. It was a simple structure with two sloping rooves, under which their tombs rested side by side like husband and wife, with an infinity chain motif circling the base. There was enough space to walk around these two prone structures. With the open sides and the pillars, and the alabaster bench I put in, I liked to think it resembled the miniature cloister of a monastery.

Ironically, one of the smaller design features gave me the most trouble and cost me the most in bribes: placing the Orthodox Cross of Greek Cypriot Christianity alongside the Crescent Moon of Islam on the double roof of the mausoleum. I am not artistic by nature, but I thought that there was great beauty in seeing the two religious symbols of Cyprus side by side. A visual reminder that Christian and Muslim could be at peace with each other. A sign also that there, in the graveyard of Bamyaköy, a Muslim lay side by side with the person that he loved the most on this earth, a Christian.

CHAPTER 44

I couldn't believe how busy we had become and how our diary had filled up in the space of the nine or so months we had been in Cyprus. The following week was to be Defne's last lecture before the spring break. And a few weeks after that, we would have the memorial service for Zeki and, against the odds, it looked as if his memorial house would be ready, right on time. The PR agent told me that we had the A -list of Turkish Cypriot society coming – including the President and his main ministers – as well as the B- and C- lists, it seemed. I hardly recognised any of the names of the few hundred people who were due to come. Defne told me not to worry – we wanted numbers for the sake of the TV cameras. I could see that she had a point. On the guest list were a few extended family members. And people I had met briefly, like Colonel Kaynar. I was not sure how I felt about that after Aydin's warning. I put the concern down to his state of health and the very obvious difference in the dispositions of the two men.

There was also Defne's book, which was going well – she thought she would be ready to send it to her agent by the autumn. And my promise to Aydin to rebuild Bamyaköy; I had a notebook into which I scribbled my thoughts, and a plan was emerging. It was an interesting intellectual challenge, and I was greatly enjoying this whole master-planning exercise. However, as a friend once told me, any fool can come up with a plan, the real genius is in getting it done. And that thought haunted me every day and pushed me to focus meticulously on the details of its execution.

CHAPTER 45

It was 25 March 2013. The date is forever fixed in my mind. We were on our way to the 'Greek' side so Defne could give her last lecture of the term. It felt as if spring had truly arrived from one day to the next. This was one of my favourite times of year in Cyprus because everything became impossibly green, as if the Almighty had just invented the colour and wanted to try it out on our little palette of land. And then onto this green came the sprinkling of wild flowers; little explosions of yellow, white and iris blue. Just a week or so before, the land was dull and brown, and by June it would be the colour of burnt copper and the flowers would be desiccated, like petals in a press of plywood and blotting paper. But right then it was nature in all its virginity.

We reached the border and crossed over. I was confident that everything would be a repeat of our previous visits. I expected her lecture to be another triumph. In my head, I had already planned a celebratory lunch at Pyxida, our favourite fish restaurant in Nicosia. In my mind's eye, I already had a steaming bowl of fish soup in front of me and, by my side, a plate full of thick slices of lemon to squeeze into the fragrant mix. But as soon as we made the crossing, we sensed, like dogs sniffing an intruder over the wind, that something was amiss. The particular sullenness of the Greek Cypriot border police should have put us on guard. But we were not yet ready to have our bubble of good humour burst. It was only after we made it through the checkpoint and found the mood was so palpably different that we could no longer brush it aside.

It was Defne who pointed out what had changed. 'Sandy, look at the trees, look at all the flags.'

From tree to tree, blue and white bunting was hanging. And from every balcony, from every pole, hung the Greek flag. It is not what we in the 'Turkish' North referred to as the Greek Cypriot flag, with its neat little representation of our island sitting on laurel leaves like an imperial dominion. It was, instead, the blue and white flag of the Hellenic Republic. A country whose capital was almost a thousand kilometres away. That day you would have imagined yourself to be in a town on the Greek mainland.

We saw young children holding hand flags and eating candy. At first, they waved their fluttering pennants gleefully at us. But then we saw some of the adults motioning their heads in our direction and particularly towards our number plate that indicated we were from the other side.

We stopped at the traffic lights, where a little boy threw a sweet at us. Then his friends joined in. And for the few seconds before the lights changed, it felt as if our windshield was being hit with hail.

'The little rascals,' said Defne, who laughed good naturedly. Nothing was going to disturb her.

I didn't say anything. Instead, I gripped the steering wheel a little tighter.

At the university, groups of young men and women were gathering on the campus steps in front of the main entrance. The police were putting up barriers. I could see, behind them, their trucks with crisscross wire shields over the windscreens. I could hear big dogs barking.

From the parking lot, we hurried towards the building. Just as we were about to make it inside, a policeman stopped us and asked what we were doing there. Defne explained and we showed our ID; after looking at them a little dubiously, turning them over as if they might be fakes, he finally waved us through. As he did so, he looked in the opposite direction as if he did not want to be seen to be associating with us.

The auditorium, which had been full the previous month, now held only a handful of students. And most of them did not seem to be Greek Cypriots, either. Out of Defne's earshot, I asked the technician what was going on. 'Oh, you don't know?' he said.

I shook my head.

'Today is Greek Independence Day.'

'But we're in Cyprus.'

He laughed in a way I didn't like and said, 'This is one of the most important holidays for Cypriots.'

'For Greek Cypriots you mean?'

He looked at me incredulously. I felt a flush of anger and clenched my fists. But I forced myself to keep a smile on my face and made my way to my usual seat in the front.

Defne, my beloved, darling woman, gave what I thought was a marvellous lecture on developing the 'interiority' of a novel's protagonist. But the applause was lukewarm, not just because of the scarcity of students but because a general lassitude seemed to be flowing through the auditorium.

'Come on Defne, let's go to Pyxida,' I said, when she had finished putting away her notes in the worn leather briefcase she'd inherited from her father – well, from Ziya Necati. She talked about him sometimes. She talked about him in a way that made me wish I had met him. He must have been a special man to have brought up Defne and for her to turn out the way she did. I sometimes asked myself if he'd have understood what I felt about his 'daughter'? But would anyone? Except for Aydin, I could never come up with another name.

I was grateful that she mostly seemed oblivious to what was going on around us. She even said, the palm of her right hand upturned as if she was presenting me with a key to open a treasure box, 'You know Sandy, as I was standing there talking about the inner life of characters it made me realise that I still had so much more to do on my novel.' She shook her head. 'Anyway, something to think about. Yes, let's go to Pyxida, I'm absolutely starving.'

The thought of the wonderful spread of food that would be waiting for us there raised my spirits. After the soup, I would have the salad, and the taramasalata spread thickly over slices of toasted bread. And then my grilled sea bass. All washed down with a bottle of nicely chilled Argyrides. However, when we made it outside, the whole atmosphere had worsened. She could no longer brush off what was going on.

The street was completely cordoned off. Behind the barriers stood row upon row of young men in black shirts. Some were waving Greek flags. Some were waving flags in support of ELAM. Others held signs written in Greek. And a few held signs in English.

When they spotted us, the young men started to bay.

The policemen, who had donned helmets with visors, were standing by the barriers, but they seemed completely uninterested in what was going on around them and did nothing to calm the situation.

I looked at the mob and felt a terrible fear as I read the signs.

'Die, Turkish Bitch.'

'Fuck Turkish Cypriot women.'

'We'll push Turks into the sea.'

'Cyprus is Greek.'

'This land belongs to Christians.'

Then they started chanting:

'The flag that I love

Oo-ray-ay

Bears a white cross

Oo-ray-ay

I will defend it

Oo-ray-ay

Until they find me dead.

I could hear Aydin's voice in my head telling me to stand tall and show no fear. I straightened up and looked at the screaming heads assembled the other side of the barriers. A mad fury started to take possession of me. Everything was slowing down. All I could see was a black haze of seething mass straight ahead. I could see neither left nor right. It was as if I was walking down a tunnel towards the hatred. I couldn't hear anything. I was filled with a desire to kick, punch and gouge. And to pummel all those who would seek to scare and hurt Defne. All those who would wish us dead. All those who would want to see people from my village, simple folk like my aunt and uncle, killed and pushed into the sea. And for what? For the crime of being a Turk.

In that instant, I was quite alone. For a moment, I felt I could see myself from above. And there, looking down, I could see someone tugging at my arm. But I didn't recognise the person, and I walked on. She walked with me. Her mouth was open as if she was saying something, pleading. Then, all of a sudden, my inner chamber of silence was pierced by a scream. I turned my head in bemusement. I looked. But what I was seeing still didn't register. Until I saw that it was Defne screaming, pleading with me. She knew what I was capable of when I was angry. I came to my senses. I turned away from the mob and put my arm around her. I turned once more to look at them, then led her off in the other direction, to the parking lot.

By the time I had us in the car, I could see in my rear-view mirror that some of the ELAM supporters had broken through the barriers. They were running towards us. The police did nothing to stop them. As we drove off, I could hear heavy objects start to land on the car. It was no longer the shrill little hailstorm of candy. The traffic was moving slowly. I feared that we wouldn't get away in time. The only clear spot I saw was the pavement. I mounted the kerb and drove off until we reached the junction. From there, I turned right and headed towards the border. Flooring the car. I remember telling myself that we could now only be safe on the 'other' side, surrounded by Turkish soldiers to protect us.

CHAPTER 46

When Defne was upset, she used to shut down. She wouldn't talk to anyone. Not even to me. She would just sit at her desk and write for hours, without break. It was as if she stepped into another world. At first, it used to upset me; made me even a little jealous that she went to this place where I couldn't follow. But, over time, I became used to it and simply let it work its way out without interfering or nagging.

After the events at the university, she went into one such mood. Predictably, she immersed herself in her writing, and I no longer existed for her. And that was fine. I was also upset. However, whereas she was productive, I sat around and brooded, trying to make sense of what we had witnessed. I started to think that maybe the old people in the village were right: only Turkey could keep us safe. Maybe I had been too quick to dismiss what I once took for simplistic nationalist rhetoric from our side. Maybe, I told myself, the stories were true about the Greek Cypriots being the aggressors in the 1950s and 1960s. I really didn't know what to believe anymore. But the sentiments swirling around my head were not edifying and, in hindsight, I am not proud of them.

I couldn't allow myself to dwell on such dark thoughts for long, as I needed to get on with supervising final arrangements for the big memorial service which was set for Saturday 16 April, just two weeks away. It would be held in front of our new house. This new iteration of Zeki's original home was an elegant white villa with arches and a large terrace. I hoped that Defne would be able to work from the outdoor space. Protected by shade, she would continue to have an uninterrupted view of the valley, although from a different angle to the one she had enjoyed at my aunt's house. And then there was the garden.

Even before the building works were finished, it was christened 'The Garden of Remembrance,' by our fellow villagers. It was easy to understand why. In the forefront of the garden, we had placed a large bronze bust of Zeki on a black granite plinth with a white marble plaque bearing an inscription in large letters, that read, 'Zeki Aziz, Beloved Son of the Turkish Cypriot People and the Village of Bamyaköy'. However, the words on the plaque were covered from sight by a curtain until the day of the ceremony. The plan was for the President to unveil the plaque in front of the press and onlookers.

Most of the time, I was pleased with what we had built. And I thought that Zeki might have liked it too. But occasionally, while it was under construction, I used to sit in the garden on an old stone basin – presumably there for washing clothes – and would think with some sadness and nostalgia for what had been there before. Before we had bulldozed the whole structure. After all, the original house was where I stayed when I first came to Cyprus – the house my father had commissioned to be built for him as a young member of parliament. At those moments of contemplation, my mind wandered back to my first interaction with Cyprus; I would think about my own particular connection to the island; its recent, and distant, past.

Recent past… already the figures of those days, my aunt and uncle principally, had passed away. But they were often with me. I could feel their presence in my bones. It was they who had done their best to make me a Cypriot when I arrived from London some seven years before, a businessman's suitcase in each hand. It was my aunt, Aysel, who broke down my aloofness, with her constant clucking and tutting, and insistence that I should eat whatever was in her cooking pot that day. I remember her wonder at my clothes. Her pride when she told the neighbours that her nephew was a real *büyük effendi*. As, doubtless, she had once said about her brother a lifetime before. Her wiping of my sweating forehead, unused to the damp thick cloud of evening heat. Her unwavering belief that I was her brother incarnate. That somehow, I would make things better for the village. How she must have gone to her grave disappointed. My Uncle Ismail: scrawny, his face scarred with cuts from his days as a bare-knuckle fighter. But, like his wife, a capacity for tenderness and a belief that I would come good. It was he who taught me the land. The landscape that Defne, to my great pride, captured so elegantly in her writing. The hills and valleys that I wished I had the talent to paint. But without having the eye of an artist I still understood what I saw, thanks to Ismail. I learnt to see what a shepherd sees: grazing, shade, water, the better path home – not necessarily the shortest. All these things were inside me; redundant, useless even, but present nevertheless. I thought, in those moments, that I was like a hunting dog run to fat and kept in comfort with no need of the skills to track and retrieve. But at least I had the instincts. I understood from what substance I was hewn; the blood that pumped inside me. I understood the peasant width of my shoulders and the hands better suited to building stone walls than typing daintily at a keyboard.

Further past was a different darker corridor altogether.... The silence of my father's house that I was confronted with during that first night in Cyprus, all those years before. Even the scattering of cockroaches and scuttling of mice could not penetrate that veil. The weight of its heavy drapes was overwhelming. Some nights I fled from it to sleep on the terrace in the care of swarms of mosquitoes whose bites I would shred to blood with my fingernails. But at others, I just lay in what had been my father's bedroom, waiting for a sign, convinced he was there. Convinced that just once he would make himself known to his son. And then when I realised at 3 a.m. that sleep was impossible, I would go to sit in his study, surrounded by his books, each one with his name and date of reading inscribed in blue-black ink. Were these neat little inscriptions there as a mark of his pride, of his ownership, a statement that said, 'I, Zeki Aziz, owned that book and read it in that particular year, in that month'? Who else for miles around would have had such a collection? 'Latin for Beginners'. 'French for Beginners'. Mathematics. Algebra.

Toynbee. Adam Smith. And amongst all the books of learning, novels by Graham Greene. Who, but Zeki Aziz, would have had such? It was in one of those books that I came across a passport photo of him. It was the one that I would come to carry in my wallet, every day. Like a nerdy, diligent schoolchild I protected it in a plastic film so it could suffer my surreptitious handling. I peered at my father's face when the mood took me. The distant past was with me, forever haunting me.

CHAPTER 47

True to form, Defne returned to the world of domestic matters by the third day. It was as if nothing had occurred. And she was full of energy. It was she who decided, there and then, that we would move our things into the new house. I would have preferred to wait until after the ceremony for Zeki. Thankfully, however, we had no more than a couple of suitcases each. But to mark this evolution in our domestic affairs, she decided that she would take a break from writing that weekend and we would do whatever we fancied without the constraints of her writing.

That Saturday turned out to be one of the happiest days I ever had with Defne. Whilst I like to think that we had many together, this one, for some reason, shines out. Perhaps by contrast with what was to happen after.

Like most happy memories, it is characterised by its banality. After a late, long breakfast at *Kemal Hussein's* – where, for once, we ate the full spread of fresh rolls, cherry jam, pine honey, omelette, white cheese, cucumbers, olives and tomatoes – we headed to one of the deserted beaches close by. There, we walked hand in hand, mile after mile, our bare feet splashing through shallow waves lapping on to the sand. Later, when we were tired from the sun and the salt breeze, we headed to the high dunes behind us and lay down to sleep under the shade of an olive tree. I woke to find her stroking my face and then she leant over to kiss me. And, without a second thought, we made love there and then. It was afterwards, when she had fallen asleep again, that I like to remember her best. Like a photograph: sleeping peacefully, the wind gently blowing through her dark hair, her body dusted with a fine icing sugar coating of sand and next to her, a wild gnarled bush full of little pink flowers. My darling Defne, I never told you how beautiful you were that day, that when I think about us in the time before, that is how you appear in my mind. I still hope that when I am in the antechamber of the hall of judgements, just at that moment before I enter to meet the Almighty, I will be able to conjure up that image and go in to meet Him for my damnation with a smile full of my love for you on my face. And then, I will be able to shout out, 'Yes, Lord, my sin was to love her!'

The next day was more domestic in nature. We decided to spend it at home fixing things up. But after I had made a terrible job with the hammer and nails, Defne shooed me into the garden where she obviously seemed to think I posed the least threat. In my temporary exile, I pottered around the garden, pretending to anyone who might spy upon me that I knew what to do. I was in the middle of checking the leaves of our loquat tree when I heard a car approaching the village at high speed. Normally, no one came to Bamyaköy fast. Neither the regular traveller wary of potholes and the tight bends; nor the traveller of leisure approaching at a snail's pace of wonder, mesmerised by the beauty of our landscape. To my surprise, the car – a silver Range Rover Sport – stopped outside our front door. First, a chauffeur got out and trotted round to the passenger rear side to open the door. And out stepped Colonel Kaynar. He was immaculately dressed in a grey double-breasted suit that might have been fashionable fifty years previously but now made him look like a film star from a 1960s B film. I hadn't seen him since my uncle's funeral. He certainly hadn't come to his brother's funeral. He looked up at me and gave me an all-white-teeth smile. I was pleased to see him. At least, at first. Perhaps it was because of what had happened back at the university.

'Colonel, we hadn't expected to see you until the ceremony next week. How are you?'

He came up the steps with a vigour that suggested a man squeezing in a little more exercise to his day's activities. When he reached the doorway, he extended his hand. As I went to shake it, he pulled me to him and kissed me enthusiastically on both cheeks. He held me in a grip from which I couldn't escape. Just like the first time we had met, his whole manner suggested an intimacy and kinship that certainly did not exist between us. Unless, that is, you counted my friendship with Aydin. Something made me uneasy. The pleasure I had experienced a moment previously. evaporated. I was uncertain how to behave towards him or what to expect.

If he noticed my discomfort he did not let on and said instead, 'Sandy *Bey*, so good to see you.'

I regained my manners. I nodded politely. And then I forced my face into a stiff smile.

'Now Aydin has gone, I've been looking forward to seeing more of you,' he said. There was no mention of his relationship to my friend.

'Come, let's go and talk.' He entered the house through the front door, without waiting to be invited.

Defne, who had been hanging a picture frame, said hello almost quizzically. I could see she was wondering who he was and by what right he was making himself at home.

'This is my wife,' I said to him. And to her, 'This is Colonel Kaynar'. For a moment I thought of saying 'Aydin's brother', but something told me to tread carefully.

'*Çok Güzel*,' he said, in the same way he might have admired some fine farm animal. 'So, you married one of your own? *Mashallah*. That's good, very good. Keep the blood pure. Keep us as Turks as Öz Turks – isn't that so, Sandy?' He laughed and slapped me on the back. I couldn't figure out if he was trying to be clever and making a play on words of what must have been his original family name, which when literally translated means 'Pure Turk'.

I smiled. But inside, he set me on edge and the very tone of his voice was making me cringe. Then I wondered how far manners and hospitality meant I should put up with his nonsense.

'I will make coffee,' said Defne.

Kaynar grunted in approval as if he expected nothing less. My loathing for the man increased.

'So, when were you two married?' As he asked, he pulled a string of worry beads from his jacket pocket and proceeded to click the little pieces of amber through his fingers. I noticed his nails were long and had ridges in them – and the tips had lines of dirt showing through.

'Last year,' I said.

'Young married couple, then?' The way he said it sounded seedy. Neither of us was young. He knew it. We knew it. I hated the fact that someone could imply, even if by the tone of their voice, that there was something abnormal about our relationship. 'How nice. Married in London, I suppose?'

I nodded. Fearing that I might sound too defensive or tell a lie so big that I would catch myself out, I realised that I needed to go on the offensive and play the card I had hoped to keep up my sleeve. So, I asked him directly, 'Is it true that you are Aydin's brother?'

'Sadly, yes Sandy.' He gave out a long sigh.

Defne brought in the Turkish coffee and set his cup in front of him. She had made the coffee beautifully. It carried a thick carob coloured foam, the *kaymak*, and the rising steam was throwing off the smell of dark roast and cardamon. On the saucer, she had placed a sugar dusted piece of hazelnut *lokum*. The old soldier nodded his head appreciatively. It seemed as if, through our play-acting, we could do no wrong. He proceeded to slurp the coffee down loudly in one gulp. And then popped the sugary gelatinous mass into his mouth and swallowed it with barely a chew. It occurred to me, as I watched him, that I would not be unhappy if he choked on it. His moustache was speckled brown and white from the coffee and the sweetmeat.

I returned to his comment about his brother. 'Why sadly? I'd have thought you would have been jolly proud of him, no?'

Kaynar clicked his tongue through his teeth. He did not need to say a word to express his scorn and dismissiveness.

I could see Defne out of the corner of my eye in the kitchen area, standing against the counter drinking her coffee and watching me. I knew she was waiting to see what I would do to defend the memory of my friend.

Deliberately, I gave him a puzzled look back, frowning for all I was worth as if trying to understand what part of the jigsaw I had missed. Perhaps he thought I was even more stupid than he had thought initially.

'Sandy, come on… you must know.' He looked at me in disbelief. 'After all you worked for him. He wasn't a real man. He was *ibne*.'

'What is *ibne*, Colonel *Bey*?'

'You know, what do they say in English? He struggled for a few moments and then proudly said, 'sodomite'.

Behind him, I could see Defne; her face in front of her mouth trying hard to stifle a laugh.

'So?' I continued, the same dazed air of incomprehension on my face.

He looked at me, shocked. Then he tried again to explain in case I had misunderstood his accent. 'You know, man who has sex with other men.' He reduced his voice to a whisper as if he did not want Defne to hear such things.

'I don't know. I don't care. He was my friend. He helped me. And I never met anyone as tough as him. My uncle used to say that when Aydin was young, he was the bravest fighter he ever knew.'

'Pfff… not a real soldier.'

'But he killed people during the fighting in the 1960s. And what about all the folk he saved in the Famagusta enclave?'

This reminder that Aydin had single-handedly attacked the Greek Cypriot forces, just before they were about to attack the refugees of the Famagusta enclave, didn't seem to please Kaynar. It occurred to me that, perhaps, he himself had not seen active duty. But then, as if he was suddenly tired of having his narrative challenged, he said, 'Sandy *Bey*, less said about my brother the better. I don't know how you got mixed up with him but now you're home and that's all that matters.' From the moment he uttered the word 'home', his voice took on an emollient tone and almost turned into a purr.

'Yes, that's all that matters,' I said, as agreeably as I could.

'So, what do you plan to do now?'

'Well, we have the memorial service for... I was about to say, 'our father' but corrected myself in time to say, 'for my father, for Zeki'. Out of the corner of my eye I could see Defne looking at me with alarm. 'Did you know him?'

'I can't say that I had the privilege. I was away in Turkey at the time, at military college. But I heard that he was a great man. An intellectual. We need those too, you see.'

'Well, given that you didn't actually know him it's kind of you to come to the memorial service next week. But after that, I have some projects in mind for developing the village.'

'Bravo!' said Kaynar in the manner of an adult praising a child for success in the most elementary mathematics at the third attempt. 'But,' and here he slapped his knee, 'a man like you has to have a political home. Especially the son of such a distinguished father. You owe him that. Think what your father would have wanted.'

I wondered if he had an inkling of who Defne was, of what she and I had achieved or, indeed, of our combined wealth. And then, out of the blue, as if trying to stir me from my moral torpor, he slammed down his cup.

I could see Defne looking aghast and trying, at a distance, to see if her beloved Selamlique ceramic coffee cup had been cracked.

'Sandy, you have grown away from us, from home. Trust me, if we'd had you as a boy, we would have made something of you.' He shook his head wistfully. 'But now, it's time to catch up and teach you about true Turkish values.'

I was about to say something about being Cypriot, but Defne was shaking her head at me. I knew she was telling me in her own way, 'Sandy, just don't go there.' So instead, I said with as much curiosity as I could fake, 'What are these values, Colonel *Bey*?'

Instead of answering me, he said, 'Do you know who Alparslan Turkesh is?' His eyes were shining as if he had drunk *rakı* for his breakfast.

'No, I'm sorry. Should I?'

He looked disappointed, as if he was just discovering that I had not completed elementary school. 'Turkesh, was probably the greatest Turkish Cypriot that ever lived. A great Turk. A great hero for us.'

'But what about Mr Denktash?' I said, referring to the TRNC's recently deceased long-standing and revered president.

'A brother – but even he would have recognised that he was not in Turkesh's league.'

'So, what did this fellow do?'

'He shaped modern Turkey.' The soldier's tone of voice was positively messianic.

'Not Kemal Atatürk?'

Once again Kaynar lashed out with his dismissive clicking of tongue against teeth. 'No, don't confuse things, Atatürk is the father of our nation. But Turkesh went on to make the ideology that shaped our republic.'

'So, what did he believe in?'

'Patriotism – there is nothing greater than love and service to Turkey.'

'Even if you are Turkish Cypriot?' I said. I could see Defne glaring at me, warning lights flashing in her eyes.

'Look Sandy, we are all from Anatolia and we are part of the Turkish Nation. Have you forgotten that young Turkish soldiers came in '74 to die in Cyprus… to save us?'

After this, the flood gates opened and there was no stopping Kaynar. He talked of Turkish culture, of family, of social cohesion, of technological dominance, of the rural classes. He went droning on until the *Dhuhr* prayer was called. I hoped this would save us. But he refused to take the cue. Instead, he paused, took a handkerchief from his top pocket and wiped his forehead.

'Look Sandy, I want you to think about what I've said.'

'Yes indeed, I will be sure to. Thank you very much for such a different perspective. We look forward to hearing more another time. Now, if you will—'

He interrupted me with a gesture, cutting through the air as if calling time. Then pointing his index at me he said, 'YOU, must return to your roots. You will find yourself surrounded by brothers and you will be safe and respected.' Then more gently, 'Just let me know when you are ready, and I will invite you to one of our meetings. You will see, a very interesting group of people. And you can be of great service to the cause.'

It was at that point, I realised that we had reached the real purpose of his visit. All his grandiose talk was his sales pitch warming us up for his big ask. I could see it all so clearly and kicked myself for believing that his calling on us had been a neighbourly social visit.

'How do you think I can be of service?' I said guardedly.

Kaynar smiled broadly at me and reached for my knee. The

touch of his hand made my flesh crawl. Perhaps he noticed my lack of enthusiasm and shot back by shouting out, 'By giving money. Lots of money!' I noticed little white gobs of spit on the side of his mouth, resting on the tiny little hairs that his razor had missed. 'A rich man like you can afford to give us what we need.' As he said this, his fingers extended over my knee and clasped it tightly.

I looked pointedly down at his hand and, thankfully, taking the cue this time, he removed it and tugged at his moustache.

I looked over at Defne. I knew we were both wondering if he had anything on us both. If he knew about us. I did what I could to suppress my fear and said, 'Well, as I told you, we have projects of our own, Colonel. For the village. I'm afraid they will take all our spare cash for a while.'

'Don't waste your time on a place like this. Look at it, it's dying.'

I wanted to remind him that once this had been his village also, but instead I said, as good naturedly as I could, 'Well hopefully we can bring it alive again. Now really, we must be—'

'Ten million English pounds, Sandy,' he said abruptly. 'That's all I want. To start with. Nothing for a man like you.'

'My goodness, Colonel, that's a lot of money. We could do so much for the village with that amount. What do you need so much for?'

'Special operations, Sandy...'

'Special operations?'

'You don't need to worry about the details. You know we have so much to do countering the vile lies of the Jews, the Armenians and the Greeks. And of course, promoting proper Turkish values.'

'What have the Jews got to do with Cyprus?' I could feel myself losing patience.

'Sandy, Sandy...' He shook his head mournfully. 'Don't you

know anything about the world? Don't you know that Jews control the media outlets around the world? That they control all the banks?'

And then I'd had enough. My first instinct was to slap him but I controlled myself and said instead, 'I am sorry, I don't agree with you. And we will not be giving you any money. I think it's best that you leave.' I stood up and showed him the door. I was ready to push him out if necessary, but looking over at Defne I could sense her willing me to restrain myself.

The old soldier stood up slowly and opened his mouth and put his index finger in the back of his teeth as if he wanted to clean out a stuck filament of meat. And then he said, 'Sandy, I suggest you reconsider your position.' He looked at me strangely. There was hint of a smile on his face. And with that he left.

CHAPTER 48

Colonel Kaynar's visit left us with a bad taste in our mouths. Now that I understood who he really was, I did what I should have done months before, when Aydin first mentioned the 'Grey Wolves' to me: I opened my laptop and went online to see what I could find out. The search results were not encouraging. 'Paramilitary', 'fascist', 'death squads', 'attempted assassination of Pope John Paul II' were the words and headlines that came up most often. I didn't share any of it with Defne. I didn't want to scare her with this nastiness. In any event, she was not talking to me. She seemed to have reverted to her mood from a few days before. Something else was bothering her, but I didn't know what. I became obsessed with the thought that maybe she had woken up and seen our relationship as how other people would: a crime against nature, plain and simple. A crime against God's laws. Against what society had codified.

I was already in a bad space because of Kaynar's visit but these other fears made everything much worse. I found myself sinking into a depression the likes of which I had not experienced since the days following my decision to get divorced fifteen years before. The normal Defne would have been able to coax me out of it. But, without her support, I just lay on the couch staring at the ceiling and listening on loop to Brian Eno's 'Music for Airports', as if some plastic sterile truth would emerge.

People knocked on our door. Presumably they had come to get clarifications and instructions for the ceremony. Neither one of us reacted. Nor did I answer phone calls or respond to text messages.

By Friday, the day before the ceremony, I thought about leaving, about walking away from everything. We had been sleeping in separate beds all that past week and I was convinced that our relationship was at an end. By evening, the air started to turn damp, and a breeze came running through the village. Out of my blackness, it seemed to me that the earth had turned up its volume and was summoning me. Everything was louder, more acute. And then it came, like a release, rolling across the valley, the sound of thunder. And I started to count. It was a habit I had, keeping tally of the seconds between each peel of thunder. Measuring the gap between them and the flashes of lightning. Determining if the storm was closing in on us or heading away.

I went out to the garden and sat under the pergola to watch the olive-sized rain drops. They splashed onto the ground and dampened it. I could feel the soil breathe. I could feel myself breathing in sync, becoming one with the land. The village was silent. The dogs, so cocksure during the day, barking at any sound or intruder that displeased them, had scuttled off with tails between their legs to find whatever shelter they could for their sorry mangy carcasses. I, on the other hand, had found some peace, my spirits were less bleak. I could feel a pleasant indifference coursing through my veins, my distance from Defne forgotten for a while. There were dozens of reasons, of course, why I should not have enjoyed such serenity. Not least that we were on the eve of our big event and, if the weather carried on like this, everything would be ruined. Despite this, I wished that the sanctuary of noise, flashes of forked lightning and falling rain, would last for ever. I curled back into my childhood; I've had a fascination with thunderstorms since I was a little boy. Ever since the day when, in a fit of capriciousness, I first forced an aged carer, blackmailed by my tantrum, to take me out on my tricycle in the middle of a storm. Perhaps, over and above the meteorological theatrics, it was the old lady's fear that I enjoyed.

For a while, my mind tried to pinpoint the precise source of my delight, but my reverie was interrupted by the sound of hurried steps on the wet and muddy stone path leading to the pergola. It was Defne. For a moment I stared, vaguely aware that she was somebody familiar – although I couldn't quite determine who at that precise moment. I remember that her mouth was making shapes that I recognised as talking. But her face was creased. I saw pain and emotion. I was torn. I didn't want to return to reality just yet. I was happy as I was. I felt so light. Tranquil. But the umbilical cord between my soul and body reeled me back in. Then her voice broke through, 'Sandy, Sandy! Do you hear me?!'

I smiled at her. I would like to think it was a serene, kind smile. But too late I realised that this was the wrong facial response.

'Sandy, it's not funny. You can't stay out here in the middle of a storm.'

I wanted to ask her why not, but then I saw that she had been crying, and I reached out for her arm. At first, she tried to pull it away, but I insisted. For a moment, we stood without speaking. The only noise was her breathing, hard breaths in and out, and the sound of the rain.

'What's wrong my love?' I asked her, finally. As I spoke, I realised that these words were the right response, at last.

Even when she responded 'Nothing', I was not phased. It was simply the opening gambit before we got to the heart of the matter. I knew I would have to try harder. Her eyes were bloodshot; the blood vessels dispersed in cobweb form across the whites of her eyeballs. I pulled her gently to me and then onto my lap. I pushed her hair out of her eyes. I held her. Her skin, normally so fragrant with the daily dab of perfume, smelt sour. Her hair was matted and strands of it stuck to her forehead. I started to hum. And as I did so, I rocked her back and forth ever so slightly. I didn't know what else to do. I remember that all I wanted was to comfort her. And then her tears started to flow. They splashed onto my face. I leant forward and rested my cheek against hers. As I did, I could feel little rivulets running down her face. Her breathing slowed and, at last, she said, 'Sandy, I'm so scared.'

'You're not still thinking about that wretched Kaynar, are you?'

She pulled away and looked at me in a way I didn't like. 'Sandy, haven't you noticed anything?'

I tried to come up with a list of things I should have noticed but drew a blank. So, I shook my head.

'Don't you know anything about women?'

'Well…'

'I'm pregnant.'

'What are you talking about?' I said, aghast.

'Haven't you realised that I haven't had my periods for the last three months?'

'But…'

'But what, Sandy?'

'I thought you were too old. And you were on the pill. I mean, nothing has ever happened before.'

'Well now it has.'

'How could it?

She turned away from me. And then she said, 'Remember that time a few weeks back I got sick and couldn't keep anything down?'

I nodded my head.

'Well after that I stopped taking the pill. The idea of taking it again just made me queasy, and I thought we might be okay. Particularly given my age and all.'

I looked at her hard and then, eventually, I said, 'What do you want to do?'

'I don't know what to do. I'm so scared.'

The rain had stopped, and the storm passed over the brow of the hill towards the sea and on towards the Taurus mountains of Turkey. The village was coming to life again. Somewhere, I heard a tractor starting up. The dogs were starting to bark again. And from Burak's coffee shop, up the empty street, I heard the clinking of glasses as the first measures of rakı were being served out. And the longer we sat there, the less I could see a problem with Defne having our child.

'Do you want the baby, Defne?'

'Yes,' she whispered, as if this was a secret so sacred that not even the trees in our garden should be party to it.

'So, let's do it then, my love.'

'But aren't you worried?'

She caught me off guard with that question. For, as I looked at her, I realised that in this matter I had no fear, no doubt. My woman was carrying our child. Full stop. What was there for me to think about? 'Not if this is what you want. I never thought I might be becoming a father at this age. I had given up all hope. But with you there is nothing I want more.'

'Aren't you frightened about how the baby might turn out?'

'I know it's not a good thing for close relatives to have children together. But I have never really looked into it.'

'Well, there are terrible risks. Recessive diseases are a possibility.' In response to my puzzled look about how she had, all of a sudden, all this medical knowledge, she said, 'I Googled it.'

'How possible? I mean, what are the odds?' As I think back to that question today, I realise that it must have sounded pretty crass, like a backgammon player figuring out the probabilities of which throw of the dice will lead to victory and which to defeat. But thankfully, she did not take offence.

'Well, because we are not full brother and sister the chances are less.'

'Give me the numbers, Defne? One in two? One in three? One

in five?'

'I just don't know.'

'And what are these recessive diseases?

'Sickle cell disease, cystic fibrosis…'

'God, they do sound pretty awful.'

'You still want to go ahead?' she said. I noted a hint of hostility in her voice as if she was testing me.

'I do, but I am worried that we are being horribly selfish. Listen, love, let's sleep on it for a while. How long before we need to make a decision?'

'Ten weeks, maximum. That's the last point at which we can do something.'

'Something, meaning?'

'Oh, for God's sake, Sandy. How can you be so thick? You know as well as I do what that means.'

She turned away from me. I did know what she meant but the thought of her having an abortion distressed me. I would rather not have had to think about it. All of a sudden, it seemed as if our innocence had come to an end; that our love was having consequences that I had never considered, and it was time to pay the price.

CHAPTER 49

I woke in a panic. It was late. At least for us. It was almost eight o'clock when we both opened our eyes. But that day, of all days, was our father's memorial service – that we had been planning for months – within a few hours, hundreds of people would be descending upon Bamyaköy. Normally, we stirred after the first call for prayer and drank coffee and made love until the sun came up properly. And, after that, we would take our bikes and ride out into the valley.

How could it have happened that, on the day of our big event, we had overslept? Slowly, it came back to me what had happened the previous night.

The prospect of Defne having our child had been like some crazy irresistible aphrodisiac and we had gone straight to bed and made love with all the frenzy of our first months together. As if the simple act of copulating would erase the reality of our predicament. As if going deep inside her would take us to some higher truth than the simple platitude of ejaculation.

I looked over at her, lying next to me in our bed. She had fallen back asleep. Her mouth was slightly open and there was the familiar throat chuckle of a snore. The young version of me would have hated this. But I was with Defne, my love, and I was overwhelmed with tenderness.

I watched her for a while – although we should have been getting ready then. But I couldn't resist the beauty of the moment. The sheets rose and fell with each breath. I kissed her eyelids and finally she stirred. She said my name. Her body was warm and gave off a gentle smell of perspiration. For a moment all I wanted to do was to kiss her body, push her legs apart and make love to her all over again. I could feel myself getting hard. I turned onto my back and took long hard breaths trying to calm down. I tried to remind myself that we should be ready by now. That I should be making coffee. Then I felt her hand on my thigh. And that was it. There was nothing that could stop us.

CHAPTER 50

In many ways, Defne and I were similar. It used to be almost like a game for me. Trying to guess what she was going to like, how she was going to react. Mostly, we enjoyed the same kinds of food, drink and smells. Sometimes I even thought our facial expressions were the same. For example, I would see her wrinkling her nose at something and I would raise my hand to my face just to check if I was doing the same. And more often than not, we were. But in one crucial respect, we were very different. She was an extrovert, and I was an introvert. Because of this nature of hers, she was looking forward to the ceremony for our father and all the festivities that were planned for after. Me? I was sort of dreading it. I was not going to let down the side or anything.

Over the years I had learnt to project myself. This was the salesman in me. In my early days when I was cold-calling and hustling for business, I overcame my reticence by repeating my little mantra that enough sales calls would lead to higher income. So, a little bit of pain and effort would lead to a bigger bonus. But that day there was no hustle. Instead, I was doing something for the memory of a man who I'd never known, yet who cast his shadow long over my life. I guess I wanted to make him proud. I wanted to make Defne proud. But the truth was that I wanted to be done with the whole event as quickly as possible. I wanted to be at the point where I could say goodbye to Zeki and be free of him, like a stone cast into the sea. In front of everyone, I would have honoured my father. They could then say that I was a good son. I no longer wanted to be haunted by him. I didn't want to be compared to him. I just wanted him to be buried and to stay dead, at last.

I didn't have the time to say all this to Defne, although I would have liked to get it off my chest. But I did not dare interrupt her. She was getting dressed and made up and we were late enough as it was. The last thing she needed was me pouring out my angst just as she was getting ready.

When she finally appeared, she looked sublime. Her dress was charcoal. She was wearing a black hat and a veil. Through its knots, I could see a dark maroon lipstick and a particularly pale make up. Her eyes were highlighted with kohl. The perfect wife of a man come to lay his father's memory to rest.

For my part, I had put on the clothes of my previous life. Grey suit, white shirt, my gold Tiffany cuff links and bright red braces. If I had to take off my jacket at some point during the day the two parallel tracks of red would show up against my white shirt like the red and white flag of the Turkish Cypriots. This would go down well with the crowd, I thought, and particularly with the President, Mr Osman Agha.

There was a canopy for the two of us, under which two velvet covered chairs had been placed. We had a large open gazebo for our guests of honour. Defne had seen to it that the President had a throne sitting higher than anyone else and that his ministers – all men, as she noted, disapprovingly – were one level down but still above the crowd.

My now friend – I had become close to the long-suffering Imam Hassan these past months – had been signed up for this event. Valiantly, and without rest, he recited the prayers for the dead, repeating them again and again. His fine voice, unfortunately, was drowned out by cars arriving and horns blaring as people desperately sought to find a place to park close to the mosque adjacent to our house.

Smoke from the roasting sheep blew over to the dais where he was standing. And so, as he recited passages of the Quran for the forgiveness of my father's soul, he was enveloped in a cloud of carbon mist – adding to the whole mystical effect. Nothing would remain on camera of the smell, but forever it would look as if he was shrouded in incense.

I watched the people gather. They had come to a party. They were smiling and laughing. They were eyeing the refreshments. Particular attention, I noticed, was given to the meat turning on various spits and the doner kebab stands. And the rows of bottles of rakı, wine and beer. I imagined that they hoped the service would be over quickly. And my heart went out to them. In the big scheme of things, I knew they were right. The only things that really mattered were the joys of a Saturday afternoon party.

The ceremony began proper when the President arrived and Defne, in her usual charming manner, led him to his place. Osman Agha was a large man. I feared that the chair we had chosen for him might not be wide enough. But against the odds, he squeezed in. He did not seem to mind. I could see from his face that he was enchanted by Defne. And all I could think was that, a few hours before, I had seen her naked in our bedroom and made love to her. That she was mine and that I loved her. And that, because of her, I was blessed to be alive and whole after so many years of half-existence.

Hassan paused for a moment and drank from the cup of water in front of him. The poor man, his throat must have been parched. He turned on the microphone and then recited the most important prayer of all for Muslims, the Fatiha. I recited its seven verses under my breath along with him. Then he finished and all of a sudden it was my turn. As I took my place in front of the crowd, I still had the Fatiha echoing inside my head, 'It is You we worship, and You we ask for help.' Even though I knew it by heart now, it still rang strangely inside of me. I wondered if, in my mind, it would ever replace the 'Our Father', if it would ever become as comfortable, familiar and comforting. But I chased the thought away as I took my place at the dais. Behind me, the door of the mosque was open. And towering above me was the newly added minaret that Mr Erdogan's government had insisted we add to our simple village mosque – as if to prove beyond doubt that we were truly Turkish, truly Muslim.

I opened my notes. My speech had been carefully crafted and written out for me by Defne. It was all about our father, or at least a version of him. She had created, out of Zeki, a mythical character. A sort of JF Kennedy for Turkish Cypriots. Those who heard of him on that day would not forget this man's story, I told myself. She had segmented the speech neatly with an introduction, a main section – with just the right number of anecdotes to pull on the audience's heart strings – and then a summary, with a closing invitation to the President to unveil the marble plaque to Zeki.

I spoke solemnly. I remembered to cast my gaze across the full one hundred and eighty degrees of the crowd in front of me. I paused, from time to time, to make them feel that I was speaking to every single one of them. I stopped at the end of every sentence to allow the interpreter the time to repeat my words in Turkish. My own spoken Turkish would not have been up to giving such a speech nor would it have done justice to Defne's craft. These forced moments of interruption to my flow gave me the chance to nod and engage more deeply with the crowd.

Defne was a genius with words, and her ability to stir up emotions through her writing was a marvel to behold. Towards the end of the speech, even I, who had read and rehearsed it many times over, was getting pretty choked up. I could feel tears coming to my eyes. My voice was cracking. But the more the waves of emotion poured out, the more I could see that I held the crowd in the palm of my hand.

She had gone full out with the story of our father's humble background; how I had been partially orphaned, and all this stuff about how I had suffered the pain of growing up without a father but found comfort in the knowledge of Zeki's love for his people, his village, and his family. I am not sure that I bought it, but the crowd did. They were definitely mine. Women and men were crying. Some even had their hands extended towards me. During one of my pauses, I turned my head towards the President. Osman Agha was sitting immobile on his dais, and I noticed that he seemed to be the only one who was not touched by the speech. What I thought I saw was resentment. But at the time I concluded that I might be mistaken.

When I finished, I descended the mosque steps to lead the President over to the wall where he would unveil the plaque. But, before I could reach him, the crowd surged forwards toward me. Hands were reaching out to touch me. People were reaching out to kiss me on the cheek. In that moment, I belonged to them. Not to Defne. Not to myself. I belonged to this mass of people, my people, with their big loving hearts. I felt subsumed into the souls of my compatriots. We were there, as Turkish Cypriots, the last of the Mohicans, dying out but still kicking. Enough energy for one last party, one last song. At that moment, I loved them back with all my being.

A couple of bodyguards felt obliged to intervene. They led the President through the mass of people to where I was waiting for him in front of the veiled memorial stone. I knew that behind the curtains was a fine piece of alabaster with the inscription we had chosen for Zeki.

Unfortunately, the orchestra got its order of music mixed up. And instead of the solemn tune that we had envisaged for this moment of unveiling, they were playing an up-tempo version of 'Kıbrısım', the Turkish Cypriot equivalent of Woodie Guthrie's 'This Land is our Land' – although I am not sure too many people there would have known the American folk singer. But 'Kıbrısım' – My Cyprus – written by Kamran Aziz is, I like to think, the unofficial but real national anthem of our community. Little could this pharmacist have known that with its few lines, her song would forever sum up a halcyon image of our beautiful land before the division, before we split into enclaves, before we became officially 'us' versus 'them'. The ballad brought a holiday mood to the gathering – some of the women were even moving their hips in time to the music and the men were singing and clapping along. I looked over at the conductor, smiled and made a cutting gesture with my hand.

Osman Agha went up to the silk curtain cord and pulled. But instead of the applause we had been expecting, a collective gasp was uttered by the crowd. Across the alabaster stone was sprayed the symbol of a wolf howling at the sky and beneath that the words:

Sandy, kardeşi Defne'yi sikiyor

Even though my Turkish was poor I understood enough to see that someone had daubed in big dripping letters that I was fucking my sister, Defne. And I also understood, there and then, who was responsible.

The President stared for a moment at what had been painted over our father's stone. He did not look surprised. For a moment, I even thought he looked pleased. He then turned and looked at me. From head to toe. He turned on his heels without saying a word. First, his bodyguards followed – one rushing ahead to open the door of his limousine. Then it was the turn of government ministers.

The momentum accelerated and more and more people left. The musicians put down their instruments. No one wanted to know us or have anything to do with us. A few people grabbed some of the food laid out on the trestle tables and headed for their cars. But it was clear to everyone that we were now outcasts.

CHAPTER 51

Like pillars of salt, we stood.

I don't know how long we remained nailed to the ground. Nor indeed how long it was before we returned to our senses. I think it may have been the sound of an empty can rolling down the street that brought me back to consciousness. When I came to, I felt suffocated, sick, winded, as if punched to the liver. But I held my ground and forced myself to breathe – in through the nose, out through the mouth. Quiet controlled breaths to give me strength. Then I looked around. The world that I returned to was not the one I had left. Save for my beloved Defne, this one seemed desolate. Even the birds, who at this time of day should have been in full afternoon chorus, were silent. The village had been abandoned.

I cast my gaze over the rows of empty chairs. Some had been knocked over as people rushed to leave. The only evidence of that other world, still there just a little while before, was the smell of smoke and lamb fat. Yet now, even that seemed acrid and rancid – like some cheap parody of the enticing aroma it ought to be.

All I could think of was the waste, and the vile desecration of our father's memorial service. That spiteful, vicious old soldier had sent us a message. There was no doubt in my mind that he was responsible for what had happened. He had attacked Defne, shamed her in public, almost as brutally as if he had shaved her head in the village square and put a sign around her neck.

She stood a few paces away from me. In exactly the same spot where she had been standing the moment before the plaque was unveiled. Coming to, and seeing her there alone, forlorn, sent electricity through my nerve endings. My limbs started to function again, and I walked over to her.

Even as I came close, my footsteps echoing loudly in the now silent village, she did not move. I lifted the black veil she had been wearing for the memorial service. Her cheeks were streaked with thin speckles of eye liner. And then like an engine kicking in, she started to tremble, and tears started to flow. I held her gently. I could feel her chest convulsing against mine and her shoulders bobbing up and down as if they had a mind beyond her command. I said all the non-sensical words of love that a man can say to a woman. They would have had meaning only for her. But, to this day, I can't remember what I said.

At that moment, I was overwhelmed by my love for Defne. My soul was hers. There was no more distance to be travelled. There could only be us. There could be no one after her, even if I lived for a thousand years and she just for another heartbeat. I could feel all her fragility and I wanted to envelope her; protect her from all the wretchedness of the world. And then it dawned on me that another emotion had taken hold. One just as potent. Hatred. Pure, unadulterated hatred for Colonel Kaynar. Hatred for men who would harm those whose only crime was to love in their own way.

It was at that moment, that I truly understood Aydin. I understood all the terrible things he did after the death of his beloved Tassos. But if part of Aydin died at the suicide of his lover, I still had life. I still had Defne, and I had money. A sugar rush of vengeance flowed through my veins. It was exhilarating for a brief moment. I decided there and then that Defne and I would have our day, would have our vengeance.

CHAPTER 52

I caught sight of a lone osprey, making its way across the late afternoon sky. I watched it fly towards the brow of the hill. From there it would glide down to the sea below where it would feed from the shoals of mullet that dart back and forth through the turquoise water. Perhaps, I said to myself, it would first take a few moments to rest and gather its strength in the very cove where Defne and I liked to go. And later, when fully ready and primed, it would head off for its predatory flight above the waves. I never tired of watching these birds soar through the air, then dive to pluck, rip and tear their twitching prey.

As I watched the bird disappear, Defne moved in my arms. She came to life again. I continued holding her. I could feel the warmth of her body as it swelled and subsided with each breath she took. I looked over at the nearby garden, for so long abandoned, with its unloved, unpruned, fruit trees – pomegranate, fig and mandarin. And beside them, glorious bushes of prickly pears. Within arm's reach there was an assortment of desserts and refreshments fit for an emperor of antiquity. I started to hum in my own tuneless fashion. I fear now that it must have seemed like a pale imitation of some liturgical dirge. But it made me feel better because it shut out the humiliation and the pain. And then, I started to feel my strength returning, as if this very earth, this little part of my beloved Cyprus, the very paradise in which I stood, was healing me. I stroked Defne's hair. I kissed her ear through the long strands of her hair. I kissed her as softly as I could as if I was placing my lips on the petal of a flower. I smelt soap and perfume. I wanted to clasp her hand and chase all the wretchedness of the day away. It was nature, not the hatred of men, that would one day come to triumph in this land, I told myself. Then I felt bold enough to kiss her lips. But when I touched her mouth with mine, I felt dry chapped skin and noticed that her breath had turned sour from the trauma of the afternoon.

At that moment I heard a door creak. I looked up towards the mosque. A pang of pubescent guilt overcame me, as if I had been caught in some indecent act. There, coming down the steps towards us, was Hassan. I slowly unwrapped my arms from Defne and took a half-step back.

'*Selam*,' he said. He uttered the greeting carefully and slowly like an old man who understood, after a life of consideration, the true significance of the word.

'*Selam*,' I replied. And I did feel some peace. Whether from the effect of the garden opposite or the greeting, I said to myself that they were, in any event, different sides of the same coin.

He cleared his throat and said, finally, 'It is not for men to judge you or Defne, Sandy. Only Allah can do that, and only He knows what is in your soul and whether you are evil or mortally pure.'

As he spoke, I wondered what he believed, what he guessed about Defne and me. I saw that he was carrying something in his right hand. It was wrapped in cloth. He noticed me looking. For a moment he seemed a little embarrassed. And then he thrust the package towards me.

'It has been in the mosque for many years, and I thought it might be of some comfort to you today. Take a look at it later.'

It felt like a book. But I said nothing.

The imam turned suddenly and scurried back up the steps. A few moments later, I heard a splash of water as he did his ablutions. And then there was the muezzin's call. When the loudspeaker fell silent again, our friend started the evening prayers.

Instead of going back home, I retraced his steps and led Defne up to the fountain. We passed the dais where I had spoken. The lectern had been knocked over. My notes, or what remained of them, were blowing back and forth in the swirls of dust. Within a day, I thought, they would be found spiked on some bush or stubble where the dogs went to pee. There were damp patches on the ground around the fountain. This was where Hassan had conducted his ablutions with water from the stone jug, which now stood ready for the next believer to use. I contemplated it. For a moment, I thought about picking it up and pouring water over my feet, hands and face, as I had seen him do so often before. But in the end, I did nothing.

We walked over to the door of the mosque. At its entrance, I saw his scuffed sandals neatly placed side by side. We did not go in. Instead, we just stood and listened. A terrible sense of shame and guilt came over me. It was not, I should say, guilt for loving Defne in the way that I did. No, I could not renounce that, I could never feel bad about what I felt for her. At least, that is what I vowed to myself. Instead, I found myself, for the first time, confronted with the memory of the scorn and disdain I had so long shown towards the call for prayer from the minaret's loudspeaker; contrasting it unfavourably with the joyful once a week chiming of Sunday morning church bells back home in London. Up until then, I had considered the muezzin's call a relic of a primitive culture, a summoning for people who knew no better. But at that moment, I was confronted with the memory of my snide dismissals of the five daily reminders that, 'There is no God but God and Mohammed is His Messenger'. I wanted to say that I was sorry for my arrogance, but I couldn't formulate the right words, and if I did who would I address them to? Would it have been to Allah, or would I have said Father, or even God? I was conscious of feeling my way in the dark and I was not sure if there was light waiting for me somewhere.

At last, the prayers were over. We left before Hassan came out. I was not ready to talk to him again yet. I just wanted to hold Defne's hand and comfort her.

When we got home, we did not say a word about the day's events. Defne made some tea and we sat down on the couch with Hassan's gift between us. I guess we were both curious about what he had given us. But it was only when my tea turned cold – I had not taken a single sip – that I finally loosened the drawstring and extracted the treasure that had been protected for so long by the grimy little dust-covered cloth bag.

The book that emerged was bound in leather and tied with thick cord cut from hide. I undid the knot. As I opened the cover, the first thing I noticed was how brilliantly white the rice-paper thin pages had remained. My first instinct was to place my palm on the cover page. Just to feel the paper. But before I did so I read the title of the book. I stared at the big bold letters: 'The Holy Quran'. Below, in italics and in smaller font, was written 'Translated into English by Abdullah Yusuf Ali'. I turned the cover page. The next page was blank save for, in the top right corner, written in neat schoolbook-perfect blue-black ink 'Zeki Aziz ~ 1953'.

The sight of his handwriting sent a shiver down my spine.

I looked over at Defne and saw that she too was staring at the inscription. She reached out and ran a finger across his name.

For reasons that I don't understand, even to this day, we read out loud… page after page. We alternated. I read one verse. And then she read the next. I still have difficulty accepting that the two people we were could have done this.

CHAPTER 53

Somewhere in the night we fell asleep, like children in front of the television meaning to watch the end of an episode but drifting off before the final credits. When we woke up, we were both still fully clothed; the Holy Quran lay open between us. For a moment, I looked at it, bemused. Like – *Sandy, really? Is this you?* Then I went to make coffee. When I returned, I said to Defne, 'We can go back if you want.' For my part, I was still full of fight, but I felt that I owed her the choice.

I didn't have to say where to. Nor express the implicit defeat that this represented. But it needed to be said out loud. She needed to know that we didn't have to go on here.

But instead of saying anything, she just raised an eyebrow at me. I noticed a solitary white hair. I reached up to touch it. Then I plucked it and showed it to her. She tutted and mumbled that a visit to the hairdresser was overdue. But, when we turned from our veranda and looked down the street, we saw the remains of the previous day's party that had still not been cleared away. Unofficially, the clean-up had begun. Clusters of hooded crows with their black and grey feathers were feasting, fluttering their wings and fighting one another for the surplus of leftover food. Doubtless, rats had gorged themselves overnight. The remains of our banquet belonged to scavengers which, given the circumstances, seemed appropriate.

But to my surprise, the sight of abandoned tables, bottles, plastic cutlery, did not dismay her as it did me. She was composed. Her breathing normal. The only thing was that she nodded her head for a little while, as if having a conversation with an invisible interlocutor. And then, as I was about to lose patience, she spoke out loud and said, 'Sandy, what's changed? Really?'

'How can you say that?' As I spoke, I cast my arm in a panoramic sweep of the mess left behind in the street below.

'It doesn't matter what people say about us. Does it? Does it change the way you feel about me, or how I feel about you?'

I was not sure what to say to her. I didn't feel ready to deal with this yet. I put my hand on her neck and then rested my forehead against hers. I could smell coffee on her breath and the night's sleep on her skin. For a moment, I was back in all those hundreds of other mornings we had woken up together. I could feel her twitching and getting restless. Finally, she nudged me out of my daydream with her nose.

'No, it doesn't,' I said. As always, she was right.

'Sandy, my love, we have gone down a strange path, you and I, and I wouldn't change it for the world. Do you hear me? Do you understand?'

Then she removed her hand from my face, patted her stomach and smiled. 'And now I am going to have our baby.'

As she reminded me of this, I realised that this last day or so I had put this crucial piece of biology out of my mind. It was then that I started to panic. If the previous day had been as bad as it had, what would happen, I wondered, when they found out that we were having a child together. What would they do to the child? To Defne? My courage suddenly ebbed away. I couldn't bear the thought of anything happening to them. I could feel my shoulders start to sag. But she was not ready to accept defeat. She said, 'Hey look... think about it. It's true that Zeki's memorial service was ruined. That they tried to destroy our reputation. But so what? Have you forgotten we still have money? We have so much money. Come on, Sandy, how much did Aydin leave you?'

I was about to give her an answer to the closest decimal when she put a finger on my lips to shush me. 'You get the point. We have all that money, the money you made, my money. We will never get through it. And we have important things to do. I still have my book to finish. And you promised Aydin that you would rebuild the village. Are you about to give up on that because of a little unpleasantness? Do you think that Aydin would give up in a similar situation? Do you remember all the things he went through? And, by the end of the year, we'll be a real family. We can't give up, Sandy.'

Once again, she was right. My fear gave way to shame at my loss of nerve. I lifted my head and looked her straight in the eyes, 'I have not forgotten what I promised. And all these things you say are true.'

'But Sandy...' here her voice changed to a tone I had not heard before. 'I want revenge for what Kaynar did to us. I want us to destroy and humiliate that nasty little man and all his cronies.'

CHAPTER 54

Defne's plan for revenge was both simple and grandiose. Never, in my wildest dreams, would I have thought to act on the scale she envisaged. But she assured me that once we had implemented it, Kaynar's hateful intervention in our father's memorial service, his crass desecration of our reputation and good standing, would be as nothing. As if it never happened. And more than that, it would be him who'd have nowhere to hide from our wrath, from our attacks on all he stood for.

In essence, she wanted me to buy up one of the major newspapers and the commercial TV station. All this, incognito to begin with, so as not to give any indication of what we were planning. And then, once we had the two assets, we would combine them and leverage them to the maximum for an all-pervasive online social media campaign. This way, we would control the public narrative on 'our' side of Cyprus.

She was prepared for us to spend whatever it took to get this done.

The more I considered this idea of hers, the more I thought it was feasible and that, if handled right, it would indeed help us achieve our aims. I suppose it was because she was a writer that she understood so well the power that came from controlling the media. As she explained it to me, it was power to shape the narrative of everyday life, to elevate a person, to bring them down, to humiliate and destroy on a grand scale. But, of course, what she really meant, was the ability to strike at Kaynar. To ruin him. To punish him for daring to turn our love into something filthy and unclean – and in front of so many people at an event that was supposed to be special for us and for Bamyaköy.

CHAPTER 55

A few months on, I felt that I had taken on too much. What with Defne's plan to create a mini media conglomerate and the redevelopment of Bamyaköy according to Aydin's wishes, I was running myself ragged. I didn't complain. It would have been unfair for me to say anything to Defne because she too had been working very hard on finishing her novel. Though, I couldn't help but notice that these days we seemed to have little time for each other. I hoped it was temporary. Just a phase.

We still did some things together. Since the debacle of our father's memorial, she had started going to mosque on a regular basis. She didn't always make prayer five times a day, as a fully practicing Muslim should. When she didn't, it was because she had been too focused on her work and lost track of time. But, without fail, she made the evening prayer, *Dhur*, and it was that one I joined her for. I enjoyed going. Not just to be with her, but because I liked the beautiful airy simplicity of our village's little mosque and the soothing nature of Hassan's voice as he recited his prayers.

During those days, Defne took to reading the Quran – our father's copy, I noted with some satisfaction – and was talking about bringing up our yet-to-be born child as a proper Muslim. I was pretty relaxed about that. It seemed to me that, by doing this, we would be fully returning to our culture and that had to be a good thing. She also, during that time, started to dress more modestly when she went out in public, and stopped swearing altogether. And she stopped drinking. But this might have been to do with the baby's health rather than a requirement of Islam. Out of solidarity, I followed suit. But I was hoping that after the baby's birth, things, at least in this respect, would go back to normal and we might enjoy a glass of wine of an evening.

One night, I was out watering my olive trees and flower beds when Defne came out to see me unexpectedly. I should explain that this whole gardening thing was something I had come to enjoy and had become my own 'private time'. I would never have imagined I could derive such pleasure from something so simple. I had never had a garden before. And, back in London, I would probably have looked askew if a colleague, or someone in my entourage, admitted to being an avid gardener. I would have thought them middle aged and boring. But, over the past months I had come to understand the deep Voltairean satisfaction of tending to a garden. I had learnt how to prune and how to plant. And with Hassan's help and advice, I built a neat series of canals that connected one olive tree to another – so I could irrigate them, row by row, with minimum effort and maximum effectiveness. I admit that I also took a childish delight in seeing the water flow from one scooped moat to another.

But Defne's intrusion was not unwelcome. I was pleased to see her. I suppose, I liked the idea of showing off my rural side; my peasant skills, so proudly acquired. But she did not seem in the least interested in what I was doing. Instead, she said, without preamble, 'It's finished'.

I looked at her, blankly. But not so blankly that I didn't register that she was looking radiant. Her skin was almost translucent. Her hair, I remember it as if it was yesterday, had a beautiful gloss. And there was a look of serenity about her that I had not seen for some time, if ever. I told myself that she looked so much younger than me. Perhaps, I thought, there was some mistake; that we were not born the same year and somehow, she really was younger than me – somehow she was not my sister. But that, I realise, was delusional speculation. I came back to earth. She was there, standing in front of me, looking angelic in a loose flower dress that no longer hid the bump of her belly.

'It's finished,' she had to say a second time. I noted the impatience in her voice.

For the life of me I couldn't imagine what might be finished. I knew from her smile that it couldn't be the laundry detergent or anything banal. And then it finally dawned on me.

'Defne? Your manuscript? *The School Master's Wife?*'

She nodded and beamed.

My first instinct was to suggest we open a bottle of wine to celebrate. But, thankfully, I checked myself in time. Although memories of white wine going down my throat set my saliva glands into a frenzy – I felt like an old robot brought alive by electricity coursing through its circuitry – the better version of me took control and said instead, 'Darling, that's great! What happens next?'

'I guess I send it over to Felicity and see what she thinks.'

'That's your agent, right?'

She nodded. 'And then it's up to her.'

'Well, when do I get to read the whole manuscript?'

'Whenever you want. I've printed out a draft for you. It's waiting for you inside.'

CHAPTER 56

I washed the earth from my hands then went into the living room where her manuscript was waiting for me on the couch. It was held neatly together with two pieces of string; one wrapped width wise, the other lengthwise. I undid the knots and turned first to the dedication page. It was almost the same as on our father's desecrated memorial stone: 'To Zeki Aziz, beloved son of Bamyaköy and The Turkish Cypriot People'. And then I turned to page 1 of 283. As I did so, I heard the evening prayer called.

For the next few hours, I read non-stop – only breaking, from time to time, to refill my mug with tea. This was certainly no longer Daphne Neil writing. Defne had moved away from commercial fiction to something quite different. She had absorbed, like a sponge, all the stories she had ever heard of our village and brought them alive with profound sensitivity. There were times, I freely admit, when I was brought to tears by what she had written, particularly with regard to our father, and indeed, Aydin. She told of things that even I did not know. Here is what I can remember from the novel. Some of the lines are etched on my memory for ever.

The Schoolmaster's Wife

Back in the 1930s, the village of Bamyaköy looked, from a distance at least, similar to how it does today, with the same number of dwellings hugging the contours of the clay hillside. But instead of the ghost village it has become, with more cats and dogs than human inhabitants – at last count there were twenty-seven living souls – it used to be one of the most important and famous villages for miles around. The constant back and forth of caravans to the cities of Famagusta and Nicosia with heavily laden camels was proof of its economic importance and success. The outbound convoys carried wheat, olives, carob, potatoes and melons. The inbound, returned with manufactured goods, yarns of cloth, sacks of rice, and packets of salt.

The village's fame, or notoriety, depending on your point of view, was because of its watermelons. Those coming from one particular field had been found to be a powerful aphrodisiac. So, women from all around, Turk and Greek, made the journey on market days to acquire this precious fruit with the intention of restoring their husband's Saturday night performance. The men, for their part, never came to the watermelon stall, for they were far too embarrassed to admit that they needed any help in that department.

In those years before the Second World War, the village was a noisy place. Not because of cars and tractors – these were not to be introduced in a proper number for another twenty years. But because, from the time the roosters first called until the last dog barked at night, there was a never-ending commotion filling the air: sheep bleating, neighbours calling out to each other, donkeys trotting about with their passengers, itinerant tradesman calling out their wares, men hammering away, women scrubbing and generally doing all the hard work around the village, and children laughing and playing. It was as a village should be. And, in the case of Bamyaköy, how it had been for hundreds of years. It was one of the few 'Turkish' villages of the Karpaz. And had been so since the end of the sixteenth century, when the Ottomans invaded and conquered Cyprus. They removed the Venetians as the ruling power and sprinkled their own human stock on the island to live cheek by jowl with existing inhabitants of the island. Despite what the 1571 decree of Sultan Selim II set out to encourage – the migration of skilled artisans - the transportees were mostly soldiers, criminals and prostitutes, or those so poor that they were easily enticed with the prospect of a better life in this island backwater, whose only value was as a military staging post in the middle of the Eastern

Mediterranean.

Whilst the village was never wealthy, it was blessed with sufficient water, adequate pastoral land, fertile soil, and trees that provided a rich yield of olives, almonds and carob. Rarely did anyone starve to death. But there was poverty. Caused most often by a failed harvest that forced someone into debt, or by the untimely death of the man of the family and the resulting loss of income.

By the time Zeki Aziz was born, in 1933, there was just one wealthy family in the village: the Atabeys. They owned the land from the coast to the top of the hill and down to the fields that lined the track to Malatya – the most accessible and easily exploitable plots – almost five miles away. Many of the villagers either worked seasonally for the family or in some form of indentured servitude, or leased *donums* of the hard-to-reach meagre-yielding slopes of the hillside. The poorest families were left with wretched cropping rights, negotiated and leased out by the Atabeys every five years, on the hardest to reach olive trees – three eights here, five eights there.

The Atabeys were the first to have a tractor, the first to have a car, the first to have a telephone. They were the only family to have a horse that could be ridden. They were the only family to have pure-bred Kangals imported from Anatolia. These dogs, who often weighed as much as a grown man, were hopelessly ill-suited to the hot summers of Cyprus, during which they were to be found stretched out and panting in a scant piece of shade. However, with their long legs, strong bodies, square heads, and general air of menace, they kept the inhabitants of Bamyaköy in check. Because of this, no one ever complained to the Atabeys about the glaring inequities and sharp practices of the family. Although, if the village people had not been so intimidated by the appearance of the Kangals, they would have found them to be gruff but friendly brutes with a liking for having their stomachs scratched and, in truth, no real threat.

Significantly, for some generations, the Atabeys had been

able to afford private tutors for their children until they were of age to go away to Nicosia to the elite boys' school there. And, because of this, the family showed little interest in the village school of their fiefdom. Indeed, the beatings dished out by various schoolmasters sent over the years to Bamyaköy to inculcate some basic education, were of no concern to them. Nor, for that matter, was it of concern to the schoolchildren's parents. The prevailing view was that the boys would get whatever education they needed by working alongside their fathers as soon as they were freed from their mothers' apron strings; and that the girls, from the age of five, could already be deployed around the house. So, there was little dissatisfaction expressed at this state of affairs. There was simply not an expectation of better.

But all that changed with the arrival, to the village, on 10 November 1938, of a new schoolmaster, Erol Baysal. He arrived the same day that the great Turkish President Kemal Atatürk passed away. And because of this unfortunate coincidence, it was always known exactly how long, to the day, he had been in the village.

This young teacher was the son of a well-to-do leather merchant in Famagusta. Initially, he came to Bamyaköy with the intention of staying no more than a year or two. He planned, thereafter, to make his way to Istanbul and become a celebrated essayist who, like his hero, Pierre Loti, would scribble great discourses, drink coffee and puff narghile in some smoke-filled café on the banks of the Bosphorus. But he started to grow up when he came face to face with the children in his care. He realised that, with some nurturing and persistence, he could make a difference to them. This became his life's passion, and he was to devote the rest of it to educating the village. For the first time, girls in Bamyaköy also benefitted from education. He was known even to dip into his own pocket to help families free up their daughters for study. Thereby providing, single-handedly, a viable economic alternative to the useful work the young girls had hitherto been deployed to.

He also discovered what it was to love, as a father, a man and as a husband. In that order. His 'son' was the paternally orphaned Zeki, whose potential he spotted at an early age. People seeing the two walking together would never have suspected they were not flesh and blood, so close was the bond between the two of them. It was Erol who made sure Zeki had all the books he needed and who set him on a path that would later lead him to university in England.

Erol's love affair, when it came, was with someone no one in the village would have expected. It was with a woman called Zainab. She had been married off at the age of thirteen because she had been considered 'wilful'. Her husband, Hakan, who was five years older than her, was already respected for his capacity for hard physical work. However, his knowledge of biology and reproduction was based on casual observation of the mating patterns of farmyard animals. But it soon became apparent to him that there was rather more to human intercourse than he could have imagined. For, by the second morning of consummation, and indeed the third, fourth, fifth and sixth, it seemed to him that he hadn't managed to break his bride in yet because each morning, the dowry-given set of second-hand sheets, revealed a fresh set of blood stains. And they needed to be boiled and washed all over again. This perplexing state of affairs made his nightly rut ever more frantic as he became ever more determined to achieve the breakthrough that he imagined would staunch the bleeding and would prove that consummation was complete, and that she had truly lost her virginity to him. By the second week, she was overcome with the fever of septicaemia. By the third week of marriage, after she had been saved by an English doctor, from the colonial service – local doctors would have refused to treat someone so poor – her husband divorced her, convinced that his bride was cursed. In fact, he was so certain that he concluded that had she been a farm animal it would have been better to put her down rather than waste money on her feed.

So, not yet fourteen years old, she was already a divorcee, a failed woman, and to make matters worse she was repudiated by her family. Her situation was precarious. It was only thanks to the two village prostitutes, Berna and Dilara, who took her in, that she did not have to leave Bamyaköy. Despite their occupation, or perhaps as a result of it, they had no liking for men. They did what they did, on the twice weekly market days when there was a reliable flow of male customers from the villages around. The rest of the time, they tended to their chickens and the little plots of land they had each inherited. Some of the other women in Bamyaköy envied them for their slightly better standard of living, their lack of husbands and children. Others, however, pitied them for being without family. But whatever opinion was held, the two prostitutes were, to their credit, not subject to sexual jealousy or pettiness. This was because they maintained a strict policy of not touching men from Bamyaköy itself. And if a man should try and knock at their door surreptitiously after a night's drinking at the café, they would be shooed away and told to return to their wife (name specified) in a voice so loud that it could be heard the length and breadth of the village. This was a powerful deterrent. As for the pubescent boys, who could hardly keep their erections in check as they passed them in the street, the two women jeered at them, to avoid any false ideas. Inevitably, the tongue lashing had the desired effect of shrivelling, for a few minutes at least, the adolescent tumescence.

For the first few months, Zainab did not understand why Berna and Dilara shared the same bed at night. Nor why they held hands at the end of the day when the evening dishes were washed and put away. After a while – though the matter was never discussed – it became something she took for granted. But more than this, for the few years she lived with them, she felt safe. At first, she helped out around the house and worked in the fields with the two women. And a little later, she helped them get ready for market day: preparing the olive oil they used in small, measured quantities to soften their skin – particularly their hands to prevent the build-up of calluses; laying out the pots of perfume and make-up they bought from Nicosia once a year; setting out the frayed clothes with large, easy to undo, brass clasps. And, in the evening, when the clients had gone, she prepared hot water for the copper tub in which the two women bathed and scrubbed themselves clean of all the slobber and semen. By the time of her sixteenth birthday, the two women, determined Zainab would not follow in their footsteps. So, they found her an apprenticeship in nearby Malatya with an old lady who specialised in the hand-stitched Lefkara lace for which the Karpaz region is famous. This woman had learnt the technique from her mother, who in turn had learnt it from her mother. Some said the tradition of this beautiful intricate stitch work, which made up any self-respecting bride's trousseau, went back all the way to the Venetians: an attempt by Cypriots to ape the finery of their wealthier, and thought-to-be more sophisticated, Italian coloniser. Zainab herself had no such item for her wedding. Other than the set of second-hand sheets, freshened up, with her initials stitched in red cotton, she had received nothing. However, she felt no bitterness and was delighted at the thought that another woman would have something so special for her wedding. She soon proved herself to be skilled at needlework, quickly surpassing the old lady in terms of dexterity, skill and originality of designs and, as a consequence, was soon able to earn a respectable living and eventually have her own home next to Berna and Dilara.

By the time Zainab came into contact with Aydin properly, she was, at thirty-two years old, a spinster and 'finished' in the eyes of the villagers. The men thought this because they were stupid and could be relied upon for such idiotic assessments; the women did so because a single and, objectively speaking, not unattractive woman, was always a threat and needed to be reduced to non-person status as quickly as possible.

Zainab knew the thin and awkward-looking boy from a distance because, unlike the other children, he was most always by himself. But it was the day she came back to her house to find him on the steps of the empty house opposite hers, balled up and shaking like a beaten chimpanzee, that her life changed in more ways than she could ever have imagined. When she went over to him and unwrapped him, hand by hand, elbow by elbow, she was confronted with an emaciated but beautiful face that was bruised and bloodied. Aydin's father had been having another of his attempts at 'making a man out of him'. She took the teenager in, washed him, gave him a blanket, and sat him down in front of her fireplace. She fed him okra and lamb stew from the big pot she had prepared for the week. And, in every bowl, she ladled big scoops of yoghurt that she had made the previous day with Berna and Dilara.

Aydin returned a couple of weeks later. He was in a worse state than before. This time, his father had broken his jaw. And, most likely, a rib or two, given the difficulty he was having in breathing. This time, she refused to let him go back to his home. Even when his father came to reclaim him. But just as Mehmet was mouthing off that Zainab was a whore, and that his son had no place being with her, the two real prostitutes turned up. And they weren't about to waste their breath in dialogue. Berna produced a shotgun from under her shawl. She opened it and slowly put in two cartridges. She clicked the barrels shut and spat to one side. She did not take aim at his head or chest. Instead, she lowered the sight of the shotgun in the direction of his groin and made a move towards him.

'You crazy bitch. *Seni manyak orospu.*' The insult and the labelling of her profession was the extent of his argument in favour of his son's release. He then turned on his heels and returned to his house. That night, the whole village heard the cries of Aydin's mother being beaten. Or perhaps it was his brothers and sisters. Or maybe it was the whole household. But nobody intervened. The men thought it was none of their business to interfere in someone else's marriage. Erol, the one man who would not have tolerated such cruelty, was in Famagusta visiting his parents that night. The next day, Aydin's father was seen skulking off to the hills with his sheep, where he stayed several days.

Zainab, for her part, was determined that she was going to make something of this boy. He was the first person she'd had a chance to care for, a being even more vulnerable than she once was. So it was that she turned to the schoolmaster to enlist his help. For this purpose, she brought with her, tied in a red polka dot kerchief, all the coins she had saved over the past three months.

'Will this be enough?' she said as she laid the little cotton bundle in front of the teacher and untied the knot.

For a moment, he said nothing. He felt himself overcome with emotion. He turned his head away from Zainab.

She said, 'I can get you more if you need.'

'No, not at all, Zainab *hanım*.'

The use of the term *hanım* and the respect with which he pronounced the word took her aback. And she looked at him. No longer as a teacher but as an unfamiliar creature full of gentleness.

'I will help him. Don't you worry. And keep your money for you and the boy.'

It was not an easy task that Erol took on. Years of humiliation, beatings, and days of schooling missed to help his father with his flock of sheep, had taken their toll on Aydin. And, to add to this, he had a frustrating tendency to jumble up his letters. But with patience and help from Zeki, who by this time was also Erol's unofficial but very useful and capable teaching assistant, Aydin did learn the basics of writing and even mental arithmetic, for which he showed quite some ability. Zeki was a couple of years younger than Aydin but if you closed your eyes you would never have guessed it because of his seriousness and maturity. Zeki was also clever enough to understand that, while Aydin's ability to learn and retain information was painfully slow, he had intelligence. Often, he was surprised at how quickly his older friend understood the things he told him about from the books he devoured each day. Aydin was grateful for the respect given to him by Zeki. A few years later, when Zeki's mother was scraping every last penny together to get her son what he needed for his trip to England where he was due to take up his scholarship at the London School of Economics, it was Aydin who, unbeknown to his friend, made up the quite considerable financial shortfall. By the age of fourteen, Aydin had started his first business, hawking his wares to the villages, and was starting to earn a respectable living even by the standards of a grown-up. And, soon after, he had his own café. Aydin believed in Zeki. He thought of him as his better side. The person he would like to be. He was convinced that Zeki would 'become someone', a '*büyük efendi*', an equal if not a better to the Atabeys. He was proud of his friend and loved him.

Somewhere towards the end of the 1940s Erol and Zainab became lovers. And because Erol was much loved and Zainab had become accepted in the village again – having shown her abilities as a mother, even if surrogate – no one minded.

Their story might have ended there, to the extent that they could have continued for years making love in quasi secrecy – so as not to officialise their sin – and Erol could have increased his girth year by year with all the good food Zainab cooked for him. And that might have been a fine ending. Indeed, in those first years of physical intimacy, she discovered what it was to make love. She never discussed what she and Erol did together with anyone else. Not even with her best friend, Eminé, Zeki's mother. But she knew that it was different and special. When the other women in the village spoke of what they did at night with their husbands it was about frequency, stamina, or, if they were feeling particularly tired, the best ways to finish their husbands off as quickly as possible so that they could get right back to sleep. With Erol, she did things that should have made her blush. Maybe, once upon a time, before him, they might have.

He was not wise to the ways of the world and had known few other women before her. However, he had found a book on 'Eastern' practices in a second-hand English bookshop in Nicosia. Together, they practiced the various contortions that were depicted, from beginning to end, like good students, and discovered joys that went beyond mechanical penetration. Zainab, quite rightly, believed herself the luckiest woman in the village.

But there were three more chapters to their life together.

The first of these was the day he found her thumbing the copybooks of his pupils and crying in frustration and humiliation at not being able to read what an eleven-year-old boy could. During the following months, Erol taught Zainab how to read and how to write. To his delight, she quickly outgrew the school text books and he could introduce her to poetry, particularly to the verses of his beloved Nazim Hikmet – by this time in jail for being a member of Turkey's communist party.

The second chapter was the day he went to her house in broad daylight and entered her dark little kitchen where she was rolling wafer thin pastry for the baklava he loved so much. Teasingly, he had her hold the sheet of pastry to the gas light and, from his pocket, he produced a scroll of paper. Through the veil of the pastry, she was able to read, in brush-stroke calligraphed words of black Indian ink: *Benimle evlenir misin*?

After he dried her tears, they stepped out into the daylight to tell all and sundry that they were to wed. Erol was to be married to an educated woman as he had always hoped and never expected to find – certainly not here up on the Karpaz. Zainab was the first woman in the village to be able to read and write – and to recite with ease verses from any number of poets. Thanks to him, by her wedding day she had her own bookshelf, filled with the works of Yurdakul, Seyfettin and Karay. But pride of place was given to the works of her husband's beloved Nazim Hikmet. She would have had these even if she had not liked the poetry.

The third and final chapter began on 23 December 1963, a period which also became known as 'Bloody Christmas'. Where did it end? With the massacre of Avrigadou? With Aydin leaving the village? With Zainab's heartbroken journey to her own death a few months later? Or was it all put to rest with Aydin's own death?

Two days before the Christian holiday, Erol was taken by 'national' guards at Boğaz and marched off to the nearby chalk quarry. He was herded into something resembling a sheep pen, along with all the Turkish Cypriot men that the young Greek Cypriot soldiers had rounded up. The teacher was still clasping his brown paper package of books – that he had bought earlier that day in Famagusta for Zainab – when they led him and the others out of the enclosure. They were made to line up. And then, from behind, the soldiers kicked the backs of their legs, forcing the Turkish Cypriots to their knees. The officer in charge pulled out his pistol and shot each of the prisoners in the back of the head. Some of them cried out for Allah and some for their mothers. Erol did neither. His last thoughts were of Zainab and, instead of a prayer, he murmured a poem for her. The bodies were left where they had fallen. In front of each corpse a crimson red spurt stained the hard white chalk soil.

By the time of Erol's murder, Aydin was no longer the shivering teenage boy that Zainab had rescued. By this time, he too had lost someone he loved. And, along the way, this young businessman had learnt to kill without remorse. It was Aydin who led a group of men in the reprisal raid against the police station in the neighbouring Greek village of Avrigadou. Zeki had volunteered to join his fellow villagers, but Aydin thought it wiser to take his friend's brother-in-law, Ismail, instead. He thought that, given Zeki's importance to the community, he should not get involved in case they were caught, or something went wrong.

It is said that Aydin killed a lot of men the day he went to avenge the beloved schoolmaster's death. That he showed no mercy. That he used grenades and his old trusted Sten gun, stolen from the British, on men still sleeping on the camp beds of their barracks.

Only one of his companions minded, and that was Ismail. The rest of the men slept easily ever after because they saw it as just retribution. But, for Ismail, it was different. And all because of one of the men that Aydin killed.

In the spring of 1946, Ismail had thought he was invincible. He had just demobbed from the British Army and brought back all the boxing skills he had learnt thanks to the good-natured coaching of Sergeant Major Eddie Garwood. Ismail cleaned up in all the local fights at the village fairs and won good prize money. But one opponent brought an end to his career and was later to destroy his self-respect.

It shouldn't have been that way. There was a big fight in the offing. Big money. More than he could hope to earn in two years of hard work. The purse was sponsored by the Keo Brewery of Cyprus. For the last three years, it had been claimed by Helios, the blacksmith of Avrigadou. The Greek fighter was strong and determined; qualities not to be under-rated in a boxer. But he was slow, heavy, and untrained in the finer aspects of boxing. Although in his personal life he was known to be quiet, a good family man, and was much respected in Avrigadou, in the ring he was arrogant. He tended to drop his guard and strut around like a prize rooster lapping up the spectators' admiration. But with Ismail he was up against a totally different class of fighter, and it would have been better for both if he had stayed home sick on the day of the fight. What the skinny Turkish Cypriot lacked in strength and weight he made up for with speed and elegant footwork. How Eddie Garwood would have loved to see his protégé dance around the blacksmith, feint, jab, test defences and then go forwards with an explosive set of combinations. But here is the thing: this was a bare-knuckle fight. And the damage on each man was terrible. Ismail knew to hit the soft parts of a man's body. And the most obvious were his opponent's two large grey eyes. The fight ended with Ismail victorious but leaving Helios blind in one eye. Ismail knew that the blacksmith, with his big heart, didn't deserve that. He was sickened. He never wanted to hurt someone like this again and gave up the boxing there and then. And, with it, every chance he ever had of making good money.

But he was to face Helios one more time. Up there in Avrigadou.

The day, years later, when the men from Bamyaköy went to take revenge.

Helios, as brave as ever, had come out into the village square, wakened by the sound of gunfire at the police barracks. He lumbered out like Cyclops ready to defend his village and home with his bare fists. It didn't matter to him one jot that he was facing men armed with automatic weapons. He just made the sign of the cross and asked the Virgin Mary to protect him. And then he recognised Ismail and his shoulders fell. He could not believe such treachery and cowardice from this man. The two looked at each other. One could not believe his eye. The other was merely ashamed. Helios went forwards to fight Ismail one more time. But Ismail's heart was not in it. He told Helios to go home. But the large Greek still kept on coming. And that was when Aydin stepped in and machine gunned the blacksmith down, and then went over and kicked the body to make sure he was really dead.

Ismail and Aydin caught up with the other men and headed back to their village. In the dark, no one could see that Ismail was crying, filled with remorse and shame at what happened to that brave and decent man. He knew now that whatever good he might do in his life it would never take away this terrible act and that he was beyond redemption.

After that night, Aydin went back to his village just once – to tell Zainab that he had avenged her husband. He did not return to Bamyaköy until he was an old man and no one was left to take revenge for the many innocent lives he had taken. By then, Avrigadou had been long since 'cleansed' of its Greek Cypriot inhabitants. In 1974, it is said the Turkish army went through the village killing, raping and threatening the inhabitants with further violence, defiling the village a second time. After this, the now derelict village was handed over to Turkish mainland settlers who set up their homes there – apparently without care or guilt at the fate of those who had lived there originally – and found the abandoned church a most convenient place to house their livestock.

Aydin and Zeki were to see each other one last time. It was in the summer of 1965 on the quayside of Famagusta harbour. Unbeknownst to each other they had both decided, but for different reasons, to leave Cyprus for England. In Aydin's case he had, days before, single-handedly liberated the enclave of Famagusta by taking the enemy unawares, having dressed up as Marylin Monroe. No one thought to ask him how he had carried off such an outfit with such ease. However, the brutality of his actions should themselves have been a death sentence – even though there were no witnesses amongst Greek Cypriot soldiers, for he had taken care to kill every single one of them.

In Zeki's case it was different. A profound lassitude had overtaken him. Cyprus was finished as far as he was concerned. The dream of an independent and free Cyprus, one that was safe for all, was crashing down around them. He thought if he could only make it back to Britain, he could start again. There his wife, Caroline, had family. Her father, founder of one of the leading advertising agencies in Britain, had been keen to employ him a few years before. He hoped he might still be prepared to offer him a job. Caroline seemed to think that he might.

That morning, when the two men met again, the world seemed to be filled with a little hope; an expectation that the madness of Cyprus could at last be put behind them.

But it was then too that Zeki finally understood that Aydin would not be having a wife and family. First, it was a look of horror that had crossed his face when Aydin told him – almost defiantly. And then, the realisation that it was only friendship that mattered between them. Aydin never forgot the moment Zeki turned towards Caroline to take her hand and introduce her to his friend. He was to play it over and over again in his head for the rest of his life. The instant that the sniper's bullet hit Zeki in the head. The blood all over Caroline. Blood on his own cheek. His friend's blood, trickling into his mouth. He did not think to clear it away. Instead, his first thought was to protect Caroline with his own body. He had to prise her away from his friend's body. She kept on screaming out Zeki's name. In the end, he picked her up in his arms and ran with her towards the ship and carried her up the gangplank.

Only when he was sure she was out of harm's way did he return to Zeki. There was no one around him. Everyone had taken cover in case the sniper took aim again. But Aydin knew that the gunman was long gone – no professional would hang around and risk a second shot that would give away his position. Already the flies had started to feast on the blood and grey sludge. But he didn't care. He held his friend. And cried out at the top of his lungs, '*Neden*? It should have been me.'

CHAPTER 57

'What did you think?' I heard her say.

I did not reply because I was not ready to talk. My mind was still lost; away in her story. I was looking out over the valley, thinking about the things she had written. My thoughts were with the ghosts that I lived with. The very ones she had so poignantly committed to text. Going forwards, they would be known to people who would never know us or our village. They would become public property. Because of that they would live on. And I was profoundly grateful.

Mostly, these ghosts I refer to, left me alone. But there were days in Bamyaköy when it rained so viciously, when you could mistake the rain for sleet as it fell onto the ground, that I liked to sit and just watch the downpour. Watch the rain as it splashed off the rooftops in cloudy explosions, hitting the ground like drops of mercury. It was in those moments, when the thin veil between this world and the next was torn, that I fancied that I saw the grey shadows of those souls the village had lost over the years. My father, his friend Aydin, Erol, Zainab, my uncle, my aunt, and all those who knew the Bamyaköy that once was. I didn't feel afraid of them. I knew that one day Defne and I would also take our place in their curtain call. But now they had been summoned back for me in her story, that they were there for anyone who opened the pages of her story, I felt overwhelming sorrow. Something was going on beyond my control. I feared that, despite anything Defne and I might do, we Turkish Cypriots were dying out. But now, our identity was to be preserved in the pages of Defne's novel. At least there would be a trace that we existed once.

'Sandy, what did you think?' she said again.

This was not Daphne Neil asking me. That person would never have cared what someone like me thought. It was Defne that was asking. I turned and looked at her. Her face was anxious, expectant.

I owed her a response. I forced myself to speak. At first, I simply told her how moved I was. How she had captured the essence of the village. But then I saw a look of disappointment cross her face. And I knew that I had not said enough, not said it right. This was not just a writer asking for an opinion. This was the woman I loved. She had made herself vulnerable to me. I went over to her and took her hand and looked into her eyes. Then I kissed it and held it against my chest. I kissed her on the eyes like my aunt used to do to me. 'I am so proud of you Defne,' I told her. This was the truest thing I have ever said. I went on, 'I love you. You've made me complete.' I felt like an ass as soon as I had spoken. I thought I was getting soppy and overdoing it. But it was all true. I couldn't stop this stuff coming out of me. If I had been in London, I would have wanted to take her out to some fancy restaurant. There, if I took her out, it would have been to *Kemal Hussein's*, where we always ate. So, instead, I went to the kitchen, squeezed some oranges and then brought her a glass full of the juice, which she drank with relish.

CHAPTER 58

I set in motion Aydin's project – the rebuilding of Bamyaköy. By the end of that year, we would own more than half the village. The remaining half was either inhabited by a few ageing households or consisted of empty houses belonging to people, most likely grandchildren of original owners, who were untraceable. No doubt they had shed their heritage in favour of the easier and safer mantle of being British or English.

I put the *mukhtar* on a monthly retainer and all he had to do for his money was to stamp the documents and permits that our lawyers put in front of him.

I could not find a Turkish Cypriot doctor to come and settle in the village. So, I brought one in from Turkey and added him to our burgeoning payroll. As it turned out, this was a very good move. Having a well-trained general practitioner providing services to the population free of charge brought a steady flow of patients from Malatya and the other villages. Bamyaköy was starting to come alive again. There was the noise of people talking, sometimes screeching, and the sound of cars and horns honking. Burak, the coffee shop owner, had never had so many customers. In fact, his establishment became the de facto waiting room for the doctor's surgery. His wife, Senem, opened a small grocery shop in a building that we leased to her for a peppercorn rent.

As for the rest of the plan, it came easily. We fixed and tarmacked the road that went through the village as well as the little alleys and lanes that branch off from it. We had all the houses repainted. Even those that did not belong to us. We had a developer build modern bungalows below the main part of the village – not the usual cheap and ugly stuff that was usually built on 'our side' but good quality tasteful houses that blended in with the general feel of the village.

These buildings would not have looked out of place in the smart Greek resorts of Mykonos and Santorini. I was determined that Turkish Cypriots would have the best, for once, rather than the shoddy, flimsy developments that had become the norm. But the significant detail was this: affordability. We sold these new units off-plan to families with young children – that was the stipulation – at a 40% discount off the actual cost.

Unsurprisingly, the take up was dramatic. The first new families were to move in within months. We also built a school. We hired the best teachers from Famagusta, Lefkoşa and Kyrenia and paid them a substantial premium on their previous salaries. Sometimes, when I was off for my walks above the village, I got carried away with the dream that Bamyaköy would become the beating heart of a Turkish Cypriot renaissance. A haven where we could live as Cypriots, as Muslims, as Turkish speakers. A place free from the crass corruption of Kyrenia with its casinos, prostitution and drugs. A place with our form of moderate, tolerant Islam. But each time I returned home my fantasy evaporated. I knew it would never happen. That the forces against us were too powerful. What we were doing would hold back the tide a little longer. But maybe, just maybe, with enough investment in the school, we could make a difference to the prospects of the next generation.

I had it in mind that the curriculum would focus heavily on maths, technology, sciences and agriculture. This last choice of subject was of course based on the following assumptions: that we would not get everyone to university and, consequently, the teaching we provided needed to have a vocational aspect too. A few basic changes to agricultural practices could make huge differences to food production, environmental care and water management. I didn't care if people thought I was a dreamer in such matters. I knew that they wouldn't say anything. Just so long as we provided all the money, they would nod their heads and agree to whatever I said.

We named the school, '*Erol ve Zainab İlköğretim Okulu ve Lisesi*'. I thought that Zeki and Aydin would have been pleased that the memory of this couple would be resurrected and, in a certain fashion, immortalised. We Turkish Cypriots are a community that forgets. We see our past through a fog, uncertain of what happened, when, or why. We are without teeth when it comes to speaking out against the lies told about us and our island.

In Bamyaköy, matters had been made worse because so few of the original inhabitants were still alive. That older generation vaguely knew that certain things had happened in the past. That the village used to be on the other side of the hill. That once there were Christians in the village. But they did not ask themselves why some of us were blonde haired and blue eyed. Why some of us looked Sicilian. Others Palestinian. Why so few of us looked as if our ancestry reached beyond the shores of the Black Sea. I hoped that one day we could tackle this too, with a museum or a university chair dedicated to the serious historical study of our island – free of propaganda and national narratives.

CHAPTER 59

Our plan to take revenge on Colonel Kaynar was far easier for me to execute than returning Bamyaköy to life. It was, at its most basic level, just a business thing – acquiring companies and merging them. Little different to what I had done for twenty years of my professional life. However, this time, I was prepared to pay whatever it took to acquire the businesses we were targeting. And there was also the simple fact that I did not need to worry about external funding.

First, we bought one of the local TV stations, *KK-News Today.* Then we bought a red top newspaper, *Vatansever.* The price we paid for these, while exorbitant for the island, hardly made a dent in our capital. We didn't care that the sellers were giving us the most outrageous numbers they could come up with – with absolutely no correlation to actual value, cash flow or income – for we had our own agenda and plan to follow.

I folded the TV station and the newspaper into one larger holding company, called *True News Today* and promptly re-branded both assets under the master brand KIBG – with the tag line of *Kıbrıs'ın Gerçekleri* – 'Truth for Cypriots'. Cynically, I played the nationalist card – splashing the white and red of 'our side's' flag everywhere and, wherever I could, planted quotes from Kemal Atatürk. And of course, I played to the lowest common male denominator: we hired, for the TV station, the most beautiful Turkish-speaking female newsreaders and weather presenters we could find. This deliberate crassness combined with swamping social media with our ads, doubled both the newspaper's circulation and the TV station's viewing figures, which, in turn, allowed us to charge a premium for advertising space. We took any advertiser who was willing to pay our rate card. So, every night, the different luxury hotels casinos and real estate developers, that I hated so much, competed for the prime-time spots. I had not intended this business to make money but the irony was that, with all the extra viewers, growing circulation and massive hike in ad revenues, we were well on the way to recouping our investment. My finance director even suggested that, in a year or two, we could think about re-selling our business to one of the big media groups on the Turkish mainland at five times our current valuation.

In the first months, this media vehicle of ours was relatively innocuous – at least if you had no scruples about our main advertisers. But then we moved on to the second phase of our plan. And for that, we needed the right editorial director. Someone who was going to put together a team of investigative journalists who were unafraid of going after Colonel Kaynar and dishing the dirt on him.

The person we ended up choosing, after a careful selection process, was a man called Ali Poleo. For what we wanted, he had impeccable credentials. He was a left-wing journalist and editor from Istanbul. He had already been in prison twice for, in the eyes of Turkey's High Court, having insulted the Turkish Republic and its loyal servants in government. Some of his articles accused elected officials of taking bribes. In others, he had spoken up for the right of Turkish novelists to speak freely and without sanction. And the deal-clinching article for me was where he identified a number of Turkish army officers as being covert members of the Grey Wolves.

As well as these impeccable credentials, I liked him immediately. There was something both so childlike and wise about him. He was a large man with curly hair and a taste for roll-ups. For our first meeting, he turned up wearing a stout but aged pair of mahogany-coloured brogues, a Viyella shirt with a frayed collar, and threadbare corduroy trousers. As I came to learn, his taste in clothes was inspired by a year spent at an English university doing his master's degree and, along the way, acquiring a taste for brown ale and the songs of Billy Bragg. His outfit only varied in winter by the addition of a sleeveless V neck jumper and a navy-blue pea coat.

We met him in Istanbul, at *Nişantaşı Başköşe*, a restaurant that both Defne and I liked very much. We made a point of going there each time we went to Istanbul. Normally, some of the meze and grilled meats were left over – so copious their portions and, in those days, frankly, so bird-like our appetites– but, this time, I actually had to go over to the waiter and call for more dishes to be brought to our table. Not that Ali noticed. He shovelled food into his mouth, with pieces of bread torn by his pudgy hands in a manner that I thought would not be out of place back in Bamyaköy. But when this ogre of a man spoke, his voice was that of a poet giving a reading in a smoke-filled club. It was both gentle and powerful, yet sandpaper-rough, scarred by years of cigarette smoking. As he was eating, I watched him closely. There was something touching and endearing about the delight with which he sucked his fingers – as if trying to extract every last microscopic drop of the grilled kofte's spicy fat from the pores of his skin; like a man conscious of the uncertainty of getting another meal as good as this any time soon.

'Ali *Bey*, what we want to do is bring independent journalism to Cyprus.'

'And what makes you think you don't have that now?' he said and then laughed.

I motioned to the waiter to bring the journalist another glass of *ayran*. I saw people at the other tables drinking wine and rakı and I couldn't help but feel envious. But then I looked over at Defne and the feeling went away. In the middle of the conversation, I felt happy that she was by my side. I turned back to Ali and said, 'We want to take on the Grey Wolves. We want to take on the useless government of Osman Agha. That's what we want.'

'You have a death wish?' He laughed again. 'Why don't you go back to Britain and enjoy your life?' As he said this, he scooped *cacık* on to a piece of flat bread that he had folded into a cornet and deftly popped the assembled morsel into his mouth.

'Because—'

'Because, Ali *Bey*,' said Defne cutting across me, 'we have business to settle with these people. It is for Sandy's father. It's for a friend of his. It's for us. Look, you'll have whatever budget you need. We want the best and most aggressive editorial coverage. This is your chance to have your own newspaper and for you to have editorial control over the TV station as well. You'll be protected by top lawyers. We'll take care of our presenters and our journalists. The only thing we ask is that you shame the Grey Wolves and all the corrupt people who benefit by colluding with them. All those people who operate in the shadows. You've done it before but now you can do it on a larger scale.'

He looked down at the empty plate in front of him.

'*Baklava*, Ali *Bey*?' I asked.

The journalist nodded. But his smile was gone. 'Do you really care so little for your lives?'

'I don't know how to explain this,' I reached out for Defne and rested my hand on her belly as I spoke. 'We are at peace with our choices.' I said that because I knew it was what Defne expected me to say but sometimes, I had my doubts, and sometimes I was just downright scared.

'And the baby?' he said, motioning his head towards Defne's stomach.

'The baby will be well taken care of if anything happens to us. And she, he… we don't know yet…' I turned and smiled at Defne and leant forward to kiss her cheek, 'will have parents they can be proud of'.

The journalist pursed his grease covered lips.

'You seem unconvinced' I said.

'I think this is a risky undertaking.'

At that moment, the waiter placed a large plate of fresh green pistachio baklava in the middle of the table. I served the journalist three pieces but none for Defne or me. When he had his mouth full, I said, 'Ali Bey are you familiar with Aristotle's choice between truth and happiness?'

He shook his head.

'What it means for us is that we could choose to live a comfortable, facile existence. We could buy a penthouse in the tallest tower in Dubai and spend the rest of our lives in the lap of luxury. But we choose to be back in Cyprus. To do something. To live as Cypriots. There are things we see there that we don't like. There are people who tried to humiliate us. Nasty, vicious people. The same people who are dragging our community down. So, we have chosen to do something. To use our money. To confront the corruption with truth and to do our bit to make our little community better off.'

He leant towards me and patted my shoulder. As he did so, I could smell garlic and syrup on his breath. He looked into my eyes and said, '*Tamam*' and shook my hand.

I don't know if Ali ever read his contract. It was a generous one. He certainly never got round to signing it and sending it back to me. But, within a couple of weeks of our lunch in Istanbul, he was with us in Cyprus, putting together his team of journalists. Some he recruited locally. Others he brought with him from Turkey.

Within two months his impact was very evident, from press communiqués from the presidential palace criticising him, us, and KIBG for our 'vile lies and treasonous allegations of bribes'. In one of his first articles, he exposed the award of road building contracts to companies who, hitherto, had never laid a single metre of asphalt.

By the third month of Ali's stewardship, the windows of our

main office in Lefkoşa had been shattered. Coincidentally perhaps – the day after an article laying blame at the door of the Grey Wolves for the unsolved murder of a journalist in Cyprus. The article included a bio of Colonel Kaynar and identified him as the head of the movement on the island.

We were having our revenge.

CHAPTER 60

The closer Defne got to her due date, the slower she walked. She needed my help more and more often. I was delighted to do what I could to make things comfortable for her. I had also taken the initiative to hire a maid to help with domestic chores around the house, so on that front we were good.

Her face had filled out and the clothes she wore were a far cry from the elegant outfits she used to wear. But she still looked lovely to me. She insisted that we make love as often as before. I wondered how much longer we could carry on doing this, but she told me not to worry for the baby and that it was okay as we avoided my weight on her stomach.

I tried to spoil her as much as I could. Not just flowers and expensive oils and bath gels from Floris, but wholesale quantities of Fry's chocolate cream bars that I had shipped in from England. I had remembered her telling me once that Ziya used to treat her with these every day after he picked her up from school. I thought that, at a time like that, she might enjoy such an indulgence. The look on her face when she saw the first delivery was one of those you wish you could frame and keep for ever. She used to happily chomp through three of four bars a day. Her only complaint was that they were no longer foil wrapped.

Sometimes, we talked openly about how the baby might turn out. We even spoke to a doctor friend of Defne's back in the UK, and told her the truth. To our delight, she reassured us that, given that we were only half-brother and half-sister, the risks were relatively small – no more than six percent greater chance of complications than in a non-consanguine pregnancy. As a businessman, I liked these odds. But, nonetheless, I had a knot in my stomach all the time. Though she didn't admit it, I think Defne must have been scared too. She would have had every right to be so. Even without the issue of our genetic connection, the fact that she was having her first child in her forties was a worry. To make matters worse, the news from Felicity, her agent, who had been trying to find a publisher for *Defne Aziz* was not very encouraging at that point. The two of them had worked together for years – ever since Defne was first published as Daphne Neil – and they were very close. Friends, even. But the email, in which she detailed the challenges of placing the novel, served only to depress Defne further. I myself read the email several times, thinking that maybe Defne was being dramatic given the pregnancy and all, and that there might be a more encouraging aspect to it if read with more detachment. But no amount of re-reading could change the harsh reality that she had not secured a publisher:

Daphne Darling,

Personally, I loved *The School Master's Wife*. I thought it was so interesting and so touching, and I learnt such a lot about Cyprus reading it. But the problem is that I am not sure there's an obvious market for this sort of stuff. I have tried your usual publisher. To be fair to the editorial team there they did think about it very hard, but it really doesn't fit in their model for mass market fiction.

I have tried a few of the smaller more avant-garde publishing houses – and I'm still to hear back from Picador – but I think we need to prepare ourselves for the fact that it's going to take rather more time to get it published than I originally hoped. Anyway, if you want, we can always schedule some time to have a quick call about this.

Love,

Felicity

I think the problem was that Defne was not used to rejection anymore. Every year, she used to produce a new book and get it accepted right away, and usually with only the mildest of edits, if any.

I wanted to tell her that all she needed at that point was to focus on the baby. But even I had just enough emotional intelligence to realise that would not have helped the situation. So, I just listened and absorbed her angst. Although, whatever else I was worrying about, I had no doubt that a publisher would come through for her eventually.

CHAPTER 61

Defne was two weeks away from her due date. We hadn't tried to find out if it was a boy or a girl. We had, however, come up with names.

The choice for a boy was relatively easy. The name that we kept on coming back to was 'Zeki', although we did briefly consider 'Aydin'. However, in the final analysis, it seemed to us that my old friend had lived his life fully and our father had not. And so, his name deserved a second lease of life through a grandson – if a grandson it was to be. The choice for a girl was far more difficult. Sometimes we lent towards Zainab, sometimes towards Aysel – my aunt's name – and, at others, we tried for names that could be bi-cultural. In the end we chose 'Lara' which we felt would work well both in Turkish and English.

By then, the first families were starting to move into the stylish new houses on the lower slope of the village. For the first time in a long while in Bamyaköy, there was the sound of children playing. At lunch and dinner time, you could hear the clink of plates and cutlery. Sometimes, if I was feeling grumpy and churlish, I wondered if I would not prefer the village to return to the way it was before; before we embarked on the redevelopment programme. But when I admitted these thoughts, Defne told me that we were doing something beautiful; we were giving life back to the village, and Zeki and Aydin would be proud of what we were doing. She also insisted that I had a proper playground built for the village children. I liked this idea, for I could imagine taking our own child there one day.

CHAPTER 62

Ali Poleo did such a good job, both with the quality of the editorial and the quality of the team of journalists he put together, that the idea of expanding into other markets crossed my mind more than once. But each time I raised it with Defne, she reminded me that our mission was Cyprus, our part of Cyprus, the Turkish-speaking northern part of the Island, and that we should stay focused on our targets. Our journalists did an outstanding job in this regard. They were absolutely the attack dogs we had hoped for. Rarely a week went by that Colonel Kaynar was not featured in the pages of *Vatansever*. Either it was for the lunacy of his ideas, the opaque source of his party's finances, or because our cartoonist, Fatoş Feran, delighted in drawing him with a Hitler brush moustache, a peaked hat, jackboots, jodhpurs and a big jacket with brass buttons and epaulettes.

No one ever mentioned the debacle of our father's memorial service. I had taken the liberty of having references to what happened that day scrubbed from the internet. I think it was safe to say that we had been rehabilitated. We were sought after again, socially. But we had no interest and Defne, quite reasonably given the advanced stage of her pregnancy, preferred that we stay in Bamyaköy most of the time.

For my part, to my amusement – having always thought of myself as an ardent capitalist – I was solicited by one of the leftist parties to run for election. While I had no intention of doing so, I did allow our newspaper to nurture the rumour. My intention was to put as much pressure on the President as we could. He had tried some sort of reconciliation by inviting me to join a thinktank of businesspeople who were to advise him on transforming the economy. But I had no interest in helping him. The memory of his scorn, and rapid exit from our father's memorial was still raw and vivid in my memory. And besides, I had no advice to give him, and the other kleptocrats, save for him to resign and leave Cyprus as quickly as possible. But I knew he was running scared. Not only did we have the have the money and the media pull to swing an election contest in our favour if I was to run, but he could have little doubt what our position would be when it came to corruption, and how I would go after the thieves who had bankrupted our people.

It was because of this, perhaps, that the President's counter-briefings against us were turning more ludicrous and vitriolic. In one of these, his press officer alleged that we were Zionist agents in the employ of Israel and, if we got elected, we would turn the Turkish part of Cyprus into a giant refugee camp for Palestinians. In response, we revealed payments the President himself had received from an Israeli investor for the authorisation to develop a luxury resort up on the Karpaz. After that he dropped his attacks on us.

Defne and I stayed close to the editorial decisions throughout. In fact, we still made the effort to go to Lefkoşa every Monday morning, just to sit in on the start-of-the-week meeting that Ali held with his journalists. It was the one outing Defne insisted on – even right up to that last meeting, a week before her due date.

They were usually held at the office, but occasionally Ali held the meetings around the corner in a bookshop café. When the weather allowed, which was most of the time, we sat outside, in the bookshop's walled garden where the journalists could freely smoke. We were fortunate that the owner was sympathetic to our cause and made sure we were given all the privacy we needed.

That last meeting – it was the second Monday of December – you could have been forgiven for thinking that we were in October. The sky was clear and there was warmth to the sun. I remember thinking that with this kind of weather I could never return to London and its low grey winter sky. I felt happy. It seemed to me that I had things under control. That within days I would be a father. That the woman I loved was going to have our child.

These were the thoughts going through my mind as I looked at the agenda for that day's meeting – the main topic of which was how we were going to tackle the government's catastrophic mismanagement of the environment, water resources and fire prevention. These might have seemed trivial matters to people outside our island – and perhaps hardly newsworthy – but in Cyprus, where fresh renewable water supplies were scarce, it was a major issue. Over the summer, large swathes of the Beshparmak mountain forest had burnt down. Even that morning, as we drove to Lefkoşa, we saw the once verdant mountainside reduced to a desolate moonscape of ash and stumps. Despite the car's air conditioning system, we could not escape the bitter sooty smell that still hung in the air.

Before Ali started, I let him and his colleagues know that we would be doubling their editorial budget for the following year. I also explained that I had the intention of putting our main rival out of business or acquiring the company. I saw nods of approval around the table. And with that, I gave the floor to Ali.

Just as he was about to speak, I became distracted by a noise coming from the street. I was not the only one. Ali had cocked his head. Defne was looking up at me. And, one by one, the journalists put down their coffee cups. At first, I couldn't determine what the noise was. And then I recognised the sound of large motorbikes. It grew louder. The building started to shake and even sitting out in the garden, we could feel the reverberations coming up through the ground. Ali looked at me, then at Defne. I could see he was worried.

'Give me a moment, I'll take a look,' I said, as casually as I could muster.

'No, Sandy *Bey* just leave it. I'm sure it's nothing,' he said, with little conviction.

'Let me just take a look,' I repeated.

I walked quickly through the bookshop and out into the street and heard Ali shuffling behind me. He started to wheeze as he tried to keep up. When I made it to the pavement everything became clear.

In front of us a convoy of Harley Davidsons had pulled to a stop with their engines still running. The riders were dressed in leather and denim. Some had pennants of the Turkish Flag on their bikes. The lead rider, however, had something different. From his antenna fluttered a blue and white flag. In the middle of the flag was an image, in white, of a wolf baying to a crescent moon. The biker turned his face towards me. It was covered with a bandana so all I could see were his pale blue eyes. He made a small gesture with his hand. The bikers behind him revved their engines until the street filled with grey smoke. The noise was deafening. And then, as one, they each made a fist in the air with their little fingers and indexes raised. Then they cut their engines and started to chant 'Turkey is our motherland; Turkey is our motherland!'

I turned back into the bookshop to find Defne. But by now the doorway was full of people come to see what was going on, so I had to push my way in. As I went through the throng, I noticed that Ayla, one of the photojournalists, had her camera out and was snapping pictures as fast as she could.

Just as I reached the garden, I heard shouts coming from the street and then the sound of breaking glass. Defne was looking at messages on her phone when I reached her.

'Come sweetheart, we must get out of here,' I said. But I looked around and couldn't see any way out other than back the way I had come. I spotted an exit sign for a door giving out to a side street, pulled Defne behind me and made my way towards it.

By now, we could hear people crying out in pain. And more glass breaking. Our friends were out there but there was nothing

I could do for them. And I thought I could smell smoke. Other people were heading back to the garden trying to escape.

I turned the handle on the door, but it wouldn't budge. I tried putting my shoulder against it, but still nothing happened. I felt Defne being pushed onto me by the crowd behind her. I kicked the door. It shook. Then I kicked it again and, at last, it swung open. But, as I was about to lead Defne through it, the crowd behind us surged forwards and pushed her to the ground.

I shouted for people to stop. I tried to help her up, but I too was knocked over. The bookshop's customers kept on rushing past us. Finally, I was able to get up and turned to help her. 'Defne, Defne...' I kept repeating. My poor darling had blood on her face from the fall. I tried to wipe it with my handkerchief, but she brushed my hand away and cried out, 'Sandy, the baby...' She kept placing her hand on different parts of her stomach as if she was trying to feel the heartbeat of the foetus. I could hear the motorbike engines come alive again. And then the bikers started to honk their horns; they put their machines into gear and rode off. There was silence. It felt like forever but was probably only a few seconds until I heard sirens in the distance. They grew louder as whatever vehicles were projecting the electronic howl came closer. I couldn't tell if it was police or ambulance.

In the event, it turned out to be both.

All this time, I was sitting next to Defne on the ground, holding her hand. Eventually, policemen came. They talked to the owner but did nothing else. They did not even take notes. I even saw one of the officers pick up a book and turn it over in his hands. There was a look of bemusement on his face as if he was handling something he had seen once before, long ago. Two ambulancemen came through, carrying a stretcher. They walked past Ayla, who was lying inert on the pavement in front of the shop. Somebody had drawn a blanket over her face. I could hear someone sobbing. I think it must have been Ali. But it could have been any one of the journalists.

'Sandy, I can't feel the baby.'

Defne lifted her head and looked down the length of her body and kept patting her stomach. Her eyes were wide open and bulging. Damp strands of hair were stuck to her forehead. I reached forward to brush them away. She tried to say something more, but the words stuck in her throat. The ambulancemen lifted her gently on to a stretcher. I walked next to her as she was taken to the ambulance. We passed the bookshop owner, who was now sitting on the floor surrounded by broken glass and books torn from the shelves. His face was covered with his hands. His thin shoulders were shaking.

CHAPTER 63

No one would explain anything. Ali was sitting next to me on the wooden bench of the waiting room. Neither of us uttered a word. Under the 'no smoking' sign, he lit up. He did not stop smoking until his pack was done, a few hours later.

Finally, a doctor came in. She was wearing a headscarf. She didn't seem to notice the cloud of cigarette smoke. She must have seen the look of anguish on my face for she immediately said, 'Your wife is all right.' But the sound of her voice was flat and I could see from the expression on her face that there was more. She sat next to me. Her eyes were gentle and full of kindness. She was about to say something but hesitated.

'What is it, doctor?'

She did not look thirty yet, but she had dark patches below her eyes and was developing a fine web of crow's feet at the sides.

'Your wife has had a severe placental abruption.'

I nodded, but in truth I had no idea what 'severe placental abruption' meant. I saw her looking hard at me. I was not sure why. So, I said what I thought was the right response, 'How long will it take her to recover?'

'There is vaginal bleeding,' she continued.

I am squeamish about blood, but this was my darling, Defne, so I just nodded again, as if I understood everything that was being said to me; as if I was unperturbed, in charge, in control of my emotions. Then it dawned on me, in acute and painful embarrassment, that there was one question that I had neglected to ask. 'What about the baby?'

'That's what I was trying to explain...' she took a deep breath. 'Your wife has lost the child.'

CHAPTER 64

They kept Defne under sedation for a week. I only left her, to return to the village to bury our child – a tiny baby boy. His body fitted in a wooden casket smaller than a shoe box. I buried this 'Zeki' next to Aydin and Tassos' mausoleum. I no longer really knew what I was saying or who I was talking to. But I started conversing with my old friend. I said to him, 'Look Aydin, I'm putting my boy next to you so that you and Tassos can keep an eye on him. Promise me he doesn't get lonely when we're not here. Promise me that.'

I felt Hassan and Frankie try to take hold of me. But I refused to budge. I thought to myself that my son's tiny grave would be sheltered from the wind and dust that blows up the valley, here next to my friend's mausoleum. The shadows from the big, beautiful marble building would keep him from getting too hot in summer. I thought I must have a water tap installed next to him. And that I would have flowers planted around his grave. After a long while, I allowed Hassan and Frankie to lead me to my little boy's own headstone. It read, 'Zeki Bligh-Smith.' And seeing that name, so foreign, there in the graveyard, made my heart break a little more. I hated myself. I thought – this is my punishment for having loved my sister. But did the price have to be so high? Why couldn't it have been me? My poor little boy. I never got to hold him. I was dying but I was still alive. It felt as if God was ripping out my soul and dangling it in front of my eyes like a bloody extracted heart, as if to say, 'Here is what happens when you transgress.' I couldn't argue with my sentence. I knew I was guilty. It was right for me to be punished. But little baby Zeki…? And Defne? 'God, how could you do this to them?' I cried out, sobbing, hysterical.

When Defne finally came out of hospital she did not speak. She stared at the ground all the time and her shoulders were hunched. From that day on, she wore black. We even had black rings made for us with his name engraved inside and one date: the day he suffocated in his mother's womb. When Defne looked at me, it was as if she was looking through me. I didn't complain. I knew I had no right to. Even though I too was going mad with grief.

Our TV station and newspaper ran nonstop coverage of the events; of the criminals whose actions led to the death of an unborn baby, the murder of a young female photographer, and the destruction of a famous bookshop. And of course, the unsatisfactory response of the police.

But none of that was any consolation. Perhaps the perpetrators thought this would break Defne and me. But it only strengthened our resolve. It seemed to me, looking back at those events, that if the memorial service was the beginning of a war of wills, then the death of baby Zeki was the point of no return. We were all in. And would go after Colonel Kaynar and his associates even more aggressively in future.

But, between Defne and me something had broken for good. Everything was different. She didn't say so, but I felt sure she was blaming what happened to our child on the nature of our relationship. I tried, once, to make love to her – it was an accident, a middle of the night thing when I had forgotten for a moment all that had happened – but she just lay there immobile as if she was waiting for me to be finished. So, I just gave up. Embarrassed, humiliated. And accepting. I couldn't blame her. I was stupid. This was all my fault.

One evening – it must have been three months or so after I buried our son – we were sitting in silence in our garden after Maghrib prayer. The valley was dark; in the distance I could see the lights of Malatya – they looked like a distant constellation. Once, I reflected, this would have been a moment of peace and we would have held hands, taking in the jasmine-perfumed air. But that night, the flower's smell felt cloying and unclean – reminiscent of the unholy sweetness of decaying flesh. And the evening warmth was a damp and oppressive blanket depriving us of oxygen.

Out of the blue, Defne said, 'We can't go on like before, Sandy.'

I thought, rather bitterly, that 'before' had long since gone, but I knew what she meant, and she was right. I knew that, by then. I felt defeated. Everything we had built together as a couple was now in shreds.

'We need to atone for what we have done.'

'How?' I was a loss to see what we could do to make things right.

'We need to see Hassan. He will understand. It is only by making the profession of faith that we can be re-born.' She said this with a certainty that I found frightening. I knew she had been reading the Quran a lot recently. She had been learning everything she could about Islam. I should have expected this, but it still came as a shock. When I had tried reading the Quran, I found it complicated, and a lot of the time I simply didn't understand the messages it contained. But that was my problem – not hers. I owed her this if she felt it would lessen the weight of her sin. I would do whatever it took. But I was not convinced that it would do any good.

CHAPTER 65

The next day we went, as agreed, to see Hassan. We had two witnesses with us: the *mukhtar* and Burak. We arrived in time for Dhur prayers. The wind swirling around the ablutions fountain carried the smell of hay and woodsmoke from one of the village's few remaining outside clay ovens. One of the old inhabitants must have been baking bread. I thought back to my aunt and wondered what she would make of my relationship with Defne. But, if I was thinking there might be a friendly smile of absolution, I was deluding myself. I knew that, for her, I would have been in the wrong. Perhaps the only way was for me to fully return to my father's religion and make the Muslim profession of faith. Perhaps this would save me. I tried to convince myself that I was ready with that thought. It pushed me forwards to take the step despite my doubts, my hesitation. But, irrespective of what I truly believed, for Defne, I would do it. For the chance, however remote, that she at least might be saved, I would do it.

After prayers, we stood side by side and proclaimed our creed and our submission to 'Allah the Most Merciful, the Most Compassionate' in front of Hassan and our witnesses: 'There is no God, but God, and Muhammed is His Messenger,' we said in unison. We then took our leave and went to wash ourselves clean. Clean of all our sin. Reborn, whole: this is what I was supposed to feel, at least. It might well have been so for Defne, because I saw she had a strange light in her eyes. It made me more uncomfortable than I already was around her. It was as if part of her was somewhere else. But for me? In truth, I felt the same as I had the previous day. No, that's not even true. My nostalgia for what we had been became multiplied many times over. I resolved to say nothing about this. I would just continue by her side, faithful to our mission to attack the corrupt, the foul, all those wretched men who had polluted our little part of Cyprus. This sliver of land where we Turkish Cypriots should at least have been safe. Where a better world could have been built for our tiny community. Why else did the Turkish army come? Why else did all those men die defending our enclaves?

CHAPTER 66

Somewhere inside, I knew she was still the woman I loved. Occasionally, in the middle of the night, I woke up tormented with the memory of our passionate intimacy. The touch and embrace before we slept. The waking in the middle of the night to reconnect. The arousal in the morning. The contentment. Now we just slept side by side in twin beds, like children, like the brother and sister we really were. But at least we were talking again. After she made her vows as a Muslim there was an easing of tension.

Some other things returned to how they were before. Coffee in the morning. Conversation about the business. My updates to her about the developments going on in the village. But the lack of physical intimacy was eating me up. I didn't know what to do. I hated myself for wanting sex with her, but I did. I told myself that only the most wretched and base of creatures could feel this way after everything we had been through.

CHAPTER 67

We had been intensifying our attack on Kaynar. Apart from the stuff in the press about him, I hired the investigation firm, Kroll, to look into his finances. When their work was completed, and we had even more details of his corrupt dealings, we would go public. But there was another initiative afoot. This one was particularly covert. Not even Defne was aware of it.

I had recently returned from Tel Aviv where I retained the services of a rather special firm made up of ex-IDF cybersecurity experts. I paid them a lot of money and vowed I would continue to do so until the Grey Wolves in Cyprus systems had been hacked, broken, infected with viruses and destroyed; until their bank accounts had been emptied and the funds transferred to various charities of my choice around the world.

My associates in Israel managed to infiltrate Kaynar's phone, and those of his cronies. Now, we could track them and read every one of their supposedly encrypted messages. My point of contact at the Israeli firm, Uri Engelman, informed me that Kaynar and his crew had started using a new, and supposedly secure encrypted app – Telegram – but Engelman's team had cracked this also. The old soldiers' gang would no longer be able to communicate or function in any proper sense. This really would be the end of the Grey Wolves in Cyprus.

CHAPTER 68

'I can't do this anymore,' I told myself. I needed a drink. Just one drink. I knew there was a bottle of red wine in the food cupboard hiding behind the olive oil. I didn't care what Defne thought. I was going to open it and drink the whole bottle in one sitting. But, as I headed over to the kitchen, I went past the bathroom. The door was slightly ajar. I heard a strange noise. It sounded like someone using garden shears. I pushed the door open. And there in front of the mirror was Defne, standing completely naked. I couldn't remember when I had last seen her this way. She had a pair of kitchen scissors in her hands. At her feet was a pile of her long black curls.

'What are you doing, Defne? What are you doing?' I bent down to pick up her hair from the floor. I was no longer thinking straight. I had some mad idea that I could fix it back on.

She started to laugh.

'Defne, what are you doing?'

Instead of answering me she returned to her grotesque task, chanting 'Allahu Akbar' as she did.

For a moment, I wanted to grab and shake her until I made her see sense. But I knew she was too far gone. There was nothing more for me to do. I headed to the kitchen and grabbed the bottle of wine. I spent the next hour out in the garden, drinking its contents by the tumbler full. God, how good it tasted. How I had missed the alcohol coursing through my veins.

After a while, I felt normal enough to put on a Spotify playlist and I filled the garden with the sound of Miles Davis. And then, later, I went back to the kitchen where I found a half bottle of brandy. I drank that too and fell asleep in the garden. I woke in the morning, my clothes damp with dew, to find Defne looking down at me. She was dressed to go to mosque. There was a glass of water in her hand that she held out to me. I could see the disappointment on her face. Then she was gone, and a little while later I heard the call for prayer. Followed by Hassan reciting his prayers. I felt utterly alone.

CHAPTER 69

The stories that Ali and his team came up with had never generated so much interest. Our paper's circulation was sky high and kept growing. We were even selling copies south of the border, on the Greek side. And I knew that some left-wing groups over there were begging us to do the same – to name which of their politicians were taking bribes, as well as members of the Orthodox Church involved in various degrees of electoral and business corruption. If it gave us the opportunity of going after ELAM, given what had happened at the university months ago, I thought that I might yet agree to help out. We had already run articles showing the world the rottenness of the Orthodox Church in Cyprus – with its hatred of Turks and complicity in the 1950s' and '60s' massacres. This was not with any intent to hurt decent God-fearing Greek Cypriots, but to lay the ground for open debate on all the factors that had caused the wrenching apart of our island – our shared homeland, our different communities. But our main focus at that time remained Kaynar. And because of this, things were hotting up for Defne and me. Although I was the only one who seemed to care.

After one particularly aggressive article against Kaynar we received an envelope with two 9 mm bullets in it. But we did not lessen the ferocity of our campaign.

Then came a letter saying, 'No more warnings.'

That was a month ago.

I felt we had nothing left to lose. So, we went full out. And we were starting to see results. Many of the MPs who we targeted in investigative reports had resigned. Young Turkish Cypriots were clamouring for justice. People were fed up with all the rottenness and corruption. They'd guessed at it before and now the efforts of our journalists delivered the confirmation. They had seen what happened in Egypt and Tunisia. They knew they could bring down the government. The authorities were scared and were talking about dialogue and creating 'citizen forums'.

The Grey Wolves had become a spent force, just as we intended. They could no longer operate in Cyprus. Many of the men close to Kaynar were arrested. The police chief could not ignore them, especially after we showed him the file we had on him – which amongst other quite interesting details, outlined the source of funding for his villa, swimming pool and brand-new S-Class Mercedes.

There was talk that Kaynar was to leave the island. But I knew, deep down, it was merely talk. At least for now. He wouldn't leave us be. He couldn't. Not after what we had done to him. Things had gone too far. I also knew, from Ali, that there was a strong and credible rumour that men had been hired from Istanbul to come and kill us. And Uri confirmed its veracity.

Ali begged us to leave the island. But we wouldn't. Because Defne refused. He also begged us to hire a bodyguard. I ought to have, I really ought. But she didn't care what happened to her. She even muttered something about martyrdom once.

Me? I was getting tired. I was ready to let go, so long as I had Defne by my side for the time we had left. The life that I loved, the one that was full of the joy, of our physical and emotional intimacy, had gone. We were left like two husks: rough fibrous memories of something once potent and fertile.

I had only a few regrets. But they gnawed away at me, night and day. I understood now, like never before, the concept of purgatory.

I wished that Defne and I were not related by blood. That we had met a long time ago and had a proper family.

I hoped still that I might be around to see her name in print. But I didn't think that was likely. *The School Master's Wife* would now be published by the summer. After several months of sending the manuscript to various publishing houses, her agent, Felicity, had secured a deal with a young and hip new publisher: 'Write Back to the Empire Ink'. Their logo was a black clenched fist with barbed wire around the wrist. But Defne displayed no joy when we received the contract. It was as if she had given up her connection to the material world. I kept my pride in her for myself. There, in a little room in my mind, I kept my treasured memories of Defne. I went there for solace, more and more often. I thought our father would have been pleased that her true Turkish Cypriot name, Defne Aziz would appear on the cover of the book. I hoped that our fellow Turkish Cypriots would be proud to be celebrated in print. That we would become, at long last, a people who told their own story, and not one whose fate was only to be described by foreigners. That come what may, to us, there would be some trace of our passing on earth. That one day, when we were no more, when we had finally been subsumed into Mr Erdoğan's Turkey and lost all memory that we were genuinely Cypriots with our unique complex cocktail of DNA, there would be a fine piece of literature to commemorate us.

Defne didn't know, but I had left a letter with my lawyer instructing him to send a copy of *The School Master's Wife* to Fatma, in case something happened to us before it finally appeared in print. I wanted her to see what her daughter had written. Perhaps she might see that Defne's time with me was not entirely wasted.

I wish I could be there to see the completion of the building works around Bamyaköy and see the *Erol ve Zainab İlköğretim Okulu ve Lisesi* on its opening day. I would have liked to see the children coming and going but I know I will never see any of it. I set aside the money needed and appointed a man I trusted to oversee our various projects. He will be paid handsomely when all is done.

The rest of our wealth is set aside for the foundation we set up. Some of it, at Defne's request, will help promote moderate Islam and interfaith dialogue. And the rest of it will go to funding education and healthcare for the poor of the Turkish-speaking part of Cyprus.

Chapter 70

I look across my father's valley. I am struck, as I am each and every day, by its beauty. This is my land. This is where I am from. I am a Turkish Cypriot. My father's family has lived here for hundreds of years, and I will die here. I am home. I am back. They will bury us near our son. And that is as it should be. There is much that I still haven't come to terms with. I now understand that life doesn't allow you to tie up loose ends. And I think I am at peace with that. I have told you my story and I hope that you won't judge me too harshly. I am guilty of having loved. Pick up your stone and throw it at me if you dare.

CHAPTER 71

My phone rings and breaks me out of my reverie. It's a +972 number. Uri is calling me from Tel Aviv.

'Sandy, they're coming for you and Defne.'

I don't need to ask who. Nevertheless, I say, 'Are you sure?'

'We're tracking them now from their mobile phones. There are four of them and we have connected to the microphones on their devices. We can hear every word of their conversation. You need to get out now, *chaber.*'

'How far away are they?'

'At the speed they're driving, we are guessing twenty minutes at most.'

I hang up and go back inside to see Defne.

'We need to leave now my love.' I implore her.

'Why?' her gaze is vacant.

'Kaynar and his men are coming.'

'We can't leave Zeki,' she says.

For a moment, I wonder which Zeki she means. And then of course it is all too clear. She means our son. I am hit with the realisation in this instant that there never was a Zeki, our father, for her. Except vicariously, through me, through my obsession. It was out of her love for me that she cared. It was me she was loving, humouring. All my stupidity becomes suddenly crystal clear to me.

'He's dead, sweetheart. We can still make it out of here. We can take the coastal road and make it to Kyrenia.' I can see that road in my mind's eye. It is clear of traffic, all the way. Just one big, beautiful road with the Beshparmak mountains on one side and, on the other, the turquoise Mediterranean Sea with its little white crests reaching out towards the Taurus mountains.

Now my instincts are to flee. There is an alternative. We can make it out of here.

'No, I am not leaving, Sandy. They can kill me here. I will die a *şehit* and buy back the soul of our child and right the wrong I have done.'

There is no more 'us' but I don't have time to dwell on that.

'There are other ways Defne… we don't need to do this.' I am still hoping against hope that she will change her mind.

'No Sandy, this is the only way. Say your prayers and you will know that I am right.' Her voice rises at the end of the sentence. I note a touch of hysteria. It cuts right through me. I no longer recognise the spirit of this person.

I look at the face I love. Her skin is dry and there are little flecks of dried flesh around her lips and cheeks.

I don't want to die. At least not like this. Not now. My mind runs wild. I want to run. I want to live. I want to make love to her again. I want to make love, full stop. I want to give up all this work and fussing about getting stuff done. I want to enjoy all the money we have. If I make it to Kyrenia, I can get away. I can go anywhere.

Enough, I tell myself. I will give up Cyprus. I will give up our fight. I will go to America. I will go to Montana. I will buy a small ranch and forget about everything. Just live a quiet life. I will give up this folly. What was I thinking? I try to turn away from her and make for the door. I see my car keys on the side table. I really do want to get out of here. But my legs won't carry me. And then, all of a sudden, I know that I won't run. I can't. I won't leave my sister alone. An invisible umbilical cord has wrapped itself around us both. We are indivisible. I have met my sister, and this is the only thing that counts. It's what I wanted. So here it is. It has come, but not in the form I expected. The damned irony of it.

My foot starts to shake. She is immobile. I think she is smiling. And then comes the call for prayer from the loudspeakers of the mosque. And now, when I look at her face, I am certain. She is indeed smiling. She is in rapture while I am in abject fear. I think I will lose control of my bowels at any moment.

I try to distract myself. I try reciting my times table. I go up the scales to the five times table. And then the six times table. But I am slowing at the seven times table. I falter at 7 x 8. I break it down… 7 x 4… okay, 28. And then? I double it, so… 56. I carry on for a while but come to a stop again at the eight times table. And then I move on to the comfort of the nine times table. Somehow an old favourite. I am taken back to the memory of a dusty classroom. There is sunshine streaming onto a wooden desk. 9 x 7 = 63. And I am through to the tens. I stop there. And then, as if the memory of the classroom has taken me back to childhood, I remember my mother. It does not comfort me. The thought of her makes me want to cry. Not because I am missing her love. But because it was not as it should have been. Because of the absence of love. All the emptiness. Perhaps everything would have turned out differently if I had been loved and secure. If I had not been forced into the skin of an Englishman of her world. I try to look elsewhere for comfort. I need it right now, for it seems to me that I can hear, carried over the breeze, coming up from the valley, the noise of a car driving at speed. But nothing comes to my rescue.

Instead, images flicker through my mind. At first, they go slowly. I see myself as a child. The wretchedness of the schoolyard. Alone. Still not strong enough to assert myself with my classmates. The first adolescent fumblings with girlfriends. First business successes. God, is that the only positive thing I can remember right now? Wife… divorce papers. The carousel speeds up. Now it is Defne that I see. Her book signing. Our first night together. Her beautiful apartment. God, why didn't we just stay there? And then the wheel comes to a stop. One last image is seared on to the screen. Defne, dressed in black. Her hair covered with a scarf. Indifferent to the world. Ready for martyrdom.

The sound of the car is getting closer. I go to the terrace. And, fast approaching the village, still a few hundred metres away, I can see the roaring silver locomotive fury of Kaynar's Range Rover as it makes its way up the last stretch of road.

I go back in. 'Defne…' One last try.

She is sitting on the couch, and she is rocking backwards and forwards, her arms cuddling an invisible form. To this bundle of emptiness, she is whispering soft cooing words.

'Defne…' she does not hear me. She does not hear anything, anymore.

I try to say a prayer. I try to recite one of the prayers that Hassan has taught me. But I can't remember the words. So, I just try to talk to the Almighty. I say, 'Let her be. Spare her. Forgive her soul. I am to blame. It's all my folly. It's all my stupidity.'

I can hear car doors opening and slamming shut. And then hurried footsteps up towards our door. They are kicking at the door.

I look over at Defne. She is still smiling. She is happy. She is with her God.

Afterword

One of the themes in this novel is Genetic Sexual Attraction (GSA) – essentially siblings who have grown up as strangers to each other and experience unusually deep feelings for each other. While for many this is deeply disturbing, it is a well-documented phenomenon. Those who are interested in exploring the subject further should read of the case of the German couple Patrick Stübing and Susan Karolewski – available from The Guardian newspaper archive.

Acting on GSA is, quite rightly, illegal. However, there are a couple of points to be made. The first is that it differs from traditional incest since it involves individuals who were not brought up together and had no prior family bond so to speak. And there is no coercion. They are in effect strangers to each other. Apparently, those who experience GSA do recount overwhelming feelings of attraction for the other that far exceed normal romantic feelings. The second is that whilst, thankfully, there are very few reported cases of GSA we are faced with the possibility that the number of these may increase in the coming twenty years or so as a result of unscrupulous men acting as prolific sperm donors in unregulated environments and within a relatively tight geographical radius.

For the individuals themselves who experience GSA for a sibling this is clearly a profound human tragedy. As a society our first best response should be psychological counselling to help those impacted to resist these feelings and understand the implications of their actions, rather than condemnation or worse, immediate incarceration.

In the case of Sandy and Defne – these two well educated people have clearly lost their moral bearings by succumbing to their desires. Objectively there is no excuse for their behaviour and ultimately, they pay a very high price indeed for their transgression. But as humans we are all, in our own way, capable of losing our sense of right and wrong at different times.

THE CRESCENT MOON FOX

The Crescent Moon Fox is a compassionate, heartbreaking, brutal and occasionally humorous debut novel by Metin Murat about Turkish Cypriots.

Set on the island of Cyprus during the British colonial era, it tells the tale of the inhabitants of the fictional Karpaz village of Bamyaköy, and in particular of two of its young men – Zeki and Aydin – during a time of heightened ethnic tensions with their Greek Cypriot neighbours.

Zeki, who is shaped and nurtured by the British colonial system, is destined for great things. His friend Aydin is a misfit in his community and yet, in his own complex and disturbing way, achieves distinction and redemption.

The span of the novel, from the 1930s to the new millennium, shows the life of the Turks of Cyprus, unique and distinct as a minority, in the lead-up to independence from Britain and the tragic aftermath of the post-colonial era.

It gives a voice to these Cypriot Turks, of all different backgrounds, particularly the illiterate rural women of mid-twentieth century Cyprus. The Crescent Moon Fox is also a poignant journey of discovery of one's true identity…

Metin Murat is a British writer of Turkish Cypriot descent. He grew up in a multi-cultural environment with exposure to English, Welsh, and French cultures. As a business consultant, he has worked extensively in the Middle East, developing a deep affection for the Levant. He currently lives in the southwest of France with his two dogs, Sevgi and Margot. *Meeting Sister* is the sequel to his debut novel, *The Crescent Moon Fox*.